W9-BEP-229

No Regrets

by

June Phyllis Baker

LSP

DIGITAL

© **2008** by June Phyllis Baker

All Rights Reserved. No part of this book may be reproduced, stored in a retrieval system, or transmitted in any form or by any means without the prior written permission of the author, except by a reviewer who may quote brief passages in a review to be printed in a newspaper, magazine or journal.

First Edition

Edited by
A.M. Lepri

Formatted by:
Linda Daly *(interior)*

Cover design:
Bonny Kirby *(front-cover)*
Linda Daly *(back- cover)*

ISBN-13: 978-0-9800733-8-6

ISBN-10: 0-9800733-8-3

PUBLISHED BY LSP DIGITAL

www.lightswordpublishing.com

Dedication

Lisa-Marie, Nicole, and Melissa you light up my life.
To Pamela Reese who taught me how to ask why.

Acknowledgements

To my sisters Eileen and Jeanne. You are the best!
To my publisher and friend, Linda Daly, who had the vision of what this book could become. Thank you for believing in me.
To Nancy Lepri my editor. Thank you for your patience and support.
To Charlotte Parker. Thank you for always being there especially when I wanted to quit.
To Sher Hames Torres. Thank you for all your help.
To Neva Franks. Your sense of humor got me through the rough times.
I love you all and I'm proud to call you my friends. I have *No Regrets*.

One

Another dead-end assignment! Arlene's pencil slashed across the copy article in her hand. How many times could she write about the Women's Club's latest accomplishments? *Seven years. Seven years at the Sunny Hills Gazette and the best they can give me is another boring chat with the Women's Club.* Fuming, Arlene dropped the pad on her desk and leaned back in her chair.

Blank walls stared back at her. Not a picture, just one small window staring out at the five and dime. She shook her head and sighed with frustration. *When did I settle for being a slave to the 'safe' job? What happened to all those dreams of glory, making a difference, being a headliner?*

While she was grateful for the job, and loved her work, she longed for assignments with more depth. She'd had a brief moment of glory when she had the opportunity to interview the mayor once. Instead she'd wondered aloud at how hideous his toupee was. Needless to say the mayor wasn't taking interviews with her any more.

"Let's face it," she grumbled aloud. "This is a small town with small problems." *Ergo, the Women's Club is the highlight of my week.*

She hadn't meant to stay this long. *Then why don't I just leave?* Arlene sighed. She didn't like to admit the answer, even to herself. Lance. *C'mon get over it. Leave this one horse town and Sheriff Lance Carter behind. All I'm gonna get here is a lifetime's worth of regrets.*

A knock on her office door brought her back to her monotonous present.

"Busy?" Jack Stewart asked, poking his head into her office. He flashed a smile that made women melt.

Jack was a knockout and he knew it, with his dark hair and gorgeous hazel eyes. Gratefully, Arlene was immune to his charms. After all he was a fellow reporter and sometimes a friend.

"What's up?" she asked, rolling a pencil between her palms.

"I thought I heard you talking to somebody, but I don't see anybody else in here with you. What are you raging about now?"

"Stewart, I don't know why we have Henrietta Winston doing the gossip column when we have you." She chuckled.

"Anyway, why did you say you came in?"

"I didn't." He grinned and leaned in the doorway. "How about dinner tonight?"

"I can't, but thanks for the offer. I'm just going to curl up with a good book and stuff my face with popcorn."

He grinned and winked. "That book won't keep you warm on a cold winter night."

"Thanks for your concern, but I have an electric blanket."

Jack uncrossed his arms and heaved himself away from the door jam with a sigh. "I have to go prepare for my meeting with the mayor..."

Her phone rang and Arlene put her hand up motioning for him to wait then hit the speaker button.

"Stewart in there with you?" Came the disembodied voice of their editor.

"Yes, he is."

"I figured as much when he didn't answer his phone. I want you and Stewart in here pronto."

Jack raised an eyebrow in Arlene's direction. "It must be something big if he wants to see us both."

"We'll be right over, Tom." She disconnected the call and got to her feet. "We'll soon find out."

"Hey, Boss", Arlene said, as they entered Tom Solana's office. "You wanted to see us?"

"Yeah." He motioned for them to take a seat. "There's been a robbery at the Corner Market. Esther put the call through and then she let me know. I need one of you over there right now."

"No can do, boss," Jack said with a shrug. "I've got a meeting with the mayor in less than an hour."

"That leaves you, Arlene"

"Sure, no problem." Arlene tried to look nonchalant. "Lance won't be happy at all with this. We haven't had a robbery in what? Ten years? He prides himself on having the safest town in the state. Whoever is responsible is going to be very sorry they crossed him."

Tom got to his feet and ran a hand through his salt and pepper hair. "Okay. That's all. Arlene, I suggest you leave now."

Jack followed Arlene into the hall, closed the door and fell in step with her as she marched toward her office.

"I thought you were leaving?" she said with a frown.

"Yeah, I am. I wanted to know if you wanted to switch places. You know, you go the meeting with the mayor and--" "I don't think so, Jack. You know how the mayor feels about me. I'm worse than eating spinach. Sorry. This is my story. It sure beats anything I've had for ages."

"Ah, well. You can't blame a guy for trying." He glanced at his watch. "I'd better get going. You want a lift?"

"Nice try, Jack." She grinned as she slid into her office. "I can drive."

~

The siren on the police cruiser droned into silence as Sheriff Lance Carter stepped out in front of the Corner Market. The old-timers seated on the bench in front of the barbershop across the street watched with interest, but no genuine concern. The owner of the small grocery store, Joe Monroe, nodded a greeting.

"Hey Joe, what's the problem?"

"Come see for yourself, Sheriff."

Lance followed the older man past the checkout counter, and to the right, stopping short as he entered the produce section. Henrietta Winston, all of ninety-five pounds soaking wet, sat astride a teenage boy, arms folded across her chest and bright eyes blazing.

Lance cleared his throat to avoid laughing, and brushed his black hair back from his forehead. "Just what seems to be the problem here, Miss Winston?"

"This young hooligan tried to steal my purse so I tackled him."

"That's pretty drastic action there, don't you think? Why didn't you call Joe?"

Henrietta raised her chin defiantly and jabbed her knees into the boy's ribs. "By the time Joe got here this kid would have been half way down the street. Now, what are you going to do about this criminal?"

The teenager twisted to look up at Lance, his brown eyes pleading. "Dang, Sheriff, please. Get her off. She's about to kill me."

"You are lucky I don't do worse than that to you, you little delinquent." She thumped him across the back of the head with her hand and his face bumped the floor, curly black hair spilling around his reddening face. "I don't know what's wrong with kids these days."

Lance held out his hand. "Okay, I'll take it from here. Let him up, Miss Winston."

A familiar voice called from the doorway, and Lance gritted his teeth and grimaced at the sound. "Dang it, not Arlene."

"Oh, come on, Lance. You knew she'd show up." Joe grinned.

"Frankly, I was hoping they'd send Jack Stewart."

"Yeah, but admit it, you would have been disappointed." Joe waggled his eyebrows and headed for the door.

Lance didn't answer. He was too busy watching Arlene as she walked toward him.

"Hi, Joe, I heard there was a robbery? You okay?"

"Police business, Arlene. You should probably wait outside." Lance caught the teenager by the arm and hauled him to his feet.

"Power of the press, Sheriff." Arlene smiled and brushed past him, her notepad already in hand. "So what's going on?" Her bright eyes flicked from Miss Winston to the teenager and back to Lance. "You involved in this too, Miss Winston?"

Henrietta harrumphed, eyes narrowed as she stared at the teenager in the Sheriff's grasp.

Lance cleared his throat. "Nothing major. This young man got caught purse snatching is all. Not smart, young fella. Not in my town."

"Aw, c'mon Lance, he's no worse than you were at his age," Joe said with a laugh.

"Would you mind answering a few questions?" Arlene intercepted the kid as Lance tried to hustle him out the door. "Why did you do it?"

He hung his head and looked nervously at Lance. "I just needed some money. Look, I'm sorry, lady. I just got here and I was hungry and... It doesn't matter anyway. I got no place else to go."

Lance shook his head. This wasn't a bad kid; something in his eyes spoke to Lance's heart. Real troublemakers just weren't this repentant.

"What's your name, son?"

"Gary. Gary Jones."

"How old are you, Gary? Why aren't you in school?"

"I'm...I'll be eighteen next month. And I've never been in trouble before, Sheriff, if that's what you're looking to find out. I just...aw, forget it."

"Well, Sheriff, what are you planning to do about this?" Miss Winston snapped. "It's a shame when a body can't even go to the store without havin' her purse stolen."

"Look, Miss Winston, Gary here didn't actually take anything and since…"

Miss Winston put her hand up. "It doesn't matter, he still stole my purse. He needs to be punished. Maybe a stay in jail will teach this young fellow a lesson."

"Are you saying you want to file charges?"

Miss Winston glanced at Gary, standing meekly at Lance's side, staring glumly at his feet. "I suppose not."

Gary's head shot up, eyes widening. "Oh, thank you, Ma'am."

"Just a second, young man," Miss Winston's eyes narrowed and she closed her hand firmly on her purse. "I'm not done yet. He still needs to learn his lesson, Sheriff. Maybe he ought to do some type of community service."

Lance ran his hand across his jaw. "The mayor has been wanting someone to clean up the debris in the park. Cheap as he is, he'll be glad to get it done for free. Would that be okay with you, Miss Winston?"

Miss Winston nodded. "You see that he does the job properly, Sheriff. I'll be on my way." She snatched up a small shopping bag from the counter, stopped and pointed a waggling finger at Gary. "I'll be watching you, young man. If I catch you even looking the wrong way, your butt will be in jail." She turned to Arlene. "I'll see you in the office."

Tossing her head, she marched from the store.

Joe closed the door behind her, squinted across at Arlene and rubbed the bridge of his nose as he trundled over to Lance and the boy. "Y'know, Miss Henrietta's right. I don't move as fast as I used to before my knee gave out. And there's some heavy lifting to be done around here, y'know, unpacking crates and all. I could use some help here in the store. Course I can't really afford to pay, but I have an empty room in the back..." He raised his eyebrows and waited for Gary to reply.

"Really?" the boy asked incredulously. "Would you let me do that? I won't be any trouble, I swear." Gary shot an apprehensive look at Lance, his eyes wide. "I mean, if it's all right. Am I free to go, Sheriff?"

"Well, I dunno." Lance stared at Gary and rubbed his chin. "That was attempted robbery, that's pretty serious."

Arlene nudged Lance's arm, a smile plucking at her lips. "Quit teasing him, Lance. The poor kid's scared to death."

Lance glanced down at her. Dang, she was pretty when she dropped the just-the-facts reporter act and smiled like that. He shook his head, and forced his attention back to Gary. "Well, all right. You report over to my office tomorrow, we'll get you started on the park detail. But if I ever catch you doing something like this again; your hide will be in jail, young man," Lance warned, poking his finger at Gary's chest. "Understand?"

"Yes sir." Gary turned to Joe. "When do you want me to start, Mr. Monroe?"

Joe winked at Lance and motioned to the display of tuna scattered across the floor. "You can start right now. Let's clear up this mess you and Miss Henrietta made, and then we'll see about getting you some lunch."

"You know," Arlene stepped closer to Lance, until her shoulder brushed his and he could smell the soft honeysuckle fragrance of her hair.

She glanced over at Gary busily stacking the cans of tuna, then her eyes met Lance's. "Ellie over to the diner has an opening for a bus boy. It wouldn't pay much." She dropped her voice to a whisper and Lance leaned down to hear her. "But I know she usually throws in free meals." Her eyebrows lifted, eyes wide as she nodded toward Gary with a knowing smile.

Lance pushed his hair back with one hand. Arlene never ceased to amaze him. With a chuckle he nodded. "I'll go on over and see to it. Kid's gotta eat."

~

"Hey, buddy, time to get off. This is the Sunny Hills stop."

The sound of the voice and a hand on his shoulder roused Kent Jordan from sleep. He scrubbed his hand across his face trying to get his bearings. Where was he? For a split second he didn't remember how he'd got here. He glanced around hurriedly, but it wasn't the prison work-crew bus. It all came back to him. He stood, stretched weary muscles, grabbed what few possessions he had and shoved an unlit cigarette in his mouth as he rose.

Making his way to the front of the bus he stopped short, staring out at the small, rural bus station and the narrow road with its overhanging canopy of trees. What was he doing back here? Hadn't this already cost him enough? Is it worth it, he wondered?

"Hey Buddy," the short, scrawny driver asked. "Is there a problem?"

"Nope." Kent nodded and hefted his bag. "Not a one."

He had come to do a job and that's just what he would do. Once he set his plan into action there would be no going back. He knew who he needed to find. Just one person was responsible for him being in that hellhole. If all went well he'd be in and out and no one would be the wiser.

Stepping down to the gravel parking lot, Kent dropped his bag to the ground and ran his hand over the bulge beneath his jean pant leg. Nobody but him would know he had the revolver taped where he could get it when the time came.

For now, he needed a car. That would be his next step. He knew how to get one. *And then maybe tonight I'll stop by* The Fin and Claw *and find myself a drink and a woman.* He'd gone too damn long without either one.

Two

Arlene reread her article on the purse snatching, and sighed with frustration. *Biggest story I've had all year, and no one even gets arrested. Even the 'crimes' in this town wind up being nothing.* She snatched the page from the typewriter and headed for Tom's office.

"Sorry," Jack grunted as they nearly collided in the narrow hall. He looked away sheepishly, biting his lower lip and edging around Arlene.

"Well, what are you all dressed up for?" No jeans and a t-shirt for Jack today; the sport coat and creased dress slacks told her he had a prestige assignment. *Yeah, and Tom promised me the next big story was mine. That rat.*

"What are you looking so happy about, Miss Sinclair?" Jack's voice told her he knew she was seething inside.

Arlene pasted on a tight smile. "Nothing much, just finished my article on the crime wave here in town. Where are you headed, Stewart?"

Jack fumbled self-consciously with straightening his red and navy striped tie, avoiding meeting her eyes. "Oh, nothing really. Just going to cover that conference in Atlanta."

Arlene nodded, fists balling at her sides. "The mayors' conference. Of course." Still, it wasn't Jack's fault their editor refused to assign her to the big stories. She drew a deep breath. "Have a good trip."

She brushed past him and headed for Tom's office without looking back. *Time for things to change around here,* she fumed. *I'm done taking a backseat to anyone.*

The glass in the door rattled as she rapped the door with her knuckles, then walked in without waiting for his invitation. Her editor swung his chair around to face her, the phone still to his ear, and stared as she took a seat in the wingback across from his desk and tossed her article on his desk. Legs crossed, Arlene folded her arms across her chest and stared him down.

"I'll...get right back to you," Tom muttered and hung up the phone.

There was no backing down from this one.

~

Tom Solana stared across his desk at Arlene. Everything about her body language told him this was no casual visit with her 'boss'. He tapped his fingers on the phone for an instant before stating the obvious. "You look a little upset there, Arlene. Something I can do for you?"

"There's my article for the morning paper, Tom. Want to guess what the big 'crime story' was you sent me on?

She wrinkled her nose and grimaced. "It was a purse snatching. That's all. Stewart is headed to Atlanta to cover the Mayors' Conference and the highlight of my weeks' assignments is a purse snatching?" Her voice rose in pitch as she uncrossed her arms and leaned toward him. "Darn it, Tom. I could have handled that story and you know it."

Tom rubbed the bridge of his nose and scanned the article she'd flung before him, studiously avoiding her challenge. "Purse snatching, huh?" His eyes widened, eyebrows crawling upward. "Henrietta Winston?"

"Yep, looks like we're providing our own news now." Arlene sat back. "Check it out. Not quite the prim, proper gossip columnist this time," she chuckled.

"Well I'll be," Tom grinned, shaking his head as he finished reading. "Who would have thought the old girl had it in her?"

"Nice change of subject, but ummm...how is it Stewart got the story in Atlanta and not me? You told me the next important assignment was mine."

Tom ran his hands through graying hair and rose to his full height to stare down at Arlene. "I'm the boss around here, Miss Sinclair. Or did you forget that? I make the assignments according to who I think is best for a job, and frankly, the idea of turning you loose in Atlanta among a few hundred politicians strikes me as asking for trouble."

"Oh really? And why do I think there's way more to it than that, boss?" Arlene clenched her fists and returned his glare. "Why do I have that gut feeling that tells me our illustrious mayor had more than a little input into your decision?" She cocked her head to the side and stared at him with narrowed eyes. "That's what Jack's meeting was really about wasn't it?"

"Dagnabit, Arlene. Look, plain and simple, Jack is better suited to this assignment. It's more than the fact the mayor winds up running for a bottle of antacids every time you come within a mile of him." Tom shook his head with a wry smile. "You can turn a tea party into a full-scale inquisition. Let it be, Arlene. Your big break you're always barking about will come.

"But this isn't it." He jerked his head toward the door. "Now let me get back to work."

Arlene sighed heavily as she rose. "I deserve a decent story to work on Tom, and you know it."

"Yeah. I know it." He waited till her hand was on the knob before dropping back to sit behind his wide desk. "And Arlene?"

She turned and looked back.

"You might want to get things closed up around here.

We have weather advisories--big storm coming this way. I want everyone home before it gets here."

"That bad?" She lifted a skeptical brow.

"That bad." Tom stared at her solemnly. He knew her too well. "Go home."

~

What's the big deal? Not like we haven't had storms before. Gees, Tom sometimes reminded her of father. Arlene glanced up warily as thunder pealed beyond the window and died away. The office lights flickered ominously as a sharp ring stabbed through the sudden silence. Arlene jumped, snatching the phone up on the second ring.

"Great, some star reporter you are," she chided herself. "Jumping at phone calls." She cradled the receiver to her ear. "Arlene Sinclair."

Silence.

"Hello? This is Arlene Sinclair's office."

Still nothing. Could be the storm was affecting the phone lines already. Arlene dropped the phone back onto its cradle. Outside, the wind picked up, whipping through the trees, its mournful howling adding a sense of foreboding.

Maybe Tom was right after all.

~

Lance scrubbed his hands over his face. Hard to remember another day when he's felt so drained. He closed the folder and stared at the name on the tab.

Gary Jones.

The fear he'd seen in the kid's eyes today roused old long-buried memories of his own youth. He'd been scared too, the day Joe caught him stealing a candy bar from the Corner Market. It had been a long time since that day. The Sheriff and Joe had been fair with him back then. He hoped Gary would be able to say the same one day.

Lance chuckled. To this day he couldn't even look at that particular candy bar.

He stared out his office window at the leaden skies. Looked like rough weather coming. With a heavy sigh, he swiveled back to his desk and ran his finger down the list of names in the phonebook. Jones. There were at least ten Jones' listed in Shrewsbury. How the heck was he going to figure out where Gary belonged?

He called one of his buddies on the Shrewsbury police force and left a message with the switchboard for them to contact him with anything they might have. Not that he really expected a record. Not for this kid.

Enough for one day.

"Night, Debbie." Lance dropped the folder on the secretary's desk.

Debbie moved her wheelchair back and deftly filed the report with the ease of long experience. "Rough day, Sheriff? Not like you to be leaving so early."

"Yeah, thought I'd call it a day while things are quiet." A clap of thunder rattled the windows. "Tyler knows he's on call tonight?"

"Sure does," Debbie rolled around to face him. "Need me to call him for you?"

"Nah, just checking. Listen, it's looking pretty bad out there. Why don't you get on home? Tyler'll call me if he needs anything."

~

Heavy drops of rain pattered to earth as Lance ran up the front steps of his house. Dark clouds had rolled in and the town seemed to be holding its breath in anticipation of what was to come.

Lance glanced through his mail, pausing to draw a crisp white envelope from amidst the bills. His sister's return address was neatly stamped on the back flap.

Huh, what would Peggy be sending me? He opened it carefully and grinned as he glanced over the enclosed card.

"Well, I'll be--she's gonna marry him."

A wedding invitation. Funny how things had changed. His baby sister was leading the way now. He'd always figured he'd be the first one married. She never wanted to settle down. Shoot, she couldn't wait to grow up and leave Sunny Hills. He'd been the 'good big brother', warned her about the dangers of big city life. Tried to keep those fancy city fellas away from his little sister.

And now she's marrying her country western singer she's been dating all this time. Isn't that something? Good for you, Peggy.

Heck, when did he have a date last? He couldn't remember. *Maybe it's time I started.* Lance tossed the mail on the kitchen counter and stared at the contents of the fridge. *Not that there are all that many prospects here in town. Let's see...* There weren't many single women in town. At least none that appealed to him. Except for one very pretty reporter...

No way. Don't even think it, Lance, old boy.

~

Arlene shivered and pulled the covers closer around her as sheets of rain pelted her windowpane. Her big chocolate lab, Coco, watched without lifting his head from where he lay curled at the foot of the bed.

"Yeah, you big baby." She leaned forward and rubbed his broad head. "It's a good night for staying close, isn't it?"

His tail thumped a merry rhythm on the blanket, and Arlene tried to focus on the book she was reading, but the words insisted on blurring together as her attention wandered to the storm, the white flashes of lightning, the way the house shuddered with each crack of thunder.

With a sigh, she marked her page and put the book on her nightstand. Arlene caught a nervous breath as the lamp flickered. *Darn storm is making me nervous as a cat.*

A blazing blue-white light filled the inky sky, then the room pitched into darkness as the lights went out. Along the street, Arlene saw the familiar glow of streetlights disappear. *Must have taken out a power line.*

Coco bolted from the bed, hackles raised, growling at the window. It wasn't like him to be afraid of storms.

"Coco, that's enough." Arlene threw back the covers and edged across the room, feeling her way toward her dog's insistent barking. Grasping the edge of the curtains in one hand, she seized his collar in the other. "Get on back to bed, maybe we should just close this. No more storm watching for us."

Lightning flared across the sky, forking a jagged rip through the night. Illuminated in its glow, a man's face peered through the window.

Arlene gasped, jumping back. Her heart pounded as she scurried across to her bedside and grabbed the flashlight. Returning, she searched the darkness beyond her bedroom. There was nothing. No shadows. No reflection. No one.

She flicked on the flashlight, its bright beam lost in the rain. For a moment she caught her breath. *Don't be silly. It was just your reflection. Who would be out in this kind of weather anyway?* With fierce determination she yanked the curtain closed.

"Okay, that's enough for one night. C'mon Coco, let's go to bed."

~

Arlene yawned and opened one eye, glaring blearily at the bedside clock. 7:37? Coco whimpered and scratched at the bedroom door, eager to get out. *What is going on?*

A steady pounding bored into her still groggy mind. Someone was knocking. Coco looked over his shoulder expectantly as she reached for her rose pink chenille robe and slid her feet into her soft slippers. *Who in the world would be here this early on a Saturday morning?*

"All right, all right, I'm coming," she muttered, Coco bouncing ahead of her toward the front door. "Only days I get to sleep in. Whoever you are, you'd better have a good reason--" Looking through the peephole she found a familiar figure standing outside. *Lance? What's he doing here?*

Arlene slid the chain off and opened the door. "Lance?"

"Good morning...or should I say good afternoon." Lance grinned and glanced down at his watch.

For a moment Arlene stared at the man on her doorstep, trying to make some logic of what was happening. "Afternoon?" She heard herself mumble.

"It's after twelve, sleepy head." He leaned close and whispered, "Are we going to talk out here or are you going to invite me in?"

The scent of his after-shave made her breath catch. *Whoa, girl. There'll be none of that.* "Really? My clock still says seven. I guess the power was out a long time last night?"

"Yeah, blew a transformer and some power lines went down I guess." His gaze moved slowly upward from her feet and when he met her eyes he grinned again. "Well are you going to invite me in? I'm quite sure your neighbors are more than a little curious as to why the sheriff is standing at your door."

Heart racing, she stepped aside so he could enter. "By all means, Sheriff," she managed, with considerably more courtesy than she was really feeling at the moment.

Lance looked around with friendly curiosity. As far as Arlene could remember, he'd only been here one other time, and that was with her brother, Dusty.

He had on jeans that emphasized his strong build, well-worn brown cowboy boots, and a white tee shirt with the sleeves rolled up. He pushed a strand of thick black hair back from his forehead and paused to scratch Coco's ears. As he straightened the lock fell forward again and Arlene caught herself hoping he would leave it...wishing she could be the one to push it back from his face.

Oh no! No, no, no! Her mind was taking her places she didn't dare to go. *No way, don't even think it.* Her fingers gripped the doorknob as she regained control of her voice and wandering mind. "Coco, go on out." She closed the door behind her dog. "So, what's the reason for this visit, Lance?"

"Your mother couldn't get you on the phone last night or this morning." He cleared his throat, obviously amused with the information. "She said she had a one of her bad 'feelings' and that something might have happened."

Arlene sighed and shook her head. "Caroline Sinclair, 'psychic momma' strikes again." She felt a flush of embarrassment. "I'm sorry, Lance," she said apologetically. "Momma just worries a lot since Dusty has been stationed overseas. You know we thought--well, we haven't heard from him since he wrote to say they were being sent home." Arlene frowned. As good as she was at finding information; there was nothing she could find out about her brother. It was hard on everyone, not knowing. "We just hoped he'd be home by now."

Lance nodded sympathetically. "Well, we miss him around the department too. He's my right hand man, you know." He smiled engagingly.

Arlene felt a smile of relief brightening her somber mood. "I know. Dusty's told us how you keep in touch, writing him and all. He really appreciates it. It was a nice thing for you to do, Lance."

"Ahh, it's nothing." He cleared his throat and looked around. "So, everything is all right here, then?"

Arlene picked up the receiver to the kitchen phone and heard the steady buzz of the dial tone. "Seems fine now. Maybe the phone was out for awhile last night with the storm and all."

Lance nodded, his warm gaze returning to her face. "Well, glad you're okay. You might want to call and let your mother know." He winked and strode toward the door.

Three

Lance parked the cruiser in front of the Sunny Hills Diner and glanced over at his young passenger. Gary hadn't said a word since Lance picked him up in front of the Corner Market, just stared out the window, gnawing nervously at his lower lip.

"Now son, there's no need to be scared. Miss Ellie is a nice lady. C'mon, I'll introduce you and we'll get some breakfast before you start work."

Gary opened the door. He stopped as he started to slide out and looked over at Lance.

"Thanks, Sheriff."

"No problem. You just do your job, everything'll be fine."

~

"Morning, Ellie," called a deep voice as the chime on the diner door jingled.

Arlene glanced up from her coffee and homemade blueberry muffin and watched as Lance wound his way through the Monday morning breakfast crowd toward the counter where she was seated.

"Morning Sheriff," Ellie called with a wave, setting a loaded breakfast plate before a customer. "Ya'll go ahead and sit down; I'll be right with you."

Arlene managed a tight smile as Lance motioned the teenager to the stool on Arlene's right, while he slid onto the end stool to her left.

Lance met her eyes, frowned, and dropped his gaze, searching the countertop with sudden intensity. "Ellie, menu when you get a chance?" he called.

With a sigh, Arlene handed him the menu tucked between the sugar dispenser and napkin holder in front of her. "Never mind Ellie, he's got one."

"Thanks," Lance mumbled, and pretended to read it.

Ellie arrived, set a steaming mug of coffee in front of Lance and smiled at Gary. "You must be Gary. The Sheriff told me he'd be bringing you on over this morning." She smiled and tucked the pencil behind her ear. "What would you like for breakfast?"

Gary looked nervously from Ellie to Arlene, then leaned forward to peer anxiously at Lance. "I--I dunno, ma'am, what am I supposed to have?" He scooted closer, whispering around Arlene. "Sheriff, I don't have any money."

"It's all right, I told you I'd get you some breakfast," Lance reassured the boy.

"You'll get meals every day you work here, so don't you worry about that." Ellie topped Arlene's coffee and stared expectantly at Lance. "What about you?"

Arlene glanced toward him and caught him staring directly at her. He jerked around, glowering at the menu before he slapped it closed and shoved it past Arlene to Gary. "The usual, thanks Ellie."

"Could I have pancakes?" Gary grinned tentatively.

"Sure thing." Ellie slid the menu back into its place in front of Arlene. "OJ or milk?"

"Orange juice would be great. Ummm, ma'am, what exactly will I be doing here?"

"Well, soon as you finish eating, the late morning crowd will be arriving. I need you to bus tables, take the dishes to the kitchen, wipe off the tables. Don't you worry, we'll show you what to do. You'll get the hang of it. Let me go get your food."

"When you aren't working here," Lance said as Ellie headed for the kitchen. "You still have community service over at the park for the rest of the month. Don't forget."

Gary shook his head, a shock of dark hair falling over his forehead. "No sir."

"You did good work this weekend. I heard from Zeke over at the park, he was really pleased with how you pitched in."

Lance's piercing blue eyes sparkled as they met Arlene's, and for an instant she forgot how to breathe.

"I'm real glad Miss Sinclair remembered Ellie was needing someone here." He looked back at Gary. "It's gonna work out fine."

Arlene forced herself to exhale slowly and swallowed the last of her coffee. *Don't stare at him.* His thick black hair was tussled from the summer breeze and those lips...*Okay. Time for me to leave, this place is getting a little too warm.* She laid her money beside her plate and smiled at Gary as she got to her feet. "I'm sure I'll see you around here again." She saw Lance's sidelong glance. "I've got to get going. Nichole Branch is receiving the teacher of the year award over at the High School. Wouldn't want to miss covering her big moment."

~

Lance watched Arlene walk across the diner. Her blonde hair swayed in time to the beat of her pace. The clicking of her high heels marked each measured step toward the door. He let his gaze wander from her dressy white heels, up shapely legs to the mesmerizing swing of her hips.

Damn. Why did the only woman in town that took his breath away have to be Arlene?

~

Arlene tapped her notepad with the eraser of the pencil. Mayor Harvey nodded cordially when he spotted her in the front row prior to his speech. *His toupee is still silly looking. Looks like a cat died on his head.*

She stifled a giggle and tried to focus on Principal Scott's chubby, smiling face as the woman meandered through her speech on the importance of teachers like Mrs. Branch.

Midway through the ceremony the principal's secretary edged on stage and handed the mayor a message. A scowl darkened his face and he crumpled the note, darted down the steps of the stage and slammed the auditorium door when he left. She'd never seen him move that fast.

I wonder what's got him so upset? I'm sure I'll find out. Arlene shrugged and returned her attention to the stage.

~

"I'm so glad you came, Miss Sinclair," Principal Scott beamed, shaking Arlene's hand. "I'm sure Mrs. Branch will just treasure your article when it comes out in the *Gazette*." She gripped Arlene's upper arm and leaned close to whisper. "Did you hear they are picketing down to the Town Hall? When Nancy delivered the message to Mayor Harvey I thought the poor man was going to have apoplexy."

Arlene drew a deep breath. *So that's what this is all about.* She managed not to grin at Mrs. Scott. "Why no, I had no idea."

"Well you should get right over there and see what's going on."

Arlene nodded slowly. *Exactly what I was thinking.* "You are so right, Mrs. Scott. Thank you. I'll get right on it." A man slammed heavily against Arlene as she turned to leave, disappearing into the bustling throng of children and parents who packed the small auditorium before she could catch her breath.

"Oh, sweety." Mrs. Scott plucked at Arlene's sleeve. "Looks like he tore your blouse."

Arlene grimaced at the neat slash across the sleeve. "Shoot, my best blouse too."

The Principal peered across the sea of faces. "What on earth would he be carrying sharp enough to cut it like that? Some people are so careless."

~

Arlene pulled up in front of Town Hall to find a dispersing group of townspeople and a hand full of pickets.

"Go on home, folks," Lance said firmly. "Nothing more to do here today. You heard what the Deputy Mayor said."

"And what was that?" Arlene smiled, pen poised in midair. Lance met her eyes, smiling despite himself as he shook his head.

"Why Miss Sinclair, I thought you were over at the High School."

"All done. Besides, would I want to miss the fun here?" She pursed red lips and raised her brows. "So? What did the Mayor say?"

"The Mayor didn't' say anything," grumbled Jester Riley. "He sent the Deputy Mayor out to do his dirty work."

"The issue will be addressed at the Town Council meeting tomorrow night." Lance relieved Jester of a homemade sign. "Look, I think that stop light is needed as much as any of you, but we're not going to solve it out here this afternoon. Let's see what the Mayor says tomorrow night."

Arlene scooped up a discarded sign leaning against the old elm in front of Town Hall. "Well, I'll get Marty over at the paper to take a nice photo of this, and make sure the Gazette let's everyone know about this meeting."

"About time the Mayor started listening to us." Jester grinned. "Knew we could count on you, Miss Arlene."

Lance chuckled. "Yes sir, we can always count on her to stir the pot."

Four

Council met the third Tuesday of each month in the old Town Hall. Tonight the place was packed. Miss Winston, looking prim and neat in her blue shirtwaist dress, took a seat beside Arlene in the front row. Chairs were quickly filling as the eight-clock meeting time approached.

The Mayor sat at the dais, decked out in his signature white shirt, striped tie and black suspenders, studying the gathering with narrowed eyes. Councilman Hughes and Councilman Baker sat on either side of him.

Arlene glanced at the paper listing the order for the night's meeting. The decision to put a traffic light in front of the Corner Market would be first on the agenda. Arlene took note of who arrived. Miss Johnson, the town librarian, arrived with Jester Riley. Rumor had it the two were dating. Arlene's parents, Caroline and Clint Sinclair, arrived just as the mayor called the meeting to order. Arlene's brow furrowed as Jack slid onto the chair beside her.

"Now, Arlene, don't get your knickers in a twist. You do the reporting, I'm just your cameraman tonight." Jack offered a winning smile and laid the camera on his lap. Leaning close, he whispered, "I bet the mayor will veto it again."

Arlene nodded mute agreement.

"All right folks," the Mayor said. "Let's get this out of the way. The first item on the agenda is whether or not to put a traffic light in front of the Corner Market."

Miss Winston stood, placing the glasses that hung on a chain around her neck on her nose and peering solemnly at the Council table. "Mr. Mayor, we have been over and over the issues regarding that traffic light for months. What else is there to say? We need a traffic light. What do you intend to do about it?"

"Absolutely right." Jester spoke up. "What's your problem?"

"The problem is spending unnecessary money. The town budget simply won't allow this kind of expense. The sheriff can assign a man there."

Arlene raised her hand. "Mr. Mayor, I have here a copy of the budget. It seems there's enough money to hire a temporary deputy and install a traffic light."

The Mayor cleared his throat. "There are upcoming expenditures not listed there, Miss Sinclair. I can understand how ya'll feel, but right now there are other things to consider."

Someone hollered from the back of the room. "Why are we paying taxes? Where is the money going?"

"This town has a lot of expenses ya'll know nothing about." The Mayor's face reddened. "And I am telling you right now, the answer is for the Sheriff to provide a deputy at that crossing."

~

Sheriff Lance Carter braced against the rear wall, watching the exchange as both sheriff and interested citizen. He had every reason to believe from the previous day's picketing that this meeting could get ugly if the Mayor didn't step up with some solutions.

One of his men? The Mayor's statement brought him up short. He shook his head. That solution to the traffic light problem wasn't even an option. With Dusty in Korea, he didn't have any men to spare. The Mayor thought he could order the police department around like game pieces. Well, he'd fix that little fantasy. He raised his hand. "Excuse me, Mr. Mayor? That won't work. With Dusty overseas, I'm already down one deputy. I have no men to spare."

"And, I told you to replace Deputy Sinclair."

"Can't do that, Mayor. I promised Deputy Sinclair he'd have a job when he got home."

The Mayor glared at Lance. "You'll have to find a way to make it work, Sheriff. I don't really care how you do it."

"Then I'll be needing payroll to hire a temporary man to fill in until Sinclair returns." Lance grinned. He rather enjoyed watching the Mayor squirm. "And as I recall you told me you didn't have the budget for that. So it appears we have an impasse here, Mayor. No money. No manpower."

"We'll see about that."

"My answer will still be the same."

"This is over, people. We cannot afford a traffic light." Mayor Harvey glowered at the room. "Now let's move on, shall we?"

Arlene raised her hand again. "Why is it you don't want to put a traffic light on Main Street? That would certainly seem a much preferable solution than tying up Sheriff Carter's men." A chorus of approval rose from the crowd.

The Mayor slammed the gavel down on the table.

"Order, order! We're not going to accomplish anything tonight if ya'll don't settle down and listen."

"Mr. Mayor, if I may?" offered a calm, well modulated voice.

"We recognize Deputy Mayor Richardson. Go ahead, Frank."

"Thank you, Mr. Mayor. Now, I realize I came in a little late, folks, but it seems to me there has to be some willingness on your part to consider the Mayor's generous offer of having that crossing manned by a deputy."

Lance rubbed his forehead. How many ways were there to say no?

~

"No disrespect, Mr. Deputy Mayor," Arlene offered quietly, "but I believe it is the Mayor and Council who are not showing any willingness to consider what this town wants and needs."

Councilman Hughes shook his head and leaned forward. "I wouldn't throw all of Council into that statement, Miss Sinclair. I want a light there as much as anyone. My son nearly got hit by a pickup last week. Scared the Missus half out of her mind. I just don't see how we can do it if the Mayor says there aren't any funds."

"Then this is really just a waste of time, Councilman. The Mayor doesn't seem to be willing to hear your concerns anymore than ours."

Mayor Harvey lurched to his feet, knuckles pressed against the table, face red with frustration. "That is quite enough, Miss Sinclair. I surely don't need you trying to turn Council against me. This matter is closed."

"It sure as hell ain't!" Jester knocked over his chair in his haste, and Arlene motioned to Jack as she swung around to face the livid man. Lance was already at Jester's side, trying to restrain him, his voice soft but commanding.

"That's enough, Jester. Don't do something you'll regret come mornin'."

"He's gonna wait till someone gets killed. There's more and more traffic on the State Route. Who's it gonna take, Harvey? Miss Johnson? Lyle Hughes' boy?" He looked around the room, wild eyed. "How about Joe? With his bum knee, you think he can keep dodging cars?" He balled his fists and lunged forward. "Who's gonna have to get hurt before you listen to us?"

"Got it," Jack crowed as Lance caught Jester's arm in time to prevent a punch from connecting with the Mayor's face.

Arlene nodded with satisfaction. This night might not be a total waste after all.

~

The lights in <u>The Fin and Claw</u> were kept low. To set the mood they said. The far end of the bar, shaded by a wall covered with memorabilia and old license plates, was especially dim and tonight that suited Lester Harvey just fine.

He tossed back his scotch and soda and slammed the glass down beside the previous three. Things were a damn mess. He rubbed his shoulder. Good thing Lance had stepped in or that punch of Jester's might have connected with his face instead of just grazing his shoulder.

"Jake, gimme another one." He folded his arms on the bar top and traced designs in the water rings left by his glass.

"I think this is enough for tonight, Mayor." Jake set the glass in front of him, collected the other glasses in one hand and wiped the bar. "Y'know Miss Lizzie isn't going to be happy if you come home drunk again."

"Well now, my wife ain't here, now is she? So just gimme a drink and stay outta my way," Lester growled, leaned over the bar and snatched the bottle of scotch from underneath. "Maybe I don't wanna go home right now anyway."

"Fine. You don't want to head on home, that's your business. But this is the last one. I'm warning you."

Lester Harvey glared at the bar owner sullenly as Jake walked away. This whole mess was that Sinclair's doing. Always stirring up trouble. Always snooping into things where she had no business. *Gonna have to watch my back with Sinclair nosing around.* He drained his glass and refilled it, sloshing scotch on the bar, then drained it again. *Dang reporter is like a dog with a bone. I gotta do something about that stoplight so she'll drop this.*

"That's enough, Mayor." Jake reached for the bottle and Harvey slapped his hand away.

"I said I ain't done," he muttered, his words slurred. He dragged a handful of bills from his pocket and tossed them on the counter. "Now, I done paid you, Jake. Lemme be."

The bartender shook his head. "That's enough. You want me to call your wife to come fetch you home?"

Heat rose in Mayor Harvey's face and he stumbled unsteadily to his feet and leaned across toward Jake. "I tol' you I'm not done," he yelled.

Jake nodded. "I'll have the Sheriff take you somewhere to sleep it off then."

~

Lance nodded to Jake as he entered the bar, wrinkling his nose in disgust as he made his way toward the Mayor. Lester Harvey was half sprawled against the bar, a half empty glass in one hand and an empty bottle in the other.

"Time to go, Mayor."

"Get yer hands off me," Harvey protested, obviously too drunk to even recognize the Sheriff. "I tol' ya, I ain't going no where."

With a heavy sigh, Lance caught the Mayor by the back of the shirt and lifted him bodily to his feet, steering him toward the door.

"Thanks, Sheriff," Jake called as they stepped out into the cool night air.

Lance pushed the Mayor's head down and dumped him into the back of the cruiser. "You know, Mayor, I ought to throw you in a cell to dry out overnight. Maybe that would cool you off." He slid into the front and grinned as he closed the door. "But I'm not. I figure Mrs. Harvey will have her own ways of doing that." Lance glanced in the rearview mirror at the Mayor, now passed out and drooling against the door. "I sure wouldn't want to be you come morning."

Five

Lance scrubbed a weary hand across his face and dropped to sit on his sofa. He glanced at the mail on the coffee table, but couldn't find the energy to bother to reach for it. Darn, he was tired. He stretched long legs out before him and let his eyes close and head drop back.

The phone rang.

Lance pried one eye open and glowered at it.

It rang again.

Go away. I'm too tired to care.

Third ring. *Might be the station.* With a heavy sigh, Lance snatched the phone up. "Hello."

"Lance?"

The sound of Arlene's voice brought Lance bolt upright. He cleared his throat to keep the sound of his fool grin out of his voice. "Arlene? Something I can do for you?"

"What's this about you arresting the Mayor for drunk and disorderly over to *The Fin and Claw*?"

Lance shook his head and chuckled. News traveled fast in a small place like Sunny Hills. "Well, that's not exactly what happened. Is this personal curiosity or a professional call, Miss Sinclair?"

It was Arlene's turn to chuckle. The sound of her laughter sent tingles across Lance's skin. "I suppose the newshound wins out this time, Sheriff." There was a pause and Lance would have sworn he could feel her smiling right through that phone. "So? What did happen with the Mayor?"

"I didn't arrest him, much as he deserved it. But drunk? Heck yeah, he was drunk."

"Suppose something at that meeting struck home with our dear Mayor?"

"I don't think I can speculate on that, Miss Sinclair." Lance settled back on the couch, the receiver cradled between his cheek and shoulder. "Off the record? Seems awfully coincidental, doesn't it?"

"Sure does. Okay, thanks Lance. I appreciate your talking to me."

Her honeyed voice could make a man melt, Lance thought. "My pleasure, Arlene. Good night."

"Night, Lance. Sweet dreams."

He sighed and gently returned the phone to its cradle. Any dream about Arlene was bound to be sweet.

~

Morning came far too early, and Lance observed the sleepy morning rituals of his hometown as he drove to the station. Hank Greeley was opening the barbershop, dusting the bench that sat out front, opening the red and white striped awning. He waved a friendly greeting. Across the street, Gary was helping Joe set out signs and open the market for the morning. The kid looked up and grinned as Lance drove past.

Well, at least this is working out. The mess with getting the light up at the intersection, coupled with Mayor Harvey's little drinking spree, weighed on Lance's mind. Lance felt a certain reassurance things in Sunny Hills would sort themselves out soon enough just seeing how well the result of young Gary's run in with the law worked out for all concerned.

~

"Take it lunch didn't go well, Sheriff?" Debbie asked as Lance stormed past her desk toward his office.

"Can't even eat around here without folks expecting me to have all the answers," he grumbled.

"Now you knew everyone round here is gonna want to know about the Mayor and all."

"Why don't they ask him?" Shaking his head, Lance gave her a half-hearted grin and sighed wearily. "No phone calls for awhile, Deb, okay? Don't care who it is, not even my own mother. I'm *not* here."

"Gottcha." She flashed a bright smile.

Lance turned back at the door to his office. "No one. Right? Only if it's an emergency and that does *not* include Miss Winston's cat."

"I got it, boss. I'll get Randy to handle the usual little odds and ends."

"Thanks, Debbie." Lance eased the door to his office closed. He rubbed the bridge of his nose as he slid onto the chair behind his desk. He needed to finish a couple of reports. Call over to the park and check on the work Gary was doing over there. Check and see if Perkin's had found the last of his cows that had gotten loose two days ago. Anything but answer more questions about the Mayor.

His police academy diploma hung across from his desk. Lance stared at the bright embossed seal, the neat lettering. He'd always loved this job. And when Sheriff Grant retired, it had just seemed natural to step up and take the position.

Of course, things were quieter then. But it still was a good town. *My town.* This current little batch of annoyances not-withstanding, Lance loved his work. He couldn't blame folks for getting riled up about things. Most lived here their whole lives. Heck, the Mayor drinking was big news in a town where Miss Winston's cat and Frank Perkin's cow were the usual highlight of law-enforcement discussions. Lance chuckled.

With a sigh, he shoved at the hair falling into his eyes, and opened a folder.

The buzzer on Lance's desk chirruped insistently and he slammed the folder closed and glared at the interruption. He reached for the button to see what Debbie wanted just as the sound of raised voices filtered through the office door.

"Now, you can't go in there. I'm telling you, the Sheriff is busy and is not to be disturbed."

Lance swung open the door and nearly ran into Debbie's wheelchair blocking the doorway. His deputy, Randy Taylor, bounced like terrier dog in front of Henrietta Winston who tried to slip around him.

"About time, Lancelot," Miss Winston snapped. "Now you tell these two to get out of my way. I am law-abiding citizen and I have a right to speak with the man entrusted with the care and protection of our town." She raised her head, peering at Randy down the bridge of her nose.

"It's all right, Randy. Thanks, Debbie. Hold my calls." Lance stepped to the side, holding his door open. "Come on in, Miss Winston. I'm kinda busy today, but I am sure I can fit in a couple of minutes for you." He closed the door behind her as she strode primly to the wooden chair in front of his desk. "Want to tell me what's so important?"

Hands clutching her straw purse in her lap, Miss Winston waited until Lance took a seat on the front corner of his desk before speaking. "I want to know what is happening with that Gary Jones."

"He's doing fine. Working hard. He gets to work on time at Ellie's and he's going clean up and landscaping over to the park. I think he's learned his lesson."

The daisy on her small straw hat bobbed enthusiastically as she nodded. "That's good to hear, Lancelot."

Lance grimaced. He hated her calling him by that name.

"Anything else I can do for you?"

"Well, certainly I didn't come all this way just for that, you know. I want to know what's to be done about Mayor Harvey. Will you be going over to Hilton Falls to bring him back here? If he's going to locked up here in town, well you know how folks will talk--"

"Beg your pardon, Miss Winston." Lance frowned. "What's this about Hilton Falls? Why would the Mayor be locked up? He didn't commit any crime last night, just got a little out of hand is all."

"A little out of hand," she snorted derisively. "Dang old fool ought to know better than to be out drinking and causing problems. Serves him right, having to spend the night over there in the jail and all."

"Jail?" Lance asked incredulously. "Are you sure, Miss Winston?"

"I assure you, Sheriff, I haven't lost my senses. He's sitting in a cell over to Hilton Falls jail right now. His dear wife refused to bail him out and I think she made a wise decision.

"Now, what do you have to say about this sorry turn of events?"

Lance slid to his feet, puzzling over the new information. "I can't rightly comment on anything, Miss Winston. I'll have to check this out with Sheriff Canton over at Hilton Falls. But I thank you for the information."

He moved to the door and held it open for her.

Miss Winston nodded curtly as she exited, nearly bumping shoulders with Arlene who smiled winningly as she slipped past Lance into the office.

Lance's confused and pleading gaze darted from Arlene to Debbie, who grinned and shrugged. With a sigh, Lance closed the door and followed Arlene inside.

"You trying to avoid your constituents, Sheriff?" Arlene asked with an impish smile. "Debbie told me you weren't seeing anyone."

"Well, no, not exactly," he stammered. "I surely didn't mean you." Every time he thought he had his thoughts and feelings about her under control, there she was again, looking pretty as a picture and jangling every nerve. He took a steadying breath and perched on the corner of his desk across from her as she took a seat. "What can I do for you, Arlene?"

She adjusted her jacket, smoothed her skirt, and met his eyes directly. "I'll get right to the point."

"You always do." The words were out of his mouth before he could stop them.

Arlene arched a brow. "And just what do you mean by that, Sheriff?"

Nothing could ever be easy with Arlene, could it? Lance smiled. "Nothing. Just that you're very direct. You don't waste time with fake politeness or beating around the bush. Just get right to the matter at hand." He cleared his throat. "Folks pretty much know where they stand with you, don't they?"

Now it was Arlene's turn to look strangely flustered. Her cheeks flushed slightly and she folded her hands in her lap. "Well then, I'll take that as a compliment. Thank you. As I was saying, let's get right to the point. I need a quote from you for the Gazette on the situation with the Mayor. I hear he's locked up over in Hilton Falls."

"I wouldn't know, Miss Sinclair."

"Wouldn't know what, Sheriff?"

"Whether he is or not. I can't seem to find time to call and check on the situation." He grinned. "So many folks stopping in to talk to me this afternoon I haven't had a chance to get much work done in that respect."

"I see." Her lips curved. "Well then, I should leave you to your work, Sheriff. I'll just call back say...end of the day...and see what you found out." She rose to leave.

"Arlene? Have you heard anything from Dusty? I haven't gotten a letter in, well, quite a while."

"No, no it's been weeks. I know my folks are getting a little worried."

"Well, I'm sure there's a good reason he hasn't gotten any letters through. I'll be glad when he's home." He moved to hold the door for her. "I could sure use him back around here about now."

"I'm sure you're right about that." Her hand brushed over his where he held the doorknob. "I'll be calling back."

The lingering scent of her perfume surrounded him in a heart-racing embrace. *Why is it we always want what we can't have and surely don't need?* He drew a deep breath and walked out to the front desk. "Deb, would you call over to Hilton Falls and check to see if the good Mayor really is locked up there? I'm going out for a spell. Maybe I'll drive out to Perkin's and see if he found all those dern cows."

"Sure thing, Sheriff. I'll let Randy know."

Six

Lance leaned against the hood of the car and stared across the park. Situated where it was on the outskirts of town, the park offered a haven of solitude for his frayed nerves.

Fat, fluffy clouds edged in charcoal promised rain come nightfall. Two squirrels chased across the neatly mowed expanse of lawn and disappeared in the heavy foliage of an old oak tree.

Lance looked around at newly mulched and planted landscaping. The playground looked great, neatly trimmed and decked out in a bright coat of red pinestraw. *Looking good. Gary's been working hard.*

"Sheriff?" The radio crackled to life and Lance straightened with a grimace.

Not even an hour to myself. Shaking his head, he leaned through the driver's side window and fished out the radio handset. "Yeah, this is Carter. What's up, Randy?"

"Dang, Sheriff, you aren't gonna believe it." Randy's voice rose, edged with a nervousness out of keeping with his usual quiet demeanor.

Lance felt his stomach dissolve into a thousand butterflies. "What Randy?"

"We got something going on over to Jonas' gas station. Clint Sinclair just came rushing in here. He says he thinks maybe the station is being robbed."

Lance swallowed hard, his mind racing. "Anyone call over to the station?"

"Yes sir. I tried. There's no answer."

"Okay, I'm at the park. I'll meet you out back of the station. You wait for me, Randy, you hear?"

"Will do, Sheriff."

Lance tossed the handset onto the seat, opened the door and slid in. "Damn." The engine roared to life, wheels spinning gravel as Lance roared out of the parking lot.

~

Not one robbery in ten years. Not one. Now this. Lance slammed his fist against the steering wheel, drove down the rising anger burning through him, and motioned to his deputy as he got out of the car.

"Hey, Lance," Randy whispered edging over to the car. "Nothing seems to be going on here."

"Well, we won't know till we get inside." Lance drew his service revolver and nodded to Randy. His deputy's face paled as he carefully drew his own weapon. It occurred to Lance Randy Taylor had probably never been faced with the possibility of using his gun before. "You take the back here." Lance jerked his head toward the station. "I'll go on around front, meet you inside. Keep an eye out for Jonas."

Randy nodded and edged toward the white-washed rear of the big old concrete block building.

Lance hurried around the outside toward the front. Jonas' old Ford pickup was under the tree on the side. There were no cars at the pumps. None parked in front. He recognized Jester's red Studebaker sitting to the far side near the service bay. *I told Jester he needed a new muffler.*

Otherwise it sure seemed quiet. *Too quiet.* Where the devil was Jonas? Lance eased the door open and slipped inside. His boots clicked across the hardwood floor. Stopping just past the front desk, he checked the alarm. If something had gone wrong, surely Jonas would have hit the alarm.

Cut wires. Neatly snipped, and no sign of Jonas. Lance had a bad feeling in his gut. He passed through the front and checked the small office to one side. *Empty.* The water cooler gurgled, causing him to jump. Lance caught a deep breath and walked toward the service area. The station smelled of oil, grease, and gasoline and had the usual well-organized clutter that marked Jonas' place.

Randy poked his head in from the rear, eyes wide as he met Lance's gaze. "Anything?"

Lance shook his head. This wasn't like Jonas at all; the man practically lived in this station. He wouldn't just leave it open and no one to take care of things.

A sound, a faint screeching noise, like nails against a black board, caught Lance's attention. He nodded to Randy to be ready then moved toward the small supply closet at the rear of the station. The squeaking noise repeated. Lance caught the handle and jerked the door open.

Jonas tumbled out, hands tied behind his back and a strip of silver duct tape covering his mouth. He made frantic efforts to yell, his voice unintelligible and all but inaudible as it was muffled by the makeshift gag. Rolling over, he stared up at Randy and Lance with obvious relief and quit struggling.

Lance holstered his gun, caught Jonas by the arm and helped him to sit up, then yanked the tape free, which elicited a yelp from Jonas who rubbed his hand across his mouth and cheeks.

"Dang, Sheriff, took you long enough to get here."

"You okay, Jonas?"

He nodded, scooting around sideways so Randy could untie him. Rubbing his wrists, he squinted at the two of them. "Don't suppose you caught him, did you?"

"Nope. Didn't see anyone at all. Sorry," Randy replied.

"Any idea who did this?" Lance asked.

"Nope. Things were real quiet this afternoon, finished up the work on Miss Sinclair's car, all we had left was the Studebaker, so Bill went on over to the diner to get us something to eat. Today is Miss Ellie's special on meatloaf, you know." Jonas pulled a greasy hanky from his hip pocket and wiped his hands. "Anyway, Bill went on, and next thing I know this happens." He frowned at Lance. "How'd you know anything was going on, anyway? I didn't hear the alarm go off."

"It didn't." Lance leaned against the wall, arms folded across his chest. "The wires are cut. Whoever it was, he's no amateur."

"You've got Clint Sinclair to thank for getting us here," Randy added. "He stopped for gas and something didn't look right. So he called the station."

"I'll sure have to thank him for that one." Jonas grinned ruefully.

"So what happened, Jonas?" Lance asked.

"Like I said, Bill went to get us some supper. Miss Sinclair had just left with her car--"

Lance stiffened. "Arlene was here? Are you sure she left before this happened?"

"Yep, I'm for certain on that, Sheriff. I saw her drive off myself, then I headed for the office to put the money away and somebody grabbed me."

"Did you get a look at the guy?"

"Nope. He had on this mask. Like one of them cartoon characters. That rabbit--Bugs Bunny. Like I said, he grabbed me, then he emptied the register and brought me back here."

A voice called from the door. "What's going on? Jonas?" Bill Jenkins poked his head around the doorway. "Sheriff? What in blazes is going on here?"

"Howdy, Bill. Station got robbed it looks like."

"Robbed?" Bill motioned to the bag he held cradled in his arms. "I just went to get supper. Tarnation, Jonas. You all right?"

"Yeah." He climbed to his feet and hitched his thumbs in the pockets of his overalls. "Just my dignity bruised a little. Robbed by a dang rabbit."

~

Caroline Sinclair put the coffee on to perk, took the warm apple pie from the cooling rack and set it on the counter. Clint looked up from reading his sports section of the paper and winked at her as she pulled out a chair and took a seat across from him.

"Want to read about the Sunny Hills Nuggets? Looks like the high school has a good team this year."

Caroline smiled and shook her head. "Just isn't quite as much fun for me since Dusty graduated. Thanks all the same, dear." She chuckled to herself and carefully selected the section she wanted from Clint's neat stack. Flipping it open she let her finger travel down the page in search of the correct horoscopes. Caroline skimmed her own; nothing there came as much of surprise. *Aquarius.* That was Clint and Dusty's sign.

This is an expansive day, and pretty much anything is possible. This air of opportunity will encourage bad things to happen just as much as it will encourage good things to happen, keep that fact uppermost in mind today. It's a day to carefully balance your cautious side with your more adventurous side. There will be consequences to whatever you choose to do, so make sure you choose to do something that is good for you -- both emotionally and physically.

Now what could that mean? *Bad as well as good. Well, certainly. It is a war after all.* Caroline clicked her long nails against each other in a nervous rhythm. Clint looked up at her over the top of his paper and Caroline pursed her lips and quickly flipped the page.

Her family just never understood the influence such things could have on a life. *What's this?* Her brows lifted as she read the brief editorial. "My goodness," she murmured under her breath. "Isn't this going to get interesting?" Carefully she folded the section and laid it in front of the chair beside her.

"That would be Arlene," she exclaimed with a bright smile. Clint looked up with a puzzled frown just as the doorbell rang.

Arlene hung her coat in the hall closet, then turned and gave her mother a hug before she followed her to the kitchen.

"Hi, Dad." Arlene gave Clint a peck on top of the head.

"Sit right here, dear," Caroline directed, pulling out a chair for her daughter. She tapped the folded newspaper. "Why don't you have a look at this while I get the pie and coffee?"

Caroline opened the paper and turned the page. Her accusing gaze lifted to her mother. "Momma, you been reading horoscopes again?"

Caroline heaved a sigh and flipped the page. "No. This." She pointed to the column "Henrietta Hears".

"What about it?" Arlene rolled her eyes, and looked knowingly at her father. "Momma, it's gossip."

"Just read it." Caroline pushed the paper back at Arlene. "Miss Henrietta is getting some licks in here."

"What's it say?" Clint leaned forward, shoving his sports section aside.

Caroline went to the stove and prepared the coffee and pie while Arlene read aloud.

"It's Miss Winston's gossip column, Daddy. *'Dear Sunny Hills, It is no secret that your Miss Henrietta has little patience with some of our local politicians. When we vote a particular person into office it is with the clear understanding that they are there to serve Sunny Hills and its wonderful residents and to represent us to the highest standards. Some people are not well suited to this task.*

What does Henrietta hear? Our Mayor has made quite a spectacle of himself of late. Drinking, and to excess. Getting himself thrown into the Hilton Falls jail.

Is this the image we seek for our beloved town? A drunk and a ruffian? I think not. Do we really want somebody with a beer in one hand and a gavel in the other making decisions for us? Or, as in the case of the much needed stop light here in town, perhaps he is incapable of making the correct decisions. Whatever our illustrious Mayor is up to, Sunny Hills deserves better than this.

What will our local politicians be up to next? We'll be keeping an eye on them all. Until next time, ya'll keep talking. Henrietta hears.'" Arlene took a deep breath and tried to hide her smile.

Clint nodded enthusiastically. "Now everyone knows there's no love lost between Miss Henrietta and Lester Harvey, but she got him dead to rights this time. Won't be a soul between here and the county seat who won't know about this by the end of the week."

"You know Miss Winston drives me to distraction sometimes," Arlene said. "But this is a fine editorial. And she got it right on the nose about him being up to no good. I know he's doing something underhanded, I just don't know what." She picked up her fork, grinning mischievously at her parents. "Yet."

~

"Sheriff?" Randy poked his head around the door to Lance's office.

Lance looked up from his pacing. "Got something on the robbery?"

"Yes sir." Randy draped himself across the empty chair. "Not sure what to make of it just yet, but it looks like that old rascally rabbit mighta been a little nervous before he robbed Jonas."

Lance dropped down to sit behind his desk, leaning eagerly toward his deputy. "What makes you say that?"

"We found an empty cigarette pack and a bunch of butts where it looks like someone was waiting over to the side near Jonas' truck. Jonas doesn't smoke and he doesn't like having it around the station much, and besides I've never seen this brand around here anywhere."

Lance felt his first flicker of hopefulness. "What is it?"

"Oasis. You ever heard of 'em?"

"Not rightly." Lance thought about it for a moment. "Yeah, seems to me I saw an ad for them once, but you're right no one around here carries them. That just might be something, Randy. Good job. Anything else?"

"Well..." Randy hesitated, hunched his shoulders and dropped his gaze. "Might not be anything...but, well, Jonas says where we found the butts and all...it's right over where he had Miss Arlene's car parked after he finished up on it."

"Shit." Lance bolted upright. He rubbed his chin. "You check and see where the closest places are that sell that brand. I'm going to find Arlene."

Seven

Lance dialed Arlene's number and let it ring. No answer. He slammed his fist against the desk. *Where is she? Think, Lance. She picked up the car less than two hours ago.* Sudden realization flooded through him, a welcome warmth chasing away the icy fingers of dread. He grabbed his keys and raced out the door.

"Sheriff?" Debbie called after him. "Where'll you be if we need you?"

"Call." Lance waved and kept walking.

~

"Arlene?" Clint Sinclair rubbed the back of his neck as he came into the kitchen.

Arlene finished drying the last dessert plate and hung the dish towel to dry. "What?"

"Lance is at the door, he wants to talk with you."

Her father's sly smile did not escape her notice. Arlene shook her head and wiped her hands on her apron as she untied it. "Well, I suppose I should go see what brought the Sheriff over, shouldn't I?"

"There's still pie left," Caroline called in her lilting voice. "If you'd like to invite him in..."

"Thanks, Momma. I'll be sure to let him know you asked." Arlene opened the front door, glanced back over her shoulder at her parents' smiling faces, and closed the door behind her. "Lance, nice to see you this evening."

"Glad to see you too, Arlene." He nodded briskly, cleared his throat, and jerked his head toward the driveway. "You just picked the car up over at Jonas' station?"

Curious question. Her nose for news began to twitch. "Yes, I did. So I take it this isn't a social call?"

Lance fidgeted and cleared his throat again. "Much as I wish it were, not...well, not entirely. Jonas' station was robbed just after you left this afternoon. I'd like to speak with you--"

"Robbed? Is Jonas all right?" Her hand clutched his arm, and she felt the heat rising in her cheeks at the sensation of taut muscles flexing beneath her touch. Arlene pulled her hand away and motioned to the door. "Do you want to come in?"

"No. Well, not till we've finished anyway. If you don't mind..." Lance pushed his hand through his thick hair and glanced toward her car. "Jonas is fine, wasn't hurt at all just a little spooked. But I guess you can tell I'm not real pleased at having something like this happen in Sunny Hills." He clenched his fists, drew a deep breath and visibly relaxed. "Did you happen to notice anything when you were there?"

Arlene thought for a moment, then shook her head. "No, I'm sorry, Lance. Everything seemed just the same as always."

"Car running good now?" Lance stepped back off the porch. "Mind if I have a look?"

"Yeah." Arlene's eyes narrowed slightly. "Car's fine. Jonas and Bill always do a good job."

"Yeah, that's good." Lance nodded nonchalantly and strolled toward the driveway.

A hundred little warnings bells sounded in Arlene's head and she felt the familiar tingle. *Oh yes, there's a story here. Something besides the robbery. What about my car?* She paused in mid-stride, a niggling thought occurring to her. "The...the car smelled funny though."

Lance looked up and the little detail suddenly seemed very silly. "What?" He opened the front passenger door and peeked inside.

"It smelled odd. Kinda like...smoky. But you know Jonas doesn't smoke and Bill never does when they're at the station. It just seemed...nothing," she finished lamely and shrugged. "Odd is all. And since you're asking so many questions, Sheriff Carter, could I know why? What's the robbery got to do with my car?"

Lance poked his head inside and sniffed loudly, then ducked back out and turned to face her. "It's nothing, Arlene. The robbery happened right after you picked up your car is all. Just checking things out." He offered a crooked smile. "Doing my job." He closed the front then opened the rear door. "You're right, does smell like cigarettes." He leaned into the back and she saw him touch the floor mats, then reach in and slowly withdraw. "Was this to help cover the smell?" He held out a long-stemmed rose, red as blood, petals open wide.

Arlene's brows inched upward and her gaze darted from the rose, to Lance's twinkling eyes, and back. She reached out and took the flower. "What is this doing in there?"

"You don't know?"

"No, of course not. I haven't even looked in the back today. I just picked up the car and drove right over here to have coffee. Now I wonder how this got in there."

"Maybe you have a secret admirer?" The tone of Lance's voice matched the spark she'd seen in his eyes.

Arlene felt the blush creeping across her cheeks again. "I have no idea what you mean, Sheriff. I'm sure it was just a mistake. Maybe poor Jonas intended it for Mitzy, and just dropped it when he was working on the car." She lifted her chin. "I'll just take it right back over to him."

"He's gone home for the day." Lance smiled, but she could see something hidden in his eyes. He was worried.

Arlene sobered. "Do you have any idea who robbed them?"

Lance shook his head. "Not yet. Wish Dusty was here, he has a nose for clues." He raked his fingers through his hair. "Guess that's something he has in common with his sister."

With a smile, Arlene pushed the car door closed. "C'mon in, Lance. Momma will be insulted if you pass up her fresh baked pie."

~

Kent's fingers closed on the edge of the rust-brown curtains. He glared across the run-down inner courtyard to the neon "Shady Grove Motel" sign loudly proclaiming vacancies. No doubt there were always vacancies in a seedy joint like this.

In the middle of the unkempt lawn a ribbon of huge, overgrown rose bushes blanketed in the last blooms of autumn surrounded a lone oak tree. *Yeah, real shady.* Kent yanked the curtains closed, ground out the butt of his cigarette, and backed up to sit on the edge of the bed.

Opening the drawer on the nightstand, he shoved the grinning cartoon mask into the back behind the Gideon's Bible. He'd been real lucky to find that kids' mask in the trash when they cleaned out this room. It worked fine.

Kent pulled the wad of dollars from his pocket and counted through it quickly. Wasn't a lot, but it would keep him in cigarettes and beer for a few days.

He'd almost decided not to risk taking the money. Just get in the back of the car---let things take their course. *Damn. And she sure was pretty--*

A sharp knock on the door brought him to his feet. He tucked the gun into the back waist of his pants, checked the chain on the door and eased it open a crack.

The desk clerk, belly rolling over the top of his jeans and suspenders stretched almost to the breaking point, rubbed sweat from his forehead and glared at him through the narrow opening. "Thursday. You gonna be stayin' any longer, we need next week's money."

Kent peeled off a bill and shoved it into the man's pudgy hand. "That ought to cover a couple of weeks." He slammed the door and dropped back down on the bed. There were plans to be made, and he needed to think things through.

Not that I didn't have plenty of time to think about this in the pen. All those years, mopping floors and eating swill. Things had changed some around here in those years, though. <u>Sheriff</u> Lance Carter, for one. He'd been nothing but a gopher-deputy last time Kent had seen him. Not now. *Yeah, I'm gonna have to be real careful getting my revenge. Real careful.*

He could walk into town come dark. He still needed a car. And he had a few more plans for the evening.

Kent lit a cigarette and smiled.

~

Gary looked around the diner and wiped his hands on the towel. Lights went out in small groups as Miss Ellie threw the switches in back.

"All done out here, Miss Ellie," he called, tossing the towel into the laundry bin. He sighed and stared out at the darkened street.

Everything changed when he came to Sunny Hills. *And nothing. Not any closer to finding out than when I came.*

Ellie's voice broke into his reflections. "Ya'll ready to go, Gary?"

He looked up quickly and nodded. "Yes ma'am. Got tonight's receipts and ledger done for you too." Gary lowered his head shyly. "I'm pretty good at numbers."

"Pretty good?" Ellie chuckled. "Boy, you are a flat out whiz. It woulda taken me another hour."

"Glad to help. I'd better get back to the store. I think Mr. Monroe has a few more crates I need to unpack tonight. I'll see you in the morning, first thing, though."

Ellie pursed her lips, eyeing him narrowly. Gary squirmed. It always made him nervous when she looked at him that way. It was such a "mom look".

"Are you sure you're getting enough rest? Working here mornings and nights both. Helping Joe at the store. And you still have to do community service at the park."

"Yes, ma'am. Just a few more weeks, though." He crammed his hands in his pockets. "And I don't mind. I appreciate everything ya'll have done for me."

"C'mon then. I'll give you a ride home to the store. But you promise me, if it gets too much, you let me know. We'll work something out. Okay?"

She put her arm around his shoulders and gave him a quick squeeze that drove away some of the lonely, helpless feelings. These were nice people: Miss Ellie, Mr. Joe, the Sheriff. Nice people. Maybe if he asked...maybe they could...

He pushed the thought aside. Not yet. He wasn't ready to share this yet. But maybe--maybe later.

~

Coco circled at the front door, whining. Arlene looked up from her book and sighed. "No, it's raining, Coco. Now lie down and let me finish Miss Marple."

The lab slunk across to the sofa and laid next to Arlene's feet, soft golden-brown eyes fixed on the door. Arlene reached down and scratched his ears, then tucked her bare feet under her and flipped the page.

Coco lifted his head and whimpered.

"Quiet, I'm getting to the best part. Now, shhh."

Outside the autumn rain thrummed a slow, steady beat against the roof. No downpour this time, no trembling thunder shaking the rafters, just a gentle, peaceful shower. Arlene snuggled deeper into the cushions and stifled an urge to yawn and let the story enfold her.

With a bark so fierce and unexpected Arlene dropped the book, Coco bolted for the door. Arlene leapt to her feet, trying to silence the thunderous pounding of her heart. Drawing a deep, settling breath, she strode to the door. "Fine," she said to the frantically circling dog. "You want to get wet for no reason, let's go."

Her hand froze on the doorknob, inexplicably reluctant to move forward. Another deep breath. *This is silly. It's just the book I'm reading and Coco being all weird about the rain. Now settle down."*

She pulled the door open with a determined confidence she didn't feel and watched as the big lab bounded outside. His nails clicked across the porch and he paused at the edge of the steps, hackles raised as he peered into the steady drizzle.

Arlene followed Coco to the rail and breathed deeply of the sweet scented breeze. The night air was crisp against her skin, sending shivers unbidden across her skin.

"Happy?" she asked as Coco looked up at her, slowly quieting. He made a low sound in his throat as he turned back to the steps, then brushed past her toward the door, tail slowly waving. "Great, then let's get inside and stop this foolishness."

She glanced down at a small bit of paper caught under the edge of the doormat. Reaching down, Arlene freed the torn scrap and held it up to the light.

"...your choice..."

A chill raced up her spine and Arlene glanced nervously back beyond the warmth of the porch lights into the dark night. Shaking her head, she shoved the strip into her pocket and opened the door.

"Come on, Coco. Nothing out here we need to see."

Eight

"You're that Gary boy Sheriff Carter sent to do community service, aren't you?" drawled the mayor.

Gary wiped his hands on his pants as he got to his feet. "Yes sir. Gary Jones. You're the mayor, aren't you? I saw you talking to the folks the other day outside the Town Hall. I was mulching some beds there." He smiled nervously.

"Well that's fine, Gary. Just fine." Mayor Harvey looked around the playground area. "You've done a good job here. How much of that mulch you got left?"

"About fifteen bags."

"Good. Good. I want you to load those up in the trunk of that car there while I go attend to some business." He motioned to a baby blue and white DeSoto parked at the curb. "You're going to be working off some of that service of yours over to my house for a bit. There are some community...functions...coming up and we'll need to have the area ready for my fine constituents." The mayor forced a smarmy smile. "You get to it now."

~

Arlene leaned on the glass counter top, letting one patent leather heel dangle loosely from her foot and swaying slightly to the music from the back room of the florist's shop. The small room, heavy laden with the perfume of roses, pinks, and lavender, contained an eclectic display of loose flowers in water vases, arrangements, ribbons, and other things.

"Mack? You get that for me?" called a deeply masculine male voice from the back as the door chime jangled.

Arlene smiled knowingly and turned to face Lance. "Why, Sheriff Carter. Fancy seeing you here. Come to pick something up?"

"Arlene," he acknowledged a bit breathlessly, then collected himself and leaned over the counter beside her to holler into the workroom. "Mack?" He glanced over to meet Arlene's gaze. "And no, I did not order any flowers."

"Of course you didn't," Arlene soothed in a honeyed voice dripping with sarcasm. "Big ol' man like you wouldn't be needing any little ol' flowers." She batted her eyelashes affectedly and giggled at the color rising in his cheeks.

"What brings you here?"

"Why Sheriff, I thought I was the reporter with all the questions." She slid her foot back into her pump and leaned back with her elbows propped atop the counter. "I wanted to see who might have ordered that lovely rose you found in my backseat."

"And?" Lance pulled off his hat and pushed his hair back roughly.

A sure sign I'm getting close to something, Arlene noted with satisfaction. "And it isn't one of Mack's."

Lance inclined his head, obviously waiting for the rest of the information.

"It's a homegrown one, cut right off someone's plant." She tried to avoid sounding smug. "And since it was still fresh hours later when we found it, that means..."

"Local." Lance released a deep breath. "Whoever it was, got it here." He managed a tight smile. "So, your secret admirer is a home-grown? Gonna tell me who it is now?"

Mack appeared from the back, arms laden with corsage boxes. "Sorry, Lance. Didn't hear ya come in. Homecoming game tonight at the high school, ya know. That means the dance is tomorrow night."

"Oh yeah, I know." Lance shook his head ruefully. "I'll be at the game, same as always. Just to keep an eye on things."

"Well, much as I love the business, I gotta tell ya, I'm always glad when homecoming is over." Mack smiled. "I was just telling Miss Arlene, that rose of hers--"

"Yeah, she told me. Thanks Mack." He exhaled slowly, lips tight and arms folded across his chest. "Stay out of this, Arlene. It could be dangerous."

"Me having a secret admirer?" She protested coyly, but her stomach tightened. *So that's not it at all. He thinks it might be connected to the robbery.*

A wistful half-smile curved on Lance's lips. "Yeah. Okay. I just...I wouldn't want to see anything happen to you," he finished with a whisper, then straightened and strode purposefully toward the door. "See you later, Miss Sinclair."

~

Clint planted a quick kiss on Caroline's cheek, then drained his coffee cup and set it in the sink. "All right, I'm gonna get on in to town. I'll be home for lunch."

"Clint?" Caroline wiped her hands on her apron and moved to the door. "Could you take Elm Street in today?"

His eyes narrowed. "Why would I want to do that, honey?"

She smiled tightly. "Oh, I just think it would be a nicer drive, you know."

"Caroline?" His voice deepened with accusation.

"Oh, all right. I was checking Dusty's horoscope this morning and, well, his is the same as yours you know--"

"You know I don't set any store in that nonsense."

She bit her lip and stepped between her husband and the door. "I know, Clint, but...I just have this terrible feeling something's going to happen up at that intersection on Main. And with Dusty being overseas and all..." She sniffled and dabbed at her eyes with the hem of her apron. "I just couldn't stand it if anything happened to you."

"Nothing's going to happen, honey." Clint gave her a swift hug. "You quit worrying. I'll be home for lunch. I'll bring you fudge from Bertie's." He winked and slipped past her and out the door.

"Elm Street!" she called to his back.

~

Kent took a deep drag on his cigarette, crushed the butt under his heel and released the smoke in a long breath that wreathed a plume of white before him. He shook another cigarette from the pack, then gently pushed it back with his thumb. He'd waited long enough.

Shoving the pack into the rolled sleeve of his t-shirt, Kent slid down the bank to the nearly vacant parking lot. The beat-up old blue pickup had been in this same spot for three days now. Whoever parked it probably got a bus at the depot across the street, he figured. The plates weren't local; no one would recognize it most likely.

Casting a final glance around the lot, Kent opened the door and slid behind the wheel. A minute to work a few wires, and the engine turned over with a cough. Kent threw it into gear and rumbled out onto the street headed back toward Sunny Hills.

"Now there's no place you can hide." He grinned at the thought. His quarry was getting closer all the time. It wouldn't be long now. Not long at all. And then he'd be out of that one horse town for good.

~

Clint's lips thinned as he approached the intersection with Elm Street. *Take Elm*, Caroline's voice echoed in his mind. He glanced at his watch and shook his head. He'd be late if he had to take Elm past the elementary school.

Foolishness. He ignored the turn onto Elm. "Dang you and your predictions, Caroline. It just isn't right."

It was a pleasant fall morning. Bright sunshine, crisp air, and everywhere signs and banners in preparation for the Sunny Hills High School homecoming celebration.

A gold and blue sign in a front yard proclaimed "Go NUGGETS!" and the number of the player who lived there. Ten.

That was Dusty's number. Dusty was one heck of a running back. Those were good days, Clint mused. God, how he missed that boy. Football games, teaching Arlene to drive. *Good days*.

And now... Dusty was a good soldier. *Any man would be proud to have a son like mine.* He just wanted him home again. Clint swallowed the lump in his throat.

A group of high-school kids, arms laden with books, hurried along the sidewalk. Letter jackets. Ponytails. Clint watched them with a mixture of nostalgia and frustration as he slowed for the stop sign approaching Main.

Talking and joking, the teenagers scarcely seemed to notice when they darted across the intersection in front of his car and then zipped across Main.

A loud honk startled him and Clint saw the group dance around the front of a big sedan as it screeched to a stop. The kids crossed and the sedan went on through the intersection.

Darn kids never even think they could get hurt.

He stepped on the gas and moved into the intersection, still watching the kids. A movement in front of the car caught his attention. *Joe!* Too late. Clint slammed on the brakes just before a shout, the impact, and his head whacking the windshield moved in slow motion through his awareness.

"Oh dear Lord." Clint's heart thudded. "Oh God, what have I done?" Clint threw the car into park and jumped out, nearly falling to his knees as he staggered to the front. "Joe! Joe, you all right?"

Joe groaned loudly, rolling onto his back. "I'm okay, I'm okay. Somethin's busted. Oh Lordy," he moaned.

"All right. I'm with you, buddy." Clint swiped at the blood on his forehead with his arm, and then closed his hand over Joe's.

The drone of sirens announced the arrival of a patrol car. Randy's familiar voice called orders. "Okay kids, get on to school. Come on." His hand fell reassuringly on Clint's shoulder. "Ambulance is on the way. Can you tell me what happened, Mr. Sinclair?"

Clint squeezed Joe's fingers tighter and shook his head. "Everyone was just moving through the intersection. You know the routine, they stop, you stop, they move, you move. God, I didn't even see him. I'm so sorry, Joe."

"It's okay," Randy assured, kneeling beside the injured man. "How you doing there, Mr. Monroe? It won't be long now."

"I'm okay." Joe grimaced, his face lined with pain.

"You just lay still, okay? We better get something on that cut of yours though, Mr. Sinclair. It's bleeding pretty good."

"I'm fine," Clint rasped. "Just take care of Joe."

"Yessir." Randy looked up at the sound of the ambulance's approaching siren. "And soon as we do, I'll get Jonas to pick up your car and I'll drive you on home."

~

"Clinton Sinclair," Caroline scolded, fighting to keep the worry out of her voice. "You totally ignored me didn't you?" Tears stung her eyes as she tenderly pressed an ice pack over the bandage on her husband's forehead. "What would I have done if something happened to you?"

"I'm all right, hon," he sat back in the chair with a heavy sigh. "Poor Joe. I'll never forget the look on his face. What'll happen to him now? He has enough trouble running the store with his knees and all, now a busted ankle and arm. How's he going to manage, Caroline?

"It's all my fault. I just...the other car stopped, and I just went on through. I never even looked."

"It's not all your fault, Dad." Arlene perched on the arm of his big recliner and draped her arm around his shoulders. "If we had lights at that intersection, it might have kept those kids from running in front of the other car. Joe might not have crossed in front of you. Who knows?

"But I know that intersection is getting dangerous, this proves it. Something has to be done."

"And I know what I'm going to do," Clint announced with a firmness that took Caroline by surprise. "Tomorrow, I'm going over to the Corner Market. I could run a whole company before I retired, I can help him manage that little store till he's back on his feet."

Nine

Lance walked the end-field, moving through the throng of high-schoolers, the parents fussing over the floats and their kids, the usual high-spirited commotion of homecoming. The band was a knot of blue uniforms and bright gold trim, gold horns, drums emblazoned with the school logo. Further back, Coach Lowery warmed up the football team in the field past the track. Looked like it would be a good game. Everything seemed normal enough. *Quiet in its usual noisy way.*

"You kids get down," Lance warned and a trio of youngsters jumped clear of the fence and ran, whooping about the floats, along the outside perimeter.

A flash of blonde, a familiar lilting voice and Lance smiled to see Arlene flitting among the Royal Court participants. The young men, some clean-scrubbed and in suits, others in their football uniforms looked nervously at their dates. The girls giggled and tried to look prim in their layered dresses and perfectly coiffed and tiaraed hair.

A shout rose from the stands, drowning the announcer's voice from the tiny booth high above and Lance leaned back, elbows resting atop the fence, as the band marched onto the field to begin opening ceremonies.

"Miss Sinclair," he acknowledged Arlene's demur nod in his direction and she paused, then strolled back toward him.

"Well hello, Sheriff."

"How's your dad?"

"He's all right. Upset, but he'll be all right. Thanks."

Lance nodded to the float behind her. "You having fun?"

A smile plucked at her scarlet rouged lips and she rolled her eyes. " Interviewing the Royal Court, as always." Her sigh betrayed her discontent, though her smile did not waver.

"Not what you want, is it, Arlene?" Lance straightened, crossing his arms over his chest and searching the clear green of her eyes.

"It's...it's a good town, Lance." She glanced toward the football field as a float rumbled slowly past them. "I just wanted something more. I thought by now I would be interviewing legislators and writing deep, important articles on real topics of social interest." She sighed again. "Making a difference, you know?"

Lance nodded. "I know you deserve it."

Arlene's face softened. He saw gratitude in the way she looked at him. The pink rising in her cheeks matched her soft pink angora sweater that clung to her body in all the right places. He wanted to see her smile again. A real smile. The kind that made the dimple in her right cheek show. She drove him crazy...and all he could think of was how much he wanted to kiss her.

"Thanks. That's why I want to cover the robbery. It's the only really news this town has had in years."

"Yeah, I can see that. But, Arlene, you have to know Tom is gonna want Jack on this one. I mean a robbery case...if anything were to happen..."

"I understand, but if I keep waiting for a safe story to be really newsworthy..." She closed her eyes and exhaled, lips pinched with frustration. "I guess you know I'll never make it out of here if I can't cover any real news. I want the robbery story, Lance. I need it."

"I know." Lance frowned. He didn't want to be in this place. Caught between what Arlene wanted and keeping her out of trouble. "I know you want it, and you can handle it as good as any man."

She was staring at him like she'd never seen him before. Lance looked around for something to get his attention off her. The float carrying last year's Homecoming King and Queen rumbled past, the crowned pair already smiling and waving even before they reached the field.

"And I know you are prettier than any girl on any one of these floats." Lance looked up, flustered. *What on earth made me say that?*

The sound of a fanfare announced the football team and with a roar the boys thundered past. "Guess, I'd better get back to..." He cleared his throat and shoved his fingers through his hair. "...work."

"Me too." Arlene strode rapidly toward the sidelines, pausing to glance back. "Lance," she called. "Thanks."

He grinned and watched her sashay into the crowd. That woman knew just how to get under a man's skin and make him never want to let her go. *If she just didn't have to get into every speck of trouble she could find...*

Lance shook his head and turned away. "Course then, she wouldn't be Arlene."

$\sim$

Lance chafed his hands together and took the steps up into the bleachers two at a time. Two minutes till the half-time buzzer.

"Miss Sinclair? Care to join me for some hot cocoa?"

Arlene looked up with a bright smile.

There's that dimple. He held out his hand and she closed her notebook, shoved it into her jacket pocket and laid it atop her pocketbook.

"Well, it is getting a tad nippy. That would be lovely, Sheriff Carter."

Lance chuckled. "No need to stand on formality. Shoot, I've just been Lance to you since you were in pigtails trying to swipe the popcorn from me and Dusty."

Arlene looked away, but Lance would have sworn she was sulking a bit. "Always just the kid sister to you." She turned sultry eyes on him and he felt his breath catch. "Even now?"

"Some things never change," Lance allowed, holding her elbow as he steered her carefully through the crowds gathering at the concession area. "Some things do. Two hot cocoas, please," he ordered at the window. "And a box of popcorn for the lady."

~

Kent pulled his cap lower and joined the stampede of bodies working their way across the bleachers. Half time, Nuggets ahead by seven and a boisterous crowd converging on the concession stand. The perfect opportunity was close. He could feel it.

He watched the Sheriff and Arlene Sinclair disappear into the throng at the concession stand then dropped casually down to sit beside Arlene's seat. Allowing his own worn coat to slide from his arm, it neatly covered her camel jacket and matching leather bag. Eyes fixed on his prey, Kent slid his hand underneath and searched for what he needed.

There they are. Cautiously he worked the small key ring from her jacket and slipped it into his jeans pocket. *Miss Arlene Sinclair is not so smart after all.* Picking up his coat, he rose and continued his casual progress down the bleacher steps and toward the parking lot.

He had exactly what he'd hoped to find. Just a couple more details to finish and this evening would be perfect. He leaned against the fence and lit a cigarette, watching with a tight smile as the couple strolled right past him.

So close. Reach out and finish it now.

No. Wait. Make it worth it. Make it worth every year spent in that hellhole. Wait a little longer.

~

Arlene dug through her pocketbook. "Come on, where did I put them?" Frustration mounted, she closed her bag with a snap and searched the surrounding wooden planks of seat and footboards while she felt in each pocket in turn.

Heaving a deep sigh, she tapped her foot and tried to think. Where else could she have set her keys?

"Something wrong, Arlene?"

Lance's deep voice roused her from her thoughts and she turned with a jerk to look over at him.

"What are you still doing here? Randy and I have already gotten most everyone safely back out on the roads headed home." His smile warmed her.

"I can't seem to find my keys or I'd be gone too. You didn't happen to see them, did you?"

Lance shook his head. "Can't say I did. Could you have dropped them? I can check under the bleachers."

"No, I don't think so. I think I would have heard them fall. But thanks, I guess we should look just to be sure."

"Here." Lance held her coat as she slipped it on then walked her down and around to the back. "Wait here, I'll go have a look."

"I'll come with you." Arlene ducked under the structure and they counted sections till they reached the spot below her seat. The ground was littered with bits of popcorn and candy, hot dog wrappers and the occasional cup. But no shimmer of silver broke the beam of Lance's flashlight as it swept across the dirt and straggly grass.

"No keys," Lance finally had to admit. "Okay, tell you what, how about if I give you a ride home tonight? Tomorrow you can check with the school to see if anyone found them and turned them in. Could they tell which ones are yours if they found them?"

Arlene made a wry face. "Only if nondescript is a description." She grinned in spite of the awkwardness of her situation. "Plain round ring, four plain keys. Two for the car, one for my office, one for the house. Not too noteworthy, huh?"

Lance smiled. "Remind me to buy you a key ring with some personality. C'mon, I'll take you home."

They walked across the nearly vacant parking area and Lance opened the passenger door of his patrol car for her. With an all but inaudible growl of surprise, he blocked Arlene and reached inside ahead of her, reappearing with a single short cut rose blossom.

Arlene read frustration and anger in his face for an instant before he carefully hid the emotions. Prickles of alarm tingled on her skin.

Lance looked up into her eyes with a forced half-smile, twirling the rose between his fingers. "Your secret admirer know I was going to get to bring you home tonight, Miss Sinclair?"

~

Coco's deep bark greeted their arrival on Arlene's porch.

"It's all right, you big baby. It's just me," Arlene assured him, fumbling with the lock in the darkness. "Guess I should have remembered to leave the porch lights on," she admitted sheepishly.

"Sure your mom's key works?" Lance sounded faintly amused.

"Yes..." The lock turned with a click. "There we are." She opened the door and Coco bounded out to her side, tail wagging and golden eyes darting from her to Lance and back.

"Atta boy, Coco." Lance scruffed behind the lab's ears then stepped past Arlene into the dark house. "Here, let me get some lights on for you."

"I know where my lights are, Lance." The porch lights flicked on, followed immediately by the living room. A table lamp was next. She could follow Lance's progress by the succession of lights. "You really don't need to do this."

"Just checking to make sure everything--"

"Everything is fine, thanks." She held the front door expectantly. He stared down the dark hallway toward her bedroom, but took the hint and went no further. "Really," she assured.

"If you're sure," he said reluctantly, returning to the front door. "I don't mind..."

She didn't mind either. *Quick, change the subject before you say something stupid.* "It was a good game."

Lance cleared his throat awkwardly. "Yeah, always good to win the homecoming game. You covering the win for the paper tomorrow?"

"No. Sports are Jack's area of expertise. I just get to report on the floats, who won King and Queen." She grinned ruefully. "You know, the important stuff. Thanks for the popcorn, Lance. I really enjoyed tonight."

"So did I." He nodded and stepped out onto the porch. "All right, I'll be going if you're sure you're okay."

"I'm sure the keys will show up at the school tomorrow."

"Goodnight, Arlene." He patted the lab once more. "You take good care of her, Coco."

Ten

Lester Harvey snapped the newspaper open and grunted as Elizabeth pushed a third cup of coffee in front of him. Eyes narrowed he tried to focus on the sports section over her unending chatter.

"Yeah. Yeah, Jester is dating Miss Winston over to the Gazette now? That's good." Football season was just getting going. No, no he needed a bigger win and he needed it now. *Stock cars*. Yeah, he understood car racing. Just one or two good races and he could make a killing. That would be where he could make up some of his losses. Of course football would still be there when he was back in the black.

"Lester?" The annoyance in Elizabeth's tone made him drop the paper. "Are you even listening to me? He isn't dating Henrietta *now*. He *was* dating her, now he's sweet on Clarissa Johnson, I think. Besides, I asked you what that Gary boy is doing coming over here and working on the yard and all."

"Just making things nice for you, Lizzie honey. Fall Festival comin' up and all, I know how you pride yourself on entertaining here that weekend." He unfolded his paper again and raised it like a wall between him and the missus. "Why? The boy not working out?"

"He's a nice young fellow, Lester. And such a hard worker. I just can't imagine how we're going to pay for all this."

"Now, Elizabeth, I've told you. Leave the finances to me. You have enough to do here at home and at the Garden Club and all. You stick to what you do, Lizzie, everything will be fine."

Yeah, a good run at the races is what I'm needing. No way is she finding out about this. Just a little luck, and everything will be all right.

~

Lance stood underneath the tree outside Jonas' garage and tried to piece together what had happened at the time of the robbery. *Something is missing*. He pounded his fist against the trunk. *Think, damnit. You're missing something.*

The man had stood under the tree for some time, judging by the number of butts. *But why Arlene's car? Not like he intended to take it, or why wait around? Was he waiting for her to pay Jonas? Why was he waiting? Why, why, why?*

Lance scrubbed his hand over his face and headed for the door, following once more the robber's path. He paused as he reached for the handle and Arlene stepped out into the bright morning sunshine. *When did she get here?*

"Morning, Sheriff."

"Miss Sinclair." He nodded politely. "Mind if I ask what brings you here?"

"She's trying to jump my story is what." Jack strode across the graveled drive toward them, shaking his head despite his smile. "Now, Arlene, you know the Boss isn't going to want you working a serious crime. Lance, how about you and I go someplace and I'll get your side on what happened?"

Lance saw the fire rising in Arlene's eyes, the flush racing across her cheeks. He fought to keep from smiling as he turned to meet Jack's expectant gaze. "I'm sorry, Jack. Arlene already interviewed me last night at the homecoming game. Looks like she beat ya to it. So I guess it is her story."

Jack sighed loudly, obviously none too happy, but all Lance saw was the way Arlene lit up. Her eyes danced, though she had the good grace to be gracious to her defeated rival.

"Oh, come on Jack," she soothed. "You know Tom is going to give you whatever big new story breaks around here. I think you can spare me just this one."

Jack rolled his eyes. "Dang it, you know I never could stand up to you when you sweet-talk me like that." He laughed and headed back toward his car. "But you owe me, Sinclair. And don't you forget it."

Arlene watched in silence as Jack drove away, avoiding looking at Lance. "That was nice of you," she said at last. "I appreciate it."

Lance decided to press his advantage. "So what about that interview?"

That got her attention. Arlene glanced up swiftly to meet his eyes.

"How about we discuss it over lunch this afternoon?"

She nodded. "All right. I have to get back to the paper and finish last night's article first."

"Meet you at Ellie's at say one?"

"That'd be fine. I'll see you then."

Lance watched her walk toward her car, then pulled the door open and headed toward Jonas' office to reenact the robbery one more time.

~

The awnings were already out in front of the Corner Market when Clint Sinclair arrived. It worried him a bit.

Maybe no one thought to close up for Joe last night after the accident. Surely Lance or Randy would have made sure things were locked up.

His hand lingered on the door. Before he could push, it swung open as a tall, dark-haired young man met him with a smile.

"Morning, sir. Store's not open yet for half an hour. Can I help you?"

"And who might you be, son?"

"Gary Jones. I work here for Mr. Monroe." His face grew sober. "If you didn't hear, Mr. Monroe was in an accident yesterday. He won't be back till Monday, so I'm watching things for him. Can I help you?"

Clint studied the boy. He seemed genuine enough. A nice polite young fellow. Something in his eyes seemed so familiar...

"Clint Sinclair. Nice to meet you, Gary. In case you didn't hear, I'm the one who hit Joe with the car." He ran his palm over his face, trying to hide the flush of emotion. "Joe's an old friend of mine, I figured the least I can do is help out around here while he's laid up." He held up his hand before the boy could protest. "Now I know Joe said he didn't need any help, but let's face it, son. He already has a bum knee, now with a busted ankle in a cast and his arm broken...well...you can see what I mean."

Gary nodded. "Yes sir. Yes sir, I do, Mr. Sinclair. It's really nice of you too." He looked over his shoulder at the empty store, then past Clint toward Ellie's. "You wouldn't be related to Miss Sinclair, would you?"

Clint grinned. "That's my daughter. Do you know Arlene?"

"Yes sir. She's a really nice lady. I really like her. She's always coming by here or over to the diner to check and see how I'm doing and all." Gary rubbed his palms on the thighs of his jeans. "To tell you the truth, sir, I could use some help here. I mean, I'm sure Miss Ellie would let me off considering Mr. Monroe being laid up and all, but I hate to leave her short handed."

"You work at the diner too?" Clint asked in surprise.

"Yes sir. And over at the park or the mayor's house, too. But today I just have here and Miss Ellie's. So, if you don't mind, Mr. Sinclair, once I get the store open, if you could mind things till I finish up at the diner, it sure would be a great help."

Clint smiled. It was good to see young people working hard and being responsible. He'd always tried to instill that in his children. "That would be fine. Makes me feel better to be able to help out some. Now, how about finding me one of those aprons of Joe's?"

～

"Morning, Sheriff," Debbie acknowledged as Lance headed past her desk toward his office. Something in her voice gave him pause. Lance stopped at the door, pinched the bridge of his nose with his thumb and forefinger and considered for a moment whether he *really* wanted to find out what she was about to say. With a deep sigh, he turned to face her.

"What is it, Debbie?"

"There's been some trouble over to the bus depot." She sounded almost apologetic. As if, somehow, she regretted the way things were spiraling out of control just now.

Lance felt his stomach knot. "What?"

"Someone took a pickup from the parking across from there. Seems Esther, over to the switchboard, it's her cousin's. He left it here when he took the bus up to Atlanta. And she went by this morning and it's gone."

"Great." Lance tossed his jacket to Debbie. The way things were warming up he wouldn't need it. "I'm on it. Esther down to the depot?"

"Yes sir. Call just came in."

He glanced at his watch. Nearly ten already. Still, that should be plenty of time to talk to Esther King, check out the missing truck and still meet Arlene for lunch. *Dang if I'm going to miss that over what's most likely just a couple of teenagers joy riding.*

~

"All right, Mrs. King," Lance said reassuringly, "you're sure the truck was here?"

"Right there." Esther, pointed to spot under a spreading chestnut. "Leroy left it when he went up to Atlanta, and it was here last night when I walked home after work and now, well, it just isn't." She patted her ruby hair, and fiddled with her earrings nervously.

"Are you sure your cousin didn't come home last night and pick it up?"

Esther crinkled her nose and giggled. "Well, seeing as this is his honeymoon, I'd just have to say no, Sheriff. His little Nancy is as sweet as a can be, but I'm just sure she isn't lettin' him come home early from their honeymoon." She batted her eyelashes coyly. "If you know what I mean."

Lance felt the color rising in his cheeks. "Yes ma'am, I guess he didn't come home early. All right then, what's the truck look like? I'll get Randy on it and we'll see if we can't find where it's gotten off to."

~

Lance crouched near the crushed marks where the truck had been parked in the unkempt, weedy patch. The hard ground offered no footprints or tire tracks. No easy clues to who had been there or where they'd gone.

Kids, Lance figured. *Probably a homecoming prank.* He started to his feet when a small glimpse of white nearly lost in the ragged growth caught his eye. Lance stooped, holding his breath as he studied the cigarette butt without touching it.

Could be Leroy's. Lance picked up a small twig and carefully turned the butt. *Maybe one of the high school kids'. Shit.*

Oasis. The print was small, but legible. He rose slowly, his mind awhirl with new probabilities he didn't like at all.

Eleven

Arlene shook her head in exasperation as she headed up the steps toward her house. *Good thing Momma had my spare keys.* Inside she could hear the heavy thumping of Coco's tail against the floor and she smiled. *Always nice to have someone who's glad to see you.*

Walk Coco, a quick change, call and see if her folks had heard from Dusty today, then over to the diner to meet Lance for lunch. A perfect afternoon shaping up.

The bright sunshine seemed to reflect her mood, bathing the front steps in golden light, catching a silver shimmer near the doormat--

What's this? Arlene stooped to draw a silver ring from under the edge of the mat, tinkling with the jangle of her keys. Her heart caught in her throat. Even if someone found her lost keys at the game, how did they know to return them to her? There was no name, nothing identifiable.

Calm down. She took a deep breath. *Maybe it was someone who knows me and has seen them. Like Jack. Or Libby.* Except neither of them were at the game.

Coco gave a soft bark inside, eager for her to let him out. Arlene pulled the screen door open and stared with a mixture of surprise and dismay as a rose tumbled from between the doors to land at her feet.

Cautiously she turned the knob to the front door. Locked. A wave of relief flooded through her, and Arlene carefully let herself in, holding the door open for her lab.

"Come on, Coco. Let's go." She nudged the rose with the toe of her shoe, then bent and picked it up. "Nothing unusual about this. Lance said I have a secret admirer. That's all it is."

Still, she couldn't help the prickles raising on her arms and neck as she looked around the yard and up the quiet street.

It's just plain creepy.

~

Caroline laid the final card on her tarot spread and sat back to consider what it meant. As with so many things these days, the reading was for Dusty...for any glimmer of insight into his present...his future.

His past she understood. After all, she was his mother. She gave it a cursory reading and moved forward.

Present. The death card.

A tiny prickle of pain nipped at her heart, but Caroline recognized it for the instinctive response to the word, not the card. She knew the card for what it truly was, the symbol of change. Of transformation. No literal death association to spook an experienced reader.

Very well then, a change in Dusty's circumstances. Considering the other cards in conjunction with it, this might be a very positive thing. She'd seen the same card a month ago, just before his letters stopped coming. *Maybe this means we will hear from him again soon,* she thought hopefully.

Future. Puzzling. Caroline stared at it, years of practice warring the surge of emotions she knew would sway the validity of her reading if she allowed them. *Still, there is definite change ahead. Change in his present and his future.* She allowed a small smile, a glimmer of hope.

The phone rang, startling her, and Caroline quickly swept the cards from the table, tapping them into a neat pile before picking up the receiver.

"Hello?" She wrapped the tarot deck in its dark cloth and placed it safely into the small teak box that kept it safe from the prying, and non-believing, eyes of her family.

She heard Arlene's familiar voice. "Hi, Momma. Any word from Dusty?"

"Not yet, honey, but I have a good feeling. Things are changing. We'll hear from him soon."

"Momma? You been reading those horoscopes again?" There was teasing accusation in her tone.

"As a matter of fact, no." Caroline smiled smugly and tucked the tarot box into the drawer. "Sometimes, I just know."

"Okay. How's Daddy?"

"He's over to the Corner Market. He plans to help Joe out there till he's back on his feet, you know."

"Well, that might be good for Daddy. Give him something else to do besides fuss over all of us." Arlene chuckled. "All right, I'll let you go. I have to get over to Ellie's and then back to work."

"Going to lunch at the diner?"

"I have an..."

Caroline heard the hesitation in her daughter's response. What wasn't Arlene saying?

"...an interview there. Then I have an article to work on for tomorrow's paper. Bye--"

"Who're you interviewing?"

"No one important. Bye, Momma."

Caroline hung the receiver gently up. *No one important. Oh no, not Arlene.* Caroline smiled. *Now what does she think she's hiding?*

~

"Now what?" Lance grumbled as he slowed the cruiser and pulled into the parking lot in front of the Corner Market. A knot of townsfolk gathered in front of Hank Greeley's barbershop across the street. They seemed peaceful enough, talking and gesturing with enthusiasm but not agitated.

Lance relaxed a bit as he strode across the street.

"What's going on here?" he asked Frank Perkins.

"Hank's got himself one of those new television sets for the shop. Nice one too, Sheriff. Said it set him back a good five hundred dollars. Can you imagine?" He shook his head and crammed his thumbs in the straps of his overalls. "Shoot, I could buy six or seven head of cows fer that."

"Guess you could at that, Frank." Lance slapped him warmly on the shoulder. "But could you keep them in?"

Perkins grinned jovially and scratched his chin. "Reckon you might have a point there."

"I just don't see how this is supposed to improve business," Henrietta Winston declared skeptically. "Folks come here to visit and get their hair cut. Now what possible purpose can that contraption serve except to make noise and distract a body?"

Lance chuckled and moved forward to get a look at the object in question. It surely didn't look like much sitting there just inside the window. He looked around at the gathered faces. Whatever Miss Winston thought, it did seem to be doing what Hank wanted.

It was drawing a crowd.

A sweet, teasingly honeyed voice sent a flush through Lance's whole body. "Why, Sheriff, how is it you are always in the middle of everything that goes on around here?"

He chuckled. "That's my job, now isn't it, Miss Sinclair?" He glanced sidelong to meet her twinkling eyes. "You covering the television story too?"

"Television? Oh, is that what everyone is all a-twitter about?" She stood on tiptoe and peered through the crowd. "My goodness, that is something, isn't it?" Dropping back to her normal height, she smiled coyly at him. "I guess as soon as things quiet down a bit, I could interview Hank about it." Her arm slid comfortably through the crook of his. "But right now, I believe I have an appointment with you?"

It felt so good, so normal, to have Arlene on his arm. Lance fought to keep his voice neutral and professional. "Yes ma'am. Over lunch, I think we agreed."

She nodded, blonde hair bouncing. "Over lunch."

~

Lance nodded to Ellie as they entered. "Okay if we take the back booth?"

Ellie's eyes widened with delight at the sight of the two of them and she pinched her lips together in an effort to keep from smiling. "Sure thing, hon'. Ya'll go on back and I'll send Katie right over." She reached over and stopped Arlene. "You and Libby still meeting me tonight?"

"Absolutely. Wouldn't miss it," Arlene assured, then followed Lance to the quieter rear corner of the diner.

"Sorry I was late, Lance." Arlene slid across the blue booth seat. "Found my keys though."

Lance sidled in beside her. Her tight fitting dungarees and white angora sweater more than made up for any amount of waiting, he thought. "Glad to hear it. They find them over to the high school?"

Arlene snatched a menu from the center of the table, staring at it with studious concentration. "Mmm," she replied noncommittally, then glanced up with a smile. "Would you like to talk before or after we order?"

Lance frowned, it wasn't like Arlene to beat around the bush. "Either, both. Whatever works for you, Arlene. Any idea what you'd like?"

"Hey Lance." The waitress set glasses of ice water in front of them on crisp little white paper coasters. "Hi Arlene. Special today is pork tenderloin sandwich with all the fixings, Ellie's home-fries, and your choice of side dish." She took a deep breath and pulled her order booklet from her pocket, pencil poised and tapping nervously on the edge of the pad. She bit her lower lip, looked toward the kitchen, then back at Arlene.

"You okay, Katie?" Lance asked.

She nodded a bit too energetically, pasting a tight smile in place. "Sure. Fine. Do you know what you'd like?"

"I think the special sounds great. Give me some coleslaw with it," Lance ordered, then looked to Arlene. "How about you?"

"I think I'll just have a BLT club and a strawberry milkshake?"

Lance nodded to Katie and she scribbled her notes. "What you want to drink, Lance?"

"Coke is fine."

"Gottcha, order'll be up soon." She shoved her pad and pencil into her pocket and turned away, then quickly back. Her fingers twisted the edge of her apron. "Arlene, have you...has Dusty..."

Arlene's expression softened with sympathy. "Oh Katie, I'm sorry. You haven't heard from him either?"

"Not a word. He wrote me every week, just *every* week...and now not a word. I'm just so worried about him." She sniffled, her nose pinking up and eyes over bright with unshed tears.

"We haven't heard from him, but I'm sure he's fine."

Lance's gaze darted from the blonde woman at his side to the dainty brunette and he wondered who was consoling whom here. "Dusty's smart, and he's strong. Probably he's just in a place he can't write right now. He'll be home before you know it."

Katie smiled wanly. "I sure hope that's the case, I miss him so much. He sent me his picture in his uniform. He looks so handsome." She ducked her head shyly. "I put it in a frame sitting on my bedside table where I can see him every morning and night." A blush colored her cheeks. "Kinda like he was my sweetheart. Silly I know."

"Not at all." Arlene squeezed Katie's hand. "It's sweet and I know Dusty must be thinking of you too."

"You think so?"

Arlene nodded. "I'm sure. And Lance is right, he'll be home soon, and then you can ask him yourself."

Katie brightened visibly. "Let me hurry and get this order in for you two. Thanks."

"Looks like we won't have to worry about your brother being lonely when he gets home." Lance chuckled, watching Katie hurry toward the kitchen.

"Oh quit," Arlene admonished teasingly. She laid her notebook on the table. "Maybe we'd better get this interview now, before there are any other distractions."

Lance stared at his ice water before slowly raising his eyes to meet hers. "I think you're distraction enough."

Twelve

Arlene slipped over to a quiet front corner table at the <u>Dew Drop Inn</u> and peered around the crowded little club. The place was the only really nice dance club in the whole county, the pride of Hilton Falls. And since her friend, Libby, had moved up to Hilton Falls, Arlene found herself at the <u>Dew Drop</u> a lot more often than she'd ever expected.

She smoothed the tablecloth and took a peanut from the big bowl in the center of the table. Weekends always seemed to pack out the crowd with good ol' boys looking for fun. Now if Ellie and Libby would just get here before any of the fellas spotted her sitting here alone...

Too late. Drew Donaldson strolled to the table, smoothing his greased-back brown hair as he came.

"Evenin' Arlene. Nice to see you here. Can I buy you a drink?"

"No thanks, Drew, but I appreciate the offer." She put on her best polite smile and cracked another peanut. "I'm waiting for Libby and Ellie. Girls night, you understand."

"Ummm, yeah." Drew looked away uncomfortably. "Guess, I'd better get back to my table. My buddies are starting to stare. Wouldn't want them to think there was something going on between you and me."

Arlene shook her head. "Don't flatter yourself," she muttered under her breath as he rejoined his friends. She checked her watch and leaned forward to look anxiously toward the door. "C'mon, Libby. Don't leave me here with the wolves."

As if on cue, the door opened, bringing with it a gust of cool night air, signaling Libby's arrival. She waved brightly and wriggled through the crowd headed for Arlene.

"Hey sweety." Libby dropped onto a chair across from Arlene, looking around with interest.

Arlene tapped her watch face with one manicured nail. "I have been sitting here by myself for ten minutes and the boys at the bar were getting a bit..." She rolled her eyes expressively. "Well, you know."

The jukebox clicked over to a new song, Dust My Broom, and the floor filled with couples eager to dance. Libby crossed her legs, foot swinging in time to the music, looking around the room with obvious intent.

"Okay, Lib, who are you expecting?" Arlene narrowed her eyes suspiciously, but the question died unpursued as the door swung open and a tall, broad shouldered figure made his entrance, pushing a strand of jet-black hair from his eyes and flashing a disarming boyish grin. "Oh my gawd," Arlene whispered under her breath and snapped her gaping mouth closed, whipping around to face Libby.

"Well, well, well," Libby purred, wiggling her eyebrows at Arlene who glared an icy hole through her. Libby remained unaffected. "What? Don't you suppose Lance might like to dance too?"

Arlene risked a sidelong glance and spotted Lance leaning against the bar, ankles crossed before him, looking totally at ease and, she realized as she forced a pent breath from her lungs, totally gorgeous.

~

Lance ordered a beer and leaned against the bar to have a quick look at the crowd. That was Arlene's car parked out front; he'd know it anywhere. Now, where was she and what brought her out to the <u>Dew Drop Inn</u> tonight?   The dance floor thumped with the energy of bodies moving to the upbeat rhythm of the music. Might turn out to be a pretty fine night after all. All he'd planned was a couple of beers and a game or two of pool, but... There she was. Lance took a sip of his beer. Now that he'd seen that certain spirited, vivacious blonde, his plans were definitely changed. *Course there's no way to predict how Miss Arlene Sinclair will react to seeing me here.* He straightened. Only one way to find out.

The song ended and some of the dancers drifted toward the bar or their tables, opening a path for Lance as he worked his way toward Arlene's table.

~

"Dang." A flush burned across Arlene's face at the sight of Lance approaching.

"What?" Libby asked with feigned innocence.

"Nothing. He's headed right this way," she growled through clenched teeth.

"Nothing?" Libby nodded. "That why you are making confetti?"

Arlene shot a startled glance at the shredded napkin in her lap, brushed it swiftly into her hand and crammed it into her pocketbook.

"Evenin' ladies," Lance drawled. "Libby, Arlene." He looked from one to the other as he slipped off his black leather jacket.

The sound of his baritone voice brought Arlene's thoughts to a screeching halt. She was certain she had some pithy comment prepared for him, instead she heard herself politely asking him to join them. It wasn't like she'd never heard his voice before. *He can't sit here! What on earth is wrong with me?*

Lance slung his jacket over the back of a chair and took a seat between Arlene and Libby. "Thanks. Can I get you something to drink?"

"No, no thanks," Arlene stammered. "I can...I can get my own." She stared into the smoky blue of his eyes. Bad decision. When did Lance get such bedroom eyes?

"What brings you here tonight?"

Stop it right now, she reprimanded herself. "My car." That felt better. She allowed herself to smile. "And what brought you to the Dew Drop on this fine evening?"

Lance chuckled and looked at her over the rim of his beer. "My truck."

Arlene laughed, feeling suddenly more at ease with Lance than she had in years. "Touché."

"Seriously, I am a bit surprised to see you here. Not that your presence doesn't do wonders for the ambiance of the place."

She spent so much time in an adversarial relationship with Lance the compliment took her quite by surprise. Had they come so far in just the last couple of days? "To be honest, I'm a little surprised myself." She smiled at Libby. "It was Libby's idea. She and Ellie thought I needed a night out...away from worrying about Dusty, and..." She looked away, suddenly afraid Lance would discover the source of the nervousness that kept her awake nights now. "You know, all the things happening around here." Arlene looked up and met Lance's eyes steadily. "I could use a coke, if you don't mind."

Lance inclined his head. "You want something, Libby?"

"A beer, thanks."

"Be right back."

Arlene watched him stride away, glancing back startled at the sound of another voice close by.

"Would you like to dance, Libby?"

Drew. Libby flashed a victorious smile. "About time I got out of the way here. Looks like you have all the company you need." She squeezed Arlene's hand and winked as she got to her feet. "I would love to dance, Drew. Arlene, I'll see you later."

~

"So you never did say what brought you out tonight?" Arlene nodded to Libby before returning her attention to Lance.

Lance took a deep swallow of his beer. Should he tell her he spotted her car and pulled in? That his planned social calendar had been a couple of games with the guys down at pool hall and home before midnight? Staring into her beautiful eyes he knew the truth.

"I saw your car parked out front and I figured I could stop in for a beer."

Arlene cocked her head to one side and offered a half-smile. "Checking up on me, Sheriff?"

"Well, let's just say you are a lot prettier company than I would have had otherwise." Someone dropped another coin in the jukebox and the sweet, mellow sound of Nat King Cole's "Mona Lisa" filled the room. Lance took a deep breath and held out his hand as he got to his feet. "Could I have this dance?"

Arlene dropped her eyes demurely, but her fingers slipped soft and warm into his palm and he swept her in an arcing circle onto the floor and into his arms.

"Mona Lisa" melted into "How High the Moon". She fit against his body as if she had been made just for him. His hand moved down to the small of her back, and her arm slipped up and around his neck. The warm, soft fragrance of flowers and vanilla swirled around her, intoxicating and sweet.

Lance nuzzled the edge of her hair and sniffed appreciatively. Arlene leaned back enough to stare questioningly into his eyes. Caught.

"You smell pretty." He grinned sheepishly.

"Why thank you. Shalimar, it was a gift from Dusty before he shipped out. I keep it for special occasions."

Lance dipped her gently over his arm, and she laughed, her hair falling back in loose golden waves. He couldn't remember ever having enjoyed a dance so much. "Definitely special tonight."

Where did that come from? "Unforgettable" drifted from the jukebox. *Yeah, that's Arlene.* The song ended, and for a moment Lance lingered with her there, soft and warm in his arms before he stepped away.

This had to stop right now. His thoughts were as jumbled as his emotions. Lance took her arm and steered her back to the table. "Want another coke? A beer?"

She smiled and tilted her head to the side. "Sure, thanks."

Lance got her a beer at the bar and took the moment to collect himself. Okay, time to get out of here before he said or did something.

Setting the beer before her, he leaned over her shoulder, hand planted on the table. "It was fun, but I've got to go. Work in the morning, you know."

Arlene nodded. "Sure thing. Thanks for the dance."

"Hate to leave you sitting here all by yourself."

"Oh, Libby will be back in a minute. And I saw Ellie come in a few minutes ago. Night, Lance."

He stood and pulled on his jacket. "Right. Night, Arlene."

~

Arlene watched the door close behind Lance and looked around quickly for her friends. Libby was on the dance floor and totally focused on Drew. It was nice to see Libby having fun.

Now, where did Ellie get off to?

"Where'd Lance run off to?" Ellie dropped, as if on cue, onto a chair beside Arlene.

Arlene rolled her eyes. "A Sheriff's work is never done?"

Ellie laughed. "I see Miss Libby has staked a new territory?"

"I swear, Ellie, I think she took off with Drew *just* to leave me sitting here with Lance Carter." She tried to sound annoyed, but how could she when she'd enjoyed every minute of his company?

"Really?" Ellie grinned. "I'm gonna have to buy that girl a drink."

"You two are terrible."

"Oh c'mon, Arlene. Only people who don't know you two belong together is the two of you."

Thirteen

Something roused Arlene from her deep, warm sleep. Movement? She dragged her groggy mind into wakefulness. *Must have been Coco getting up.* Was it morning already? She rubbed her eyes and turned her clock toward her. Three o'clock. She'd only been asleep for less than three hours? Darn, why would Coco be up at this time? His deep bark brought her upright in bed. Three o'clock. She'd only been asleep for less than three hours? Darn, why would Coco be up at this time?

She heard him again. "Coco?"

Grabbing her robe from the foot of the bed, she headed for the kitchen. "What's the matter with you, crazy dog?"

The dim light from over the sink cast a faint bluish glow as Arlene padded across the linoleum floor. Coco whined softly and pawed at the door.

He gave another sharp bark.

"Quiet Coco. You keep this up in the middle of the night and the neighbors will be calling the Sheriff on us."

The thought brought a smile to her lips. "Okay," she whispered to the dog. "That might not be so bad." *Especially after tonight.* When did she start thinking of Lance as more than a friend? More importantly, why did it suddenly feel as if he was thinking the same thing?

Cut it out, she reprimanded herself. *You're just two friends who happened to be at the same place, at the same time.* She sighed wistfully. *Shared the same music, the same moment, the same...*

Coco whined, his rapt attention focused on the door.

The knob seemed to turn slightly and Arlene caught at Coco's collar and pulled him back. There was an almost inaudible clicking sound. The door or Coco's nails on the floor?

Arlene felt her heart thudding hollowly against her chest. *Calm down, Arlene. Good grief, now you're imagining things. The dog wants to go out, that's all there is to it.*

She reached for the doorknob, fingers closing in a slow turn. *Just let Coco out into the yard so he can do his business.* His chocolate brown head shot up and he yanked free of her grip on his collar and bolted through the kitchen and toward the living room.

A low growl rumbled in the dog's throat as he slid to a halt at the front door. Arlene heard a soft click and her gaze fixed on the knob, waiting for it to move. Nothing.

Coco lunged at the door, barking fiercely. Arlene forced a breath into her lungs, willed herself to move toward the door. She seemed rooted in one spot. *Breathe.* Slowly exhaling, Arlene took a hesitant step forward.

The door remained silent. The knob never twitched.

Okay. She took a more confident stride forward. "Coco, be still," she ordered as forcefully as she could manage over the lump in her throat. The lab turned soulful amber eyes to her and sank to the floor with a whimper. "It's okay, buddy. I believe you." His heavy tail thumped on the floor and Arlene reached down and scratched his ears. Standing on tiptoe she peeked out into the darkness. Nothing. It was dark, silent, but she couldn't see anything out of place near the doorway. Nothing moved.

Arlene took a steadying breath and flicked the porch lights on. Everything was quiet. A gusty wind trembled in the trees out front, she could see them swaying just beyond the pale circle of light.

Maybe that's what scared Coco. The wind rattling things out there. That's all.

~

Kent heard an order from inside for the dog to be still. Brilliant plan, but too damn late. He leapt the cement steps and flattened against the side of the house as the porch lights flashed on.

Damn, the bitch and her stupid dog! He'd almost gotten the duplicate key to work. If the dog hadn't started yapping, he would have gotten in.

The lights went off again and he released a deep breath and hurried through shadows to the truck parked three houses up the street.

Back at the motel he drove the stolen truck across the dry, weeded lawn to a narrow strip behind the buildings near the garbage dumpsters. A heavy bramble hedge protected the area from view; the truck was pretty safe from prying eyes.

Inside his dingy room, Kent tossed his keys on the dresser and flopped onto the bed with his hands folded behind his head. He was tired. *Next time.* He'd just have to wait for a place when the dog was out of the way.

Next time.

~

Lance squinted up into the bright orange leaves of the maple tree and chuckled. "Fluffy, you'd better hightail it down here cat before I shoot you down." He heard Miss Winston's alarmed gasp and it made him grin all the wider.

"Lancelot! You wouldn't."

Even her using his proper name couldn't dampen his mood this morning. "All right, Randy. Whose turn is it, yours or mine?"

His deputy shrugged. "Well if you're offering, I'm sure not standing in your way. Feel free to climb right on up there."

Lance grunted, caught a branch just over his head and swung up into the tree. Two limbs further up Miss Winston's cat yowled pathetically. How many Fluffy rescues had he done over the years? More than he could count, that was for sure. Still, the sun was warm, the trees were beginning to sparkle with fall colors, and the emerald lawn below reminded him of the clear green of Arlene's eyes.

He grinned, hearing once more the strains of Nat King Cole's "Unforgettable", remembering the softness of angora beneath his hands. He reached up and Fluffy scrambled out of reach to a higher limb.

No silly feline was going to steal his good mood this morning. Lance found a foothold and stepped up. "Do that again and I'll leave your sorry hide up here." Fluffy yowled in reply and Lance grabbed the reluctant cat. "Come on, Fluffy. We have better things to do yet this morning."

Dropping to the ground, Lance deposited the animal into Henrietta Winston's waiting arms. "There ya go, Miss Winston. You let us know when he gets up there again. Who knows, we might even make it till tomorrow."

"What the heck's got you in such a good mood this morning?" Randy asked, leaning on the front of the squad car.

Lance shrugged noncommittally. "I dunno, just seems like a fine day. No sense in ruining it this early." He looked down the street. "Tell you what, you take the car, head on back to the station. I'm going to walk."

Randy's eyebrows crawled upward. "Yessir. Well, hope that good mood lasts a while. See you back to the station later."

Lance watched him drive away, then set off with long strides up the tree-lined street toward Birch. Yes indeed, it was a fine morning. About time he checked in with his folks, maybe he'd even get a cup of coffee out of it.

~

Lance sat back on the porch swing and sipped his coffee. His mother set a plate of fresh-baked biscuits and honey at his elbow and lowered herself onto one of the wicker chairs.

"You're looking good since your and Dad's vacation trip, Mom."

"Thank you. About time you came to check up on us since we got back."

"Sorry, Mom. Things have been a little crazed here lately. Reckon you heard about the robbery?"

"Did indeed. You going to catch whoever did it?"

"I'm working on it."

"Well that's good. Can't have the criminal element moving into our town. Makes folks feel safe just knowing you are going to take care of this." She folded her hands in her lap, staring

"You know Caroline called me just yesterday. They're having their annual Halloween party."

"I expected they would." The Sinclair's Halloween bash was a much-anticipated event in Sunny Hills. Kids came from all over town to run through the hay maze spook house set up in the backyard and a chance at bobbing for apples. Most of town would show up over there at some point in the evening for hot, spiced cider and Caroline's fortuneteller act. Lance shook his head. Sometimes you would swear she really might be psychic.

"You going to be joining us this year?"

"She hasn't invited me, Mom."

"Course she has. You know you have always been welcome at their house. Caroline is my best friend, why she's practically family. And you hardly ever even bother to come to anything any more."

"I have duties, Mom. I can't always make plans."

"Just for a couple of hours, I expect Randy can get along fine without you. Arlene will be there and I would hope you would be polite enough to come at least for a little while."

Lance nodded. *"Arlene will be there..."* So, his mother and Caroline Sinclair were plotting against him again. Wasn't the first time.

Except this time it didn't feel so bad. A little smile began to worm its way into his heart. Halloween at the Sinclair's had been a rite of fall since he was a kid. Him and Dusty teasing Arlene and... *Shoot, Dusty.* What would Dusty think if he knew Lance was thinking of Arlene as more than his 'little sister'? If Dusty knew how he felt when he was around her?

The memory of Shalimar scented hair...'Dusty gave it to me'... All right then, Dusty knew she was a grown woman. No little sister smelled like that, melted in your arms when you dance with her like that.

They could talk, soon as Dusty came home. Lance nodded again. "All right. I'll do my best."

His mother ruffled his hair as she passed and kissed his forehead. "That's better. Now eat your breakfast."

~

Lester Harvey pulled a chair from beneath the wrought iron patio table, and watched Gary Jones push a wheelbarrow around the corner.

"Morning, Mr. Mayor," the youngster called. "Just getting started on these back beds."

"That's fine, Gary. If you need anything, the back door here is open. You can go on in and get a drink or use the toilet there in the washroom."

"Thank you, sir. Appreciate it."

The boy started shoveling mulch into the beds bordering the patio and Lester dropped down to sit at the table, spreading his thick town finance folder in front of him. He flipped through the loose pages to the spreadsheet and ran his finger slowly down the columns. What was left?

He'd depleted the town services fund to a level he didn't dare touch the little that remained for emergencies. The thought of Jester, Henrietta and that nosey Sinclair made his blood boil. Heaving a loud sigh, he focused on the figures marching across the page. The school repair and improvement fund...that looked promising.

But the school already has a list of work to be done. Dang, how would he explain the missing money?

He slapped the folder closed. *I have to have it; there isn't any way around it. I'll just have to put it back, that's all. One good win and I'm back in the black.*

How the heck else could he get the kind of money he needed? If he tried to get a second mortgage on the house, Elizabeth would find out for sure.

There was a good series coming up at the Jackson track. The top running dog couldn't keep this up forever. Yeah, he could drive down; place his bets. That was where the money would come from.

He opened the folder again and stared at the improvement column. Yeah, first the Series gets the town funds back and then football season. He always did fine with football. How to cover using those monies till he won enough?

He looked over at Gary, kneeling to mulch around the rows of Elizabeth's beloved mums. *The boy has a way with mulch.* Lester grinned.

All right, borrow some from the school fund; get that bet in there. Start setting things right around here. A few quick strokes of the pen and the money vanished from the books, 'spent'.

The phone rang inside the house and he heard Elizabeth call, "Lester, it's Mr. Richardson."

He pushed the folder away from the edge of the table and strode into the house. "Now what?"

~

Gary wiped his hands on his pants legs and watched Mayor Harvey disappear into the house. Darn, he was thirsty. A quick glance down at his dirty dungarees and muddy shoes said he probably shouldn't take the Mayor up on his offer to just go in. Mrs. Harvey didn't seem like she'd much appreciate having her floors tracked up.

Should'a grabbed a drink on my way out of Ellie's. Now, a couple of hours later, he was feeling parched and getting hungry.

Maybe if the Mayor was still in the kitchen he would bring him a glass of water when he came out. Gary stepped up onto the patio, going between the array of potted mums and the table. Tilting his head, he glanced over the neat rows of figures. *Always did like math. What is this?* Stepping closer, he peered at the books with rapt attention. *Kinda odd.*

Shaking his head, he continued to the back door. "Hello? Mayor Harvey? Ma'am?" No answer. "Hello, it's me, Gary. Could I get a drink, please?" Vaguely he heard voices from somewhere inside, but no one answered. He looked ruefully at his shoes, then back at the shiny white floor. "Water hose," he muttered to himself as he headed back across the patio.

He paused again to consider the open book, running his fingers across the tables of figures. "This is all wrong. Didn't they teach them anything in school?" Gary shoved hair out of his eyes and looked around quickly. "There ya are," he said to himself as he spotted the coiled hose behind the big yew at the corner of the patio.

Fourteen

Arlene rested her cheek in her palm and absently drummed her keys against the edge of the desk. Her mind, a million miles from Sunny Hills, couldn't seem to focus on her story but whirled through a hundred possibilities.

Dancing with Lance. Robberies. Roses. *Too darn many sleepless nights lately, that's all that's wrong with me.*

She pulled out her pocketbook, but the key ring seemed reluctant to leave her fingers as she stared at it for the hundredth time. Why did she feel so violated? Nothing had happened. She lost the keys. Someone returned them.

With a deep breath she shoved them into her pocketbook and snapped it shut.

"Arlene?" Jack poked his head around the door, flashing a winning smile. "Saw your article on the robbery, looks good."

"Thanks." She just didn't feel up to one of his usual cat and mouse games today. "What do you want, Jack?"

For an instant he looked genuinely surprised, but he recovered quickly, hand over his heart in a dramatic denial. "Me? Why would I have to want anything, Miss Sinclair? Mightn't I just come to congratulate a fellow reporter on a job well done?"

Arlene resisted the urge to laugh at his antics. No point in encouraging him, Jack was full enough of himself already. "Hmm, in a word? No." She worried her strand of pearls, sliding them back and forth through her fingers. "Really, what do you want?"

His mock emotions disappeared along with his smile. "Nothing. What's the matter? This story getting to you? Something happen?" He dropped down to sit on the edge of her desk and all Arlene saw in his hazel eyes was concern.

"You look spent, hon. What's up?"

Arlene sighed wearily, dropping her hands to her lap so he wouldn't see how nervous she felt. "Nothing. Really, it's nothing. I'm just a little tired, that's all."

"Too many late nights?" A hint of his teasing smile warmed his face. "Have anything to do with all the time you and a certain Sheriff around these parts have been spending with each other?"

"Certainly not. And shame on you for thinking it." She shook her head and stared at the blank page in her typewriter. It wasn't like her to be at a loss for words. Ever. "Just working on a follow-up to the story, actually."

Apparently Jack didn't miss it either. "And nothing to say? Look, Arlene, if something about this story is bothering you..."

She took a deep breath and looked up into his face. Sure, Jack was the competition for big stories in this one-horse town, and sometimes he flat drove her to distraction, but beyond all that he was a trusted friend. Did she dare tell him? If he breathed a word to Mr. Solana...or worse, to Lance...

"Can I trust you?" The words slipped out before she had a chance to take them back. Arlene hated the hurt she saw flash through his eyes.

"Don't you know I wouldn't do anything to hurt you?"

She pressed her hand over his. "I know that. I just... I need to tell someone, and it probably isn't anything, but I want this story, Jack. I *need* it. Can you understand that?"

He nodded. "Promise, your secret is safe with me."

"Thanks. The thing is, oh shoot, I don't even know how to begin." Arlene stood, and moved slowly around her desk to stare out the window. "There's something going on, and somehow it's connected to this robbery. I just don't know how yet."

"So tell me," Jack encouraged.

"Coco's woken me up a couple of times in the last two weeks barking. And both times, I would have sworn there was someone outside."

Jack stiffened. "Did you see anyone?"

"No, no not really. It was just a feeling, that someone was there. Well that, and I found things."

"What kind of things?"

Arlene turned to face him. "A little scrap of paper, a cigarette butt--"

"Lot's of folks smoke."

"I don't. And neither do my neighbors. It just struck me as odd, it being there near the window."

She saw Jack's expression darken. He didn't like where this seemed headed any more than she did. Somehow that made her feel better. Maybe it wasn't all just her overactive reporter's imagination after all.

"And then there were my car keys. I lost them at the homecoming game. You didn't happen to find them did you?"

Jack shook his head, but his gaze flicked to the basket at the corner of her desk where Arlene always threw her keys. They were there as usual and he looked back at Arlene quizzically.

"Someone found them and left them on my porch."

"That was nice of them." His voice didn't sound as assured as his words.

"How would anyone know they're mine?" Arlene dangled the plain silver ring from her index finger. "No ID on them of any kind." She tossed them back into the basket.

Jack released a slow breath. "Yeah, I know. Arlene, have you reported this to Lance?"

She felt the blood rush from her face. "Oh geeze, no. And don't you dare tell him. You promised, Jack."

"This could be nothing, just like you said, but Arlene, if there *is* something going on..." He stared hard into her eyes. "What else? There's more, I can feel it in my bones. Spill, lady."

She shook her head firmly. "Not if you're even thinking you're going to tell anyone. This is between you and me, Jack. If it gets to where I need someone else to know then I'll be the one to tell them."

Jack raked his fingers through his hair. He didn't like it; she could tell he didn't. Finally he nodded curtly. "Okay. But you understand, I'm trusting <u>you</u> now. You ask for help if you need it, you got me?"

Arlene smiled. He really was a good friend.

"What else?"

"I think the person who robbed Jonas's garage was in my car when they were there. And they left a rose in the backseat."

Jack flashed his heart-melting grin. "Sounds more like you've got a secret admirer, Miss Sinclair."

"That's what Lance--the Sheriff," she quickly corrected, "said too. And you can just quit." She frowned pensively. "He didn't believe it any more than you do." Arlene lifted her chin determinedly. "Whoever it is, they left another one. On my porch."

She went back to the window, where she wouldn't have to face Jack and he wouldn't see the emotions spilling out of her heart. "My place doesn't even feel like home any more. I hate that feeling. It all just seems a little creepy. Like somehow that robbery is connected to me now. I just can't to seem to get the pieces to fit." Arlene turned to Jack. "Anyway, thanks for letting me talk. Somehow, I just needed someone else to know. To tell me I'm not just being a hysterical woman."

Jack got to his feet and crossed to stand before her. "You are the least hysterical woman I've ever known. It's real, hon, and I'm glad you told me what's going on." He gave her a quick hug. "You be careful. Any time you think something is wrong, you know to call. Call me. Call Lance. Don't try to do this alone, Arlene."

"Okay." She smiled. "Thanks, Jack."

"So, do I get an invitation?" He grinned broadly, the mischievous twinkle returning to his eyes.

"Invitation?"

"Hey, I've seen you and Lance lately. Want to make sure I get an invitation."

Arlene stared at him in confusion.

"To the wedding."

Her eyes widened and she nearly choked on the words. "Oh for pity sake, we aren't even dating."

"You blush every time someone even mentions his name. Don't you suppose that says something about what you're thinking?"

She felt the heat creeping across her cheeks.

Jack chortled. "See? There it is again."

"Enough already, Stewart." Arlene took his arm and guided him firmly toward the door. "Get back to work. I have a story to write and then I think I'm going for a drive."

~

Arlene drove slowly through town, enjoying the colors of autumn and the fall decorations. It helped clear her thoughts, and right now she needed to think clearly.

She made a left on Newton Street into an older part of town, the wide cobble street lined with mature maple trees and stretches of green lawns with large, well-maintained homes. *Goodness, how long has it been since I spent any time here?*

In school hardly a week had gone by she hadn't been over here. They were good times. She slowed, seeking familiar houses and childhood sights. A For Sale sign caught her eye and Arlene pulled to the curb.

The Davenport's. *Gees, Heather and Melissa...the three of us had such a good time here.* She had loved this house, the cheery kitchen always smelled of fresh-baked cookies, and the yard held a lifetime of memories.

When was the last time she'd seen Melissa? She couldn't remember seeing her at all since Melissa got married two years ago. And Heather... Where had Heather moved to? Had her life become so busy that she couldn't keep in touch with her childhood friends?

Now this house she loved was for sale?

Arlene jotted the realtor's phone number down and pulled away from the curb.

Talk about perfect timing.

Fifteen

Arlene stood in front of the Davenport's house and watched the realtor in her neat candy-pink suit stride down the driveway to meet her.

I can't believe I'm even thinking about doing this. She felt her pulse speed up with anticipation.

The realtor held out a perfectly manicured hand. "Miss Sinclair, I'm Abby Winslow. Glad you could come." She turned and gestured broadly to the house. "So, you're somewhat familiar with the home?"

"More than somewhat. I spent a lot of time here when I was growing up." She patted the square, solid column of the porch. The plantings were more overgrown than she remembered. The once vibrant yellow was faded and chipping, the brilliant blue trim a chalky gray, but the house still brought back the beloved emotions, the safe, warm 'home' feeling that Arlene longed to reclaim.

"Shall we go in?" Abby asked, knocking on the door.

Mrs. Davenport opened the door, her face brightening. "Arlene is that really you?" She threw her arms around Arlene in a warm embrace. "It is so good to see you, honey. Heather and I were just talking about you last time she came to visit." She looked questioningly at Abby Winslow. "Are you who's come to see the house?"

"I saw the sign out front, and Mrs. Winslow told me it was still available."

"It surely is. We actually just made the decision to sell the old place two weeks ago." Mrs. Davenport led Arlene into the living room. "With Michelle married and living in North Carolina, and Mr. Davenport retiring last year, we really want to move up there and be closer to the grandbabies."

"That sounds nice," Arlene agreed. "Although it must be hard to leave. I always loved this place."

"Well, come on into the kitchen."

It didn't smell of cookies any more Arlene noted, but sunlight streamed through the windows making it bright and cheery. The cabinets needed refinished and she could use a little more counter space. Still, such a pleasant room; she could imagine herself here.

They walked down the long hallway to the bedrooms. Arlene stopped in front of the girls' old bedroom. The door stood ajar, Arlene took a peek inside. How many times had she slept in this room? All those nights of giggling and boy-talk. Pajama parties. Swearing they were staying up till the sun rose, and falling asleep before midnight every time. With each step she took through the house another memory came floating back.

Through the screen door, Arlene stepped out into the backyard. Towering over the house, the oak tree appeared even taller than Arlene remembered. It dappled the yard with cool shade. *Coco will love it here.* Wispy beards of Spanish moss festooned its heavy branches and on the far side hung an old tire swing. She grinned as she gave it a push.

Abby Winslow moved to her side. "More fond memories?"

"Definitely. I think I love this house even more than I did as a kid. I'm almost afraid to ask but...how much?"

Had she been that obvious, Arlene wondered as Abby flipped her notebook open and held it out for Arlene to see the fact sheet on the house. *Subtle has never been my best trait.* Her gaze followed Abby's finger to the bottom figures, eyes widening as she saw the asking price.

"Are you sure?"

Abby Winslow smiled and nodded. "The Davenports have been very clear that a quick sale is most important to them and, as I am sure you noticed, the house will need some work. You should plan on some expenses in repairs, repainting and what have you."

Arlene looked toward the back porch and saw Mrs. Davenport's warm smile. *She knows I love this house.*

"I want it."

Mrs. Davenport hurried down the step, encircling Arlene in another hug. "I am so glad. That just makes us leaving it perfect."

"I'll get the papers drawn up," Mrs. Winslow offered.

"We're heading on down to North Carolina in a week. Can we get it done by then, Abby?"

"I don't see why not. Miss Sinclair has a good, steady job. Shouldn't be any problem at all."

"Good then. We'll get those papers signed, Arlene, and after that...it'll be all yours."

~

Arlene couldn't help smiling as she pushed the door to Ellie's diner open. Ellie, never one to miss such details, noticed immediately and hurried toward her with a grin of her own.

"And what canary have you swallowed today, Miss Arlene?" She waggled her eyebrows.

Arlene rolled her eyes. "Oh geeze, Ellie. Can't a girl just be happy around here?"

"Not you, my dear. Not a chance." She glanced toward the end of the counter. "Glad someone is in a good mood."

"The Sheriff having a bad day?" Arlene peered around Ellie at Lance where he sat staring into a cup of coffee from within a cloud of gloom that would have made Eeyore proud.

"You could say that." Ellie glanced sidelong at Arlene. "You gonna sit down there?"

Arlene looked around. The diner bustled with its usual early dinner crowd, but a few empty tables remained. "Looks like the best seat in the house," she whispered.

Walking to the back of the room, Arlene slid onto the stool beside Lance. "Hey, Lance. Something wrong?"

He shook his head glumly. "It's nothing. Goes with the job, I guess."

"I've never known your job to get your down like this."

"I don't have an answer on the robbery. I've checked. None of the local teens have been seen joy riding in that truck. I went to Cobbler's Bluff in case..." He cut his eyes toward her and cleared his throat self-consciously.

Arlene flashed a dimpled smile. "In case someone used it for a little spooning?" She squeezed his arm gently. "I grew up here too, remember?"

Lance's grim mood lightened. "Know Cobbler's Bluff first hand, do you?"

"Rude," Arlene quipped. "And nothing there either?"

He shook his head and resumed glowering at his cold coffee. "The Mayor wants an answer. He must call me three times a day now. Doesn't want the first 'crime wave' to hit Sunny Hills to be during his term in office."

"Mayor Harvey just wants a scapegoat, Lance. Anyone to take the attention off him. You're convenient, that's all."

"That may be, but the fact is I don't have enough clues to make heads or tails out of this. Damn, I need Dusty."

"He is good at puzzles," Arlene agreed.

"Best detective I've ever had." He slammed his fist on the countertop so hard the cup rattled and heads turned toward the commotion. "There's something I'm missing. It's there, I just can't put it together."

"I understand. Really, I do. Hey, who spends more time sticking her nose into things than I do? And I can't figure this one out." She caught Ellie's eye and motioned for coffee. "How about I get you some hot coffee? You'll figure it out, Lance. I know you will. "

Lance straightened, and Arlene saw the hint of a smile curving on his lips. "Thanks, but how about a rain check? I need to get back to work." He laid his money on the counter and nodded to Ellie. "Thanks, Ellie." Rising to his feet, he leaned for a moment close to Arlene. "I appreciate it, Arlene. More than you know."

Arlene watched him stride toward the door, enjoying the gentle swagger, the powerful grace of his movements.

Ellie filled Arlene's cup with steaming coffee, then swept Lance's money from the counter. "Well at least he's not growling now, that's something." She chuckled. "So, that good mood of yours still holding?"

Arlene considered it for a moment. She hated seeing Lance like this, hated even worse the guilt washing over her for the details she did not share with him. *He'll figure it out. There's no reason to worry him even more.*

"Depends," she answered at length. "Suppose, in a couple of weeks he'll be done sulking enough to help me paint my new house?"

Ellie's mouth fell open and she stifled an excited giggle. "House? Oh, honey! You bought a house?"

Arlene grinned. "Yep, just signed the final papers this afternoon. The old Davenport place."

"Oh, I remember the fun we all had over there. You and me, Heather, Michelle and Libby. Remember the sleepless sleepovers?" She shook her head, grinning broadly. "Those were good times. And now it's yours?" Ellie squeezed Arlene's hand. "How exciting. When are you moving?"

"Not till the end of the month. I want to get it fixed up and painted first."

"Have you told your folks?"

Arlene caught a quick breath. "Well, no. Not yet. Wanted to make it final first."

Ellie chuckled. "Afraid your momma would try to change your mind?"

"Don't you know it." Arlene nodded confidently and stirred sugar into her coffee. "But this is right, I have a really good feeling about this. Like I've finally come home at last."

~

Lester Harvey looked around worriedly before closing his car door. It wasn't a bad neighborhood, real middle class, and he'd been here plenty of times before.

Can't afford to be seen at a place like this, even if it isn't in Sunny Hills. That's all I'd need, have that nosey Sinclair get wind of this.

At the doorstep he paused again, checking up and down the quiet street. No traffic. Being after nine pm, most folks were already home. *Should be safe enough.*

He rang the doorbell. A man poked his head out the door, looking up and down the street before speaking to Lester Harvey.

"Been a while," the man muttered. "Back for more?"

"The boss in? I have money."

The guy opened the door and allowed Harvey to enter. "Good enough." They passed through the living room and down a narrow staircase to the basement. "Someone here to see you, boss."

A large desk dominated the small room. The man at the desk sat with his hands clasped before him studying Lester Harvey with the calculating coolness he might regard a bug under a microscope. He took a deep drag on his cigar, blowing a ring of smoke above his head. "What can I do for you this time, Harvey?"

"I need to make a wager."

"You're already in the hole to me."

Lester Harvey swallowed hard. "Damnit Brennan, now you know me better than that. I've done my fair share of winning, and I've never left you holding the bag."

The bookie nodded slowly. "You're in deep this time, Harvey."

Harvey bobbed his head nervously. He'd done this more than a few times. No one was scaring him off when the big money was so close to being his at last.

"I'd call this more of a business transaction." He wiped sweaty palms on his handkerchief and hoped his nerves weren't giving him away. He needed this. He had to have it. "Look, you need me to catch up what I owe you. Just give me a marker. Let me place this bet. I'll make it up. You'll see."

Brennan spread his hands over the spreadsheets covering the top of the desk. "How much?"

"First race at the Wilson Speedway. A thousand says Thomas will win."

"You got the money?" The bookie puffed on his cigar, staring narrowly at Lester.

"Yeah." Lester took out a wad of bills and laid them on the desk. "He's having a good run, this is gonna be the one. You'll see."

Brennan nodded. "I think we have a...transaction. Good luck, I know you can use it."

Sixteen

Caroline smiled when the doorbell rang. *That would be Arlene.* Her horoscope had been right all day, nothing but good news and surprises. Loved ones close at hand. *Perfect.*

She opened the door and embraced her daughter. "Sweety, I just knew you'd be coming tonight. I made extra for supper. Meatloaf and mashed potatoes."

"The men-folks' favorite." Arlene stepped out of her mother's hug. She hung her coat in the entry closet from long practice then turned to study Caroline with an appraising eye. "What do you mean you were expecting me? I didn't call. Momma..."

Caroline chuckled. "Why don't we have some tea? I have the kettle already on. Your dad won't be home for a half hour or so yet. He stays and helps Joe close up the store every night."

"How's Joe doing?" Arlene took cups from the cabinet and set them beside the stove, then took a seat at the small kitchen table while Caroline made the tea.

"A lot better. Clint says that young boy who's helping Joe out has just been a Godsend. Such a hard worker." She set the steaming cup in front of Arlene and leaned close with a conspiratorial smile. "I think your dad really likes that boy. Now tell me, what's going on in your life?"

Arlene hesitated an instant, sipping at her tea. Caroline pursed her lips but said nothing. *Keeping secrets from your mother are you? We'll see about that.*

"Nothing much really, Momma." Arlene stared at her cup. "Well, one thing, but I really wanted to talk to you and Daddy together about it."

"All right, honey. We'll wait till supper." Caroline stirred sugar into her tea. "Fall Festival is coming up soon you know."

"I know. Hard to believe how quickly this fall is going. And, of course, end of the month is Halloween." Arlene rolled her eyes playfully. "I don't suppose plans for that have changed much?"

"Certainly not." Caroline winked. "Halloween at the Sinclair's is a Sunny Hills institution."

"Daddy already loading in the straw bales?"

Caroline nodded. "And the corn stalks. And pumpkins."

"I bet by Fall Festival he'll already have the yard decorated." Arlene smiled fondly. "Always so much to do. Yep, Dusty and I carve the pumpkins, you and I make pies."

Caroline saw the wistful look in her daughter's eyes. "I know. I was hoping Dusty would be home this year too." She glanced at Arlene's nearly empty cup. A quick change of subject might just be in order here. "I know Lance was hoping Dusty would be home by now too." She pretended to be concentrating on her own tea even as she watched Arlene. "How are things going with Lance these days?"

Arlene's cheeks pinked. *Now isn't that interesting.*

"He's...busy. The robbery and all," Arlene offered, draining her cup.

Caroline quickly caught the cup from her hand and hurried to the sink. The late afternoon sun spilled into the kitchen through the window and Caroline tipped Arlene's cup to get a clear look at the dark pattern of tealeaves in the bottom. "Want more tea?" she asked absently.

Change, the tealeaves said. And...love? Caroline nodded with satisfaction. *Affairs of the heart. Well, well.*

"Why don't we get supper on the table? I hear your father coming now."

~

"The old Davenport place?" Clint Sinclair rubbed his chin thoughtfully and stabbed his meatloaf. "Didn't know they were selling the house. Where're they going?"

"North Carolina," Arlene answered, twisting her napkin in her lap. "Grandkids are there I guess." *C'mon, Arlene, you're a grown woman. Just tell them.* "Anyway, since I saw they were selling the place, I...well...I bought it."

"You bought what, dear?" Momma asked, staring at her. Her dad laid his fork slowly across the edge of the plate.

"I bought the house." Arlene took a deep breath. "It's all mine, and as soon as I get it cleaned up and painted, I'll be moving over there."

"You bought a house?" Her father's voice rose a little, but he seemed calmer than she'd feared. "I'll be. You bought a house."

Arlene nodded eagerly. "It's such a dear old place. And once I get it fixed up..." She looked from her father to her mother, who sat staring in silence. "It's not even far, you know, Momma. I used to ride my bike over all the time, remember?"

Momma nodded. "Quit twisting that napkin before it's so knotted up I can't ever iron it flat again." A slow smile wreathed her mother's face. "Good for you, honey. A house of your own. That's quite a step."

"Yes it is," Clint agreed. "Congratulations."

Arlene felt herself begin to breathe again for the first time since they'd sat down to eat. Getting to her feet, she went and gave each of her parent's a hug.

"Thanks, I really wanted you to know how excited I am about this move. Things at the apartment have just felt so"--she surely didn't want them to know all her reasons for wanting this new place--"so stressed lately. This house it's just...it's everything I ever dreamed."

"Well, soon as I can get over there, we'll make a list of the repairs the place needs." Her father nodded reassuringly and bit into his meatloaf.

~

Lance counted the rings...eight, nine...then hung up the phone. Where could Arlene be? She wasn't at the paper. She wasn't answering at home.

Dang it all, she's always around if I don't need to talk to her. Need. *Interesting choice of word there, Lance old boy.* Still, if he was going to ask her out... Lance caught a deep, shaky breath and picked up the receiver again. *Ask her out. Ask Arlene Sinclair to go on a date.*

He hung up the phone again and wiped his sweaty palms on the thighs of his slacks. How long had it been since he asked a lady out? He couldn't even remember. Fact was, there wasn't anyone else for him. Arlene had a lock on his heart.

Her folks' house. Maybe she went over there after I saw her at Ellie's.

He picked up the phone again and dialed the Sinclair's.

~

Caroline paced to the door and peeped out the side window again, shook her head and returned to clearing the table.

"What are you looking for, Momma?" Arlene stacked the plates in the kitchen sink.

Her mother sighed heavily. "I can't rightly say. Just one of my feelings, you know." She forced a tight smile and tied on an apron. "Like something is getting ready to happen. I don't know."

She glanced toward the front door again, and Arlene moved quickly to intercept her mother before Caroline could head that way again. "Here you go, Momma. I'll get the coffee started, okay?"

The phone rang and Arlene startled. *For pity sake, don't let 'psychic momma' get you jumpy as Miss Henrietta's cat,* she admonished herself. She heard her father's deep voice as he answered the call.

"Hello, Sinclair residence. Yeah, sure thing, Lance. She's right here." Clint cocked his head to one side to peer toward the kitchen and held out the phone. "Arlene, it's Sheriff Carter for you."

"Oh? Oh." Arlene stammered uncharacteristically and laid her dish towel beside the stove before she strode into the living room to get the call. *Now what could Lance Carter be calling me about?* Her father grinned, an annoyingly cat-ate-the-canary smug little grin, and Arlene snatched the receiver from him. "Hello?"

"Hi Arlene," said the deep smoky voice on the other end. "It's Lance."

"Yes, I know. Hi, Lance. What's up?"

"Not much, really. I guess." He cleared his throat. "Got Fluffy down out of that tree again tonight."

Arlene chuckled. "Maybe Miss Winston should keep poor Fluffy on a leash."

"Could be." His voice lost some of the tense edginess it carried when she answered. "Anyway, didn't mean to bother you if you're busy...with your folks and all."

"No problem," she assured. "Now, what can I do for you?" She really didn't intend the purr that rose in her voice. Sure didn't intend for it to slip out like this in front of her folks. *Dang it Lance, why do you do these things to me?*

A firm knock on the front door brought her father to his feet. "You go ahead, I'll get it." Clint sauntered toward the door with a wink.

"I wanted to ask--" Lance began.

"Caroline! Arlene!" Her father's voice was choked and filled with emotion. Her mother rushed past.

"Just a second, Lance. There's someone--"

The front door banged open and a familiar voice hollered above her parents', "Where's that nosey little sister of mine?"

"Oh my gosh!" The phone slid, forgotten, from Arlene's hand as her heart leapt. The golden curls were cut short now, but the laughter in the sparkling blue eyes was the same, and the dimple in his cheek when he smiled and threw his arms open to greet her. "Come here, soldier boy!"

Dusty strode to meet her, sweeping her into his arms and spinning in exuberant circles till her feet left the floor. He kissed the top of her head, just as he always did to remind Arlene who the 'big' brother was.

"Put me down," she protested with a laugh. Arlene felt her dad reach across her shoulder to clap his son on the shoulder.

Clint swiped roughly at the tears on his cheek as he stepped away. "Good to have you home, boy. I'm so proud of you."

Momma dabbed at her eyes, beaming as she looked at her children. "You are so thin. Didn't they feed you at all? We just finished supper, and there is meatloaf and mashed potatoes right there in the kitchen just waiting if you're hungry."

Dusty's face lit up. "Oh Momma, that sounds like pure heaven. I have missed your cooking something fierce." He hoisted the heavy duffel bag sitting outside the door. "Just let me stow my stuff away and I'll finish up everything you've got left."

~

"Why didn't you call and tell us you were coming home?" Momma wrapped one arm around Dusty's neck as she set the plate in front of him.

He shook his head, glanced up to meet Arlene's eyes and winked. "Well I figured you'd know, Momma."

Arlene laughed and her dad leaned into his hand to hide his grin.

"Oh, you are so bad." Momma narrowed her eyes at them, but couldn't hide her smile. "You could at least have let us know you were getting out."

Dusty dropped his gaze, intently burying the peas under the pile of potatoes just like he had at six. "I dunno," he mumbled, shoveling food into his mouth.

"You haven't written in weeks, Dusty. We were worried about you." Arlene touched his arm and he looked up at her with a rueful grimace.

"When they told us we were coming home--well, I didn't want to say anything till we were sure. Things are kinda crazy over there, you know? And then..." He flashed a tense smile and set to fiercely buttering a biscuit. "Well, by the time I got out of the infirmary I was headed home." Dusty looked up with a shrug. "And here I am."

"Infirmary?" Momma pressed a hand to her chest and slowly lowered herself onto a chair. "You got hurt over there? Oh my dear lord, honey."

"It's all right, Momma. I'm here now."

"You get shot, son?"

"No." Dusty looked into his father's worried eyes, then at his mother and sister. "Not shot, well not exactly. But I'm okay now. It just took a little while for me to heal up, that's all. Now, no more talk about it, okay?

"I'm home." He smiled and patted his mother's hand. "And that's just where I want to be."

"Okay." Arlene got to her feet. "How about I make us all some coffee?"

"So, how's Lance? Reckon he's still got room--"

Arlene's mouth dropped open, her eyes widening with sudden realization. "Oh my goodness! Lance!" She raced through the kitchen door and snatched up the still dangling receiver. "Lance? Lance?" No answer. With an embarrassed sigh she hung up.

Dusty chuckled, watching her through the open door. "What's going on?"

"I got so excited, I forgot poor Lance was on the phone. Maybe I should call him back."

Her mother gave her arm a squeeze as she passed, headed for the front door. "No need, I think that's him coming now."

Arlene and Dusty exchanged bemused looks, then the sound of sirens approaching filled the air. Arlene groaned and Dusty laughed aloud, wiped his mouth and got to his feet.

"Guess I can ask Lance about that job myself."

Seventeen

The siren moaned into silence as Lance pulled up in front of the Sinclair's. He stifled a gasp that changed into a chuckle. *Well, I'll be danged.*

A grin curved on his lips as he surveyed the group gathering on the front steps to greet him. Lance slammed the cruiser door and strode toward the house. Dusty bounded down the steps and met him half way. They clasped hands, but somehow, seeing his friend still dressed in his uniform grinning back at him, it just wasn't enough. Lance threw his arms around Dusty and they slapped each other on the back.

"Why didn't you call me, you son of a gun? I heard Arlene scream and then nothing...you like to scared a year's growth out of me."

Arlene approached, her head tilted to one side as she chewed at her lower lip. "Oh Lance, I'm so sorry. I just..."

She turned shining eyes to Dusty and Lance chuckled. "It's okay, I don't blame you a bit. I saw his ugly mug coming in the door I might have screamed too." He scruffed a palm over the top of Dusty's head. "How are you gonna get the girls to notice you without those pretty curls of yours?"

"I'm not worried about my girl." Dusty punched Lance in the shoulder. "But where do you think you're gonna find a girl that'd want you?"

Lance's gaze flicked to Arlene, and he turned hastily away. "Yeah, well, you might be right there, buddy."

"Now let's all go in," Caroline Sinclair said. "Getting chilly out here, and we were just putting some coffee on and I have a big pan of brownies."

"That sounds great," Dusty chaffed his hands together.

"And Lance, I am calling your folks right now and get them over here to celebrate with us."

Lance chuckled, no surprise there. "That's fine, Mrs. Sinclair. Thanks." Lance shot a glance at Arlene. How was he going to ask her now? He looked up at Dusty. Would he understand?

Dusty looked back with his familiar half-grin and Lance knew. *Yeah, it'll be okay. Now how do I ask her?*

"Coming in, Lance?" Arlene asked, pausing at the top of the steps.

He hadn't realized he'd stopped moving. "Sure. Could I talk to you for a minute?"

Arlene cocked her head to one side, regarding him with warm green eyes. She stopped on the bottom step. "Considering I left you hanging and made you drive all the way over here, that only seems fair."

Lance glanced nervously toward the house. Why did Arlene always leave him speechless? "It's great having Dusty home. He looks good."

"Yeah, I'm so glad he's home safe." She came down the last step. "But that's not what you wanted to talk about, is it?"

He swallowed hard and ran a hand through his hair. "Tomorrow night there'll be one of my favorite bands playing over at <u>The Fin and Claw</u> and, well, I had such a good time dancing with you the other night I"--he looked down then back up into her beautiful green eyes--"I was wondering if you'd like to have supper with me."

She stared at him, lips parted, those wide eyes sparkling and dancing. *Why doesn't she answer? Shoot, maybe I shouldn't have…*

"I'd love to have dinner with you. That would be very nice."

His heart started beating again. "Great. Okay, I'll pick you up at say seven?"

Arlene nodded, her blonde hair swaying with the movement. "Great." She slipped her arm through his. "Come on in. I'm sure the folks will be regaling Dusty with horror stories about my new house so I'd better be there to defend it." Her smile made him light up like Fourth of July.

"House?" His eyebrows crawled upward. Arlene had a house?

"Come on in, and I'll tell you and Dusty all about it. It's been a red letter day for me for sure." She laughed and waltzed up the stairs ahead of him and all Lance could think was he hoped he had some part in making her day special.

~

"Evening, Arlene." Lance slid into the cruiser, stretched his arm across the back of the seat and ducked his head to see his friends. "Dusty, whenever you're ready, let me know. We've missed you around the station, partner."

Arlene looked up at her brother as Lance pulled away. "Ready to get out of that uniform and just take it easy around here for awhile?"

Dusty stared after the police car with a distant wistfulness. "So you and Lance finally quit fighting it, huh?"

"Fighting what?" Arlene felt the heat creeping along her cheeks again.

Dusty shot her a sidelong glance. "Don't try to deny what you feel, sis. You wait...it could be too late." The muscles jerked in his jaw and he dropped to sit on the step.

Arlene could feel the emotions boiling just beneath his surface. "Okay, what's wrong?"

"I just...I need to know." He choked, cleared his throat and stared at the polished toes of his shoes. He wanted to say something more; the words wouldn't come. "Can you take me to see Katie?"

~

Arlene parked in front of Ellie's diner. Warm light shone from the windows breaking the coolness of dusk. Inside Gary bussed tables; Ellie worked the counter, and they could see Katie pass the window as she hustled among the few remaining tables of customers.

Dusty didn't move. His fingers frozen on the door handle he simply stared wistfully into the diner. Arlene couldn't decide if she wanted to hug him or kick him. Reaching across his frozen body, she opened the door.

"Come on, let's go in." Arlene gave her brother a shove.

"I can't. Look at her." He sighed heavily. "It's been almost two years. What if she doesn't..."

"Why are you here, Dusty? You didn't even want to take time to change."

His eyes never left Katie. "I came home for her."

"Then go get her."

He took a deep breath, straightened his shoulders, got out of the car and strode toward the door.

Arlene jumped out, opening the diner door before he could freeze again. Poking her head inside she saw Katie vanish into the kitchen. Arlene pressed her finger to her lips, cuing everyone for silence. The customers, each one a familiar face, smiled and nodded as Dusty stepped into the diner. Ellie pressed her hands together over her mouth, tears bright in her eyes, glanced back into the kitchen behind her and waved frantically for Dusty to get out of sight.

Katie reappeared, and Gary glanced from Arlene to Katie and deftly intercepted her. "Let me get it." He took the tray from her and nodded to an empty table. "Got a...ummm...party...taking that table. If you want to take it, I'll get this."

Arlene smiled appreciatively as Gary hurried past with the tray. Katie bent over the table, intent on laying out placemats and silverware.

Dusty squeezed Arlene's hand and strode back into the diner, until he was close behind her. "Katie, honey. I'm home," he whispered.

Katie bolted erect, a sound between a gasp and a whimper escaping when she saw him. Her arms flew around his neck and Dusty swept her off her feet and kissed her as the diner exploded with cheers, hollers and applause.

When he finally set her to her feet, Katie stepped back, tears sliding down her cheeks. "You didn't write...I thought something happened. I've never been so scared in my whole life."

"I'm sorry, Katie. I couldn't... I won't scare you like that ever again. I promise. I just...I just want to be here with you."

Katie swiped at her face, then threw her head back and laughed with delight as she wrapped her arms around him. "You're home. Now you're really home."

Eighteen

Gary took another nervous look around, and not seeing hide nor hair of a secretary or anyone else he at last poked his head around the door to Mayor Harvey's office.

"Mr. Mayor? It's Gary Jones. You wanted to see me, sir?"

"Come in, Gary." The mayor rose, smiling a bit too enthusiastically as he motioned for Gary to take a seat.

"Good to see you, son." He extended his hand and Gary accepted tentatively.

Why is he acting so danged happy to see me? Gary eased his hand from the man's grasp and perched on the edge of the chair.

"You've done some good work over at the park. And from what I've seen, you have a fine work ethic.

"So I have a special project for you. I'd like you to do some work on the playground over to the elementary school. It wouldn't take a lot of work, but it would have to be perfect when you're done. You up to it, son?"

"What would I have to do, sir?"

"Not much more than cleaning up and putting some mulch around the swings and the slide. See the tetherball poles get a new coat of paint. We don't want the little ones to get hurt, do we?" Mayor Harvey winked and patted Gary's shoulder.

"No sir." Something wasn't quite right, but Gary couldn't put his finger on just what it was. "When do I start?"

"Saturday morning."

Dang him. Gary sighed wearily. The Sheriff was right; he'd sure enough learned his lesson. Why was it the mayor always needed him to work on the weekend? *Once in a while would it be so bad to just have a day off? I just want to play some ball.* "Yes sir. I'll get it done."

Well, maybe I'll meet some other kids while I'm over there fixing things up. That'd sure be nice. Never thought I'd miss going to school so much.

~

Lance tossed the last stack of reports into the basket on the corner of his desk and rubbed his face with both hands. *Nothing. Not a single crime in the whole state that matches up with the ones here. I'm no closer than I was before.*

It had to be a coincidence; it didn't make sense the thief would somehow be tied to Arlene. The very thought tied his stomach in knots. Arlene didn't cover crimes... *As if we really had any before this.*

He shook his head and shoved away from his desk. He needed to get out of this office, clear his head. Something would come to him.

~

Arlene finished her article on the preparations for Sunny Hills' Fall Festival. It might be an ordinary little article, she thought with a smile, but Festival was just too much fun not to enjoy covering it.

She walked down to Tom Solana's office and dropped it in his box. "Anything else for me, Boss?"

Mr. Solana looked at her narrowly. "You seem to be in an awfully good mood today, Miss Sinclair."

"Something wrong with that, Mr. Solana?" She smiled and leaned against his doorframe.

"You'll get no argument from me," he said, holding his hands palm-outward. "We could use a filler article for page three. I'd like to see some coverage of the fall crops over to Knickerbocker's Farm and Orchard. Ox Knickerbocker told me he had a bumper crop this year."

"Do I need to take anyone with me, or would my photography be good enough on this one?"

"I trust you to take a picture of a pumpkin and some apples, Miss Sinclair." Now even Tom had to smile.

Arlene giggled and headed out the door. "You got it, Boss."

~

Arlene held her breath and waited. *Just a little closer. Come on, baby, just get right up there.*

Bright sunlight poured across the brilliant autumn colors of red and gold leaves and apples, warm browns, and bright orange pumpkins. She focused the camera. The chipmunk edged closer to the panorama of piled pumpkins in front of her, and in the perfect moment, skittered atop and sat up to munch the slice of apple she had placed there as a lure.

The camera clicked. "Perfect." She waved to Ox and his wife, Millie. "Thanks. Article should be in tomorrow's paper."

"Don't forget your cider." Millie brought the ice-cold jug to the car and Arlene tucked it in the back floorboard.

"I'll take one of those too, Millie." A familiar voice murmured behind Arlene and she whirled to face Lance as he handed the money to Millie

Knickerbocker, a gallon of apple cider clasped firmly in hand. "Finished up here, Arlene?"

She nodded. "Thought I'd stop over at my new house and...I dunno...just look things over." Arlene smoothed her skirt and slid into her car. "Would you like to see it?"

Lance smiled, and shoved his hat back. "Can't really leave the cruiser, but tell you what, I'll follow you over." His blue eyes danced and Arlene couldn't tear her gaze away. "I'd love to see your place."

"Great." She forced air into her lungs. "Let's go."

~

Arlene pulled up the driveway of the Davenport place. My place, she reminded herself. Lance parked in front and met her on the treelawn.

"Nice place, Arlene."

She glanced sidelong at him, saw that all-too-familiar 'male' look in his eyes. He was studying her house. Studying it! "What?" she demanded, hands on hips and a small wry smile twisting on her lips.

"Nothing." Lance tilted his head, still lost in his inspection. "Just...it could use some paint."

Arlene laughed. "Yes, it could. You volunteering?"

"By myself?" he asked skeptically. "You buy the paint, and feed us...I could probably round up some help for you." He flashed a heart-warming smile.

"I'll pay for the paint, if you'll buy it," Arlene offered. "But I pick the colors." She slipped her arm through his and they strolled toward the back yard.

"What color are you thinking?" Lance squinted up at the chipped and graying trim along the roofline.

"A warm, deep moss green with crisp white trim." Sheer delight colored her voice. How long had she dreamed of this moment? Her own home. And richer colors, more contrast, would set the architecture of this wonderful classic bungalow off to perfection. "And a white picket fence, all the way around," she added dreamily.

Silence from Lance. Arlene risked a glimpse. He was smiling. A warm, contented kind of smile. "Sounds beautiful, hon."

Hon? Where had that come from? Her eyes widened.

Lance must have realized what he'd let slip as well; he strode toward the back with workmanlike determination.

"Gonna have to replace these back steps too," he announced. "Tell you what, I'll come over the next day or so and get things sanded down and repaired for you. That'll make the painting go a lot faster." He cleared his throat and met her gaze. "I guess we can discuss this tonight over supper."

Arlene smiled. *Tonight*. She had a date with Lance. She looked around the shade-dappled yard, and nodded contentedly. "Yes we can. Tonight."

Nineteen

Lance looked in the car mirror and slicked his jet-black hair back smooth, then took a deep breath and got out of the car. He wouldn't be coming to this rambling old colonial once Arlene left her apartment here and moved to her new place.

From inside he heard Coco's excited bark even before his knuckles rapped on the door. He heard Arlene's approaching footsteps and instinctively straightened his shoulders and brushed his hands against the thighs of his slacks.

Looking at her, he couldn't speak. *She is so pretty*. Her golden hair was pulled away from her face to cascade down her shoulders in loose waves. He rarely saw her like this. *Not that she isn't always pretty as a picture but...wow.*

The red and white stripes of her top accentuated her breasts and a wide, black patent leather belt cinched in her tiny waist. Vertical stripes on the skirt drew his eye down the curve of her hips to shapely legs and bright red spike heels. She was a knockout.

Finding his voice at last, he managed a throaty, "Damn if you're not going to make every other woman tonight look plain as Jake's old crabs."

She pinked adorably and held out her white jacket. "Thank you, you don't look so bad yourself."

Lance held her jacket as she slipped into it, then she picked up her black patent pocketbook from inside and closed the door behind her.

~

The lights were low in <u>The Fin and Claw,</u> and the plush carpeting muted their footsteps as they followed the waitress to their table. Lance held the chair for Arlene and looked approvingly at the small, intimate dance floor only a few tables away. From the little corner stage sweet strains of "I'm Yours" wafted from the band.

Lance flashed a tentative smile at Arlene and wiped his hands on his pants legs under the table. Dang it all, he was nervous. *What the heck is wrong with me? I've known her all her life. Not like she's some blind date, some woman I just met.* He sighed under his breath, staring at the way the candlelight danced across her features and lit sparks in her hair. Then again, no woman had ever made him feel this way.

"What would you like for dinner?" Lance drained his ice water and tried to concentrate on the menu, but the entrées were swimming harder than they probably ever did in life.

"I really like their flounder here, but everything looks so good. Why don't you order for us?"

Lance glanced up at the waitress. "What would you recommend for the lady?"

"The crab-stuffed flounder is real popular."

Lance tilted his head, waiting for Arlene's response and saw her smile and demure nod. "Fine, how about we start with shrimp cocktail, then crab-stuffed flounder for Miss Sinclair, and I'd like a steak." He winked, nodding to Jake behind the bar. "Just ask Jake, he knows how I like 'em."

"And to drink?"

"A couple of drafts? Or would you prefer wine, Arlene?"

"Beer is fine, thanks."

"I'll be right back with your shrimp." The waitress collected the menus and vanished toward the bar to talk to Jake.

The band struck up the first stanza of "Because of You", the lead singer doing a decent imitation of Tony Bennett. Lance got to his feet and held out his hand. "Would you care to dance?"

He wondered if he looked as eager as he felt. Shoot, he'd thought of holding her in his arms every day since that dance at the Dew Drop Inn. She took his hand and swept elegantly to her feet.

Lance held her loosely, not daring to be forward and press her close so soon, even though he wanted it desperately. He stepped to the side, stumbled and recovered. "I'm sorry, didn't mean to step on your toes," he mumbled, looking down at her feet.

"It's okay, Lance. It's not your fault. I have a tendency to want to lead."

There was a teasing lilt in her voice that made his blood pressure soar. She looked different tonight. Or maybe it was the way he was looking at her.

~

Arlene couldn't take her eyes off of Lance. The crisp blue of his shirt brought out the blue of his eyes. The man looked deliciously handsome, she had to admit. Everything she wanted. And here he was. Her heart beat so fast it sounded like a drum roll every time he looked at her.

Lance stepped back, eyebrows raised. "What? Are my shoes untied? What?"

"Nothing," Arlene covered quickly, moving closer. Lance would really be blushing if he knew what she was thinking.

The waitress arrived with the shrimp and beers and Lance jerked his head toward the table as the music changed once more. "Shall we?"

Arlene inclined her head, then caught a short gasp and turned her face away. "Oh my. Look who's here."

"Who?" Lance peered over her shoulder toward the door just as a high-pitched voice called his name.

"Lancelot! Lancelot Carter. Goodness, imagine finding you here tonight."

Arlene bit back an urge to chuckle at the look on Lance's face at the sound of Henrietta Winston's voice.

"Miss Winston, nice to see you." He managed to sound almost cordial, in spite of his clenched teeth.

Arlene pasted on her sweetest smile and turned to face her co-worker. "Miss Winston."

"Why, Arlene." Henrietta was grinning like the cat that caught the canary off guard. "And what brings you here this evening?"

Great, this should make her column by the end of the week. Fine. Why should we have to hide? "Lance brought me, actually. Our food just came; we probably should go eat. Nice seeing you." Arlene took Lance's hand, holding her breath until he lifted his arm and moved away from the nosey gossip columnist.

"Well, certainly don't want to disturb you." Miss Winston snipped.

"Night, Miss Winston." Lance grinned at the sound of Henrietta sputtering as they walked away.

~

Lance laid his fork across his plate and smiled at Arlene across the top of his beer. Dinner had been delicious, but it wasn't what he wanted most. The band finished playing "The Glory of Love" and moved into "The Tennessee Waltz". *Perfect.*

"Would you like to dance?"

Arlene dropped her napkin atop the table and her hand slid into his as if it had always belonged there. He wasn't sure what he was doing was a waltz exactly, but it was a four step, and with Arlene floating in his arms, he didn't really care.

His hand closed naturally across the small of her back and she slipped forward a few inches closer, so close the perfume of her hair drove him crazy and the feel of her arm on his shoulder made tingles rush across his skin. He could stay here all night.

"I'll need to be getting home soon," she whispered, but she sure didn't look like she wanted to go.

Lance twirled with her, easing her even closer in his arms. "One more song?"

Arlene nodded. "Yes."

As the band moved into "Howlin' Moon", Lance left Arlene beside the dance floor and headed for the stage. One thing he knew for sure, this band knew the song he wanted. A quick gesture brought the bass player to him and he slipped him a bill and whispered his request, then returned to Arlene.

She looked at him quizzically, her green eyes dancing.

"What was that all about?"

"You'll see."

The last stanza of the song faded away and the bandleader took the microphone. "We have a request for a special song this evening for all you lovebirds out there."

Lance swept Arlene onto the dance floor and into his arms. "I think they're playing our song," he whispered as the first notes of "Unforgettable" sounded.

Arlene melted into him, and Lance held her close, swaying with the haunting melody, lost in her embrace.

~

Lance paused on the steps in front of Arlene's place.

She looked beautiful in the moonlight, all silver and gold.

Should he kiss her goodnight? What if she didn't want him to?

Only one way to find out. He ran his fingers down the side of her jaw, gently tipping her face upward. Moonlight lit sparks in her eyes. She didn't pull away.

Lance pressed his lips against hers. He intended to make it quick kiss, but once her lips met his there was no holding back. She was warm and soft and yielding. The kiss deepened.

He didn't know which of them broke away first. It didn't matter. All he knew was if he didn't leave now he never would.

He drew a shaky breath and cleared his throat. "Thank you for the evening. I'd ummm...I'd better go."

"Yeah," she said. She tried to put her key in the lock, but her hand was trembling.

Lance took the key, unlocked the door and opened it for her.

Arlene turned as she stepped inside and looked up at him. "Good night, Lance. It was lovely, I had a really nice time."

"Yeah, I did too." He stood for a moment, uncertain what he wanted to say. "I'll call you soon," he managed at last, jumped the steps and trotted the short distance to his car as Arlene eased the door closed.

~

Arlene leaned against the door and ran her fingers over her lips, reliving Lance's kiss. She couldn't remember ever being kissed that way, ever feeling what he made her feel.

Coco pressed his head up under her hand and she looked down and scratched his ears. "Dang, Coco. That man can kiss."

Twenty

Gary stood at the edge of the playground and studied his work. Everything trimmed. Tetherball poles and merry-go-round painted in the school colors. Fresh mulch under the slides, swings and other equipment.

He sighed, rubbed his hands on a rag and dropped down to sit. The sun was a warm gold on the horizon, but a cool evening breeze rustled in the trees and chilled the sweat on his skin. He couldn't remember when he'd ever been so tired.

Maybe I was wrong to come here. Maybe I won't ever find anything-- find anyone. Gary snuffled to keep the tears from coming. "Gotta try though. What else have I got?"

The mayor's car pulled up the driveway, and Lester Harvey leaned out the window. "Well, come on boy. You done here?"

"Yes." Gary got to his feet, dusted his pants with his hands. "Yessir," he said wearily. "Can I go back to the Market now? I gotta clean up before supper."

~

Mayor Harvey considered the bedraggled boy. Anyone saw him spattered with paint and covered with dust they'd ask questions. Questions he didn't want answered. Harvey jerked his head. "Get in. You can clean up over at my house."

To his credit, the kid never made a sound all the way to the house. A momentary twinge tugged at Lester's gut. He'd used the kid but...

Hell, what choice do I have? Besides, he owes me. He was caught committing a crime. Serves him right to have to do some real labor.

~

Gary slicked his black hair back from his face and looked in the bathroom mirror. *Well, at least I'm clean enough Miss Ellie won't be afraid to let me in the diner.* He smiled in spite of himself. A nice hot supper, and then he'd balance the night's books for her and get some sleep.

He padded down the hall to the kitchen on bare feet. Elizabeth Harvey looked up as he entered. "Better?" she asked.

"All done, thanks."

"Glass of juice for you on the table," she offered. "Go ahead and sit down here. You can have an apple if you want. Just watch out for Lester's books and stuff. He's left such a mess. Always leaving those things around when he knows I can't make heads nor tails of all those numbers. Just don't see why they can't put such things in plain English for a body." She fluttered her hands toward the table, untied her apron, then patted her hair. "Just let yourself out, you can walk home right? You don't need Lester to drive you home, do you? I mean we do have a dinner engagement over at Francis Buckley's."

The woman looked suddenly flustered, if not positively horrified at the thought of something...namely him...changing her plans. Gary shook his head. "No ma'am. I can walk, no problem."

"Oh good," she sighed and sashayed from the room. "Just close the door when you leave."

Gary pulled a chair away from the table and sat down. It felt good to relax for a minute before he started the walk across town. He drank the juice, tilting his head to get a better view of the long columns of numbers dancing down the pages of the ledger book. Red must mean those funds are exhausted, he mused.

"Lester, you ready? We're going to be late, honey." Gary heard Elizabeth Harvey call from the front room, followed by the Mayor's muffled reply and the sharp closing of the door.

Gary moved over in front of the books, took an apple from the fruit bowl and studied the town ledger. *Dang, what's the mayor doin' here?*

~

Dusty wiped his arm across his brow and handed the last board to Lance. "Looks pretty good," he admitted.

Lance pounded the final step into place, then met Dusty's eyes and grinned. "Yeah, not bad." He got to his feet, squinting up at the lowering sun. "We've gotten a heck of a lot done this week, partner."

"It's been good." Dusty turned to face his friend. "You still got room for me on the force?"

"Take some time, Dusty. No hurry, whenever you're ready, there'll always be a place for you. You know that."

"I've had time, Lance. More than you can imagine. I can't stand just laying around any more." He released a long breath and dropped to sit on the top step. Lance settled beside him, fiddling in silence with his hammer. Dusty knew what he was waiting to hear. He frowned, reluctant to relieve those memories.

"I'm not gonna stay on the force forever, you know," he managed at last. Lance glanced over at him curiously but made no comment so Dusty continued. "I've got some money comin' from the service and well, once I save up some, get a place of my own and all, I was thinking I'd get myself a plane."

Lance straightened. "A plane?" He stared across the wide lawn for a moment, then looked back to meet Dusty's gaze. "I figured your flying days were over now that you're home."

Dusty shook his head. "You know we made a lot of plans when we were growing up. Plans for what we wanted when we grew up. You--you always wanted to be Sheriff. From junior high on it was all you've ever wanted." He grinned. "And you're good at it, and you still love it, don't you?"

Lance chuckled and shook his head. It was answer enough.

"I like being deputy. I do. But there's something about flying...the feel of the plane...clouds like cotton candy and the sky going on forever. It gets in your blood." Could Lance even begin to understand this? Dusty looked at him hopefully.

"You get shot down?"

"Well, not exactly. I managed to land her. Just got a little torn up is all."

"And that's what you want?"

"Yeah, I do. I don't want to lose the way it makes me feel. That freedom." He smiled at the memory bringing those sensations back. He missed it.

Dusty cleared his thoughts. This was more than an idle kid's dream. Lance had to understand. "And I think I could make a living of it. Crop dusting...there isn't another crop duster for a hundred miles. Maybe even take folks on hops down to Jacksonville, or to Savannah, if they needed to go."

"Sounds like you've got it all thought out, Dusty."

"I had some time to think about things."

"You're sure you're ready to come back? We've got some stuff going on here. Hate to sound selfish, buddy, but I hope it takes you a while to make enough for that plane." Lance chuckled ruefully.

"So, what's going on?" Dusty leaned forward, elbows on his knees. "I mean how bad can it be? This is Sunny Hills."

The look on Lance's face silenced his urge to laugh. He'd never seen Lance this grim.

"Something's going on here. And I just haven't got all the pieces yet." Lance jumped to his feet and started pacing the small brick semi-circle leading from the steps to the back walkway. "Someone robbed Jonas' service station. They didn't get much, but whoever he was he gave Jonas a pretty good scare."

"Any leads?" Dusty's brow furrowed. Lance continued to pace, pausing only to accentuate his words.

"Nothing I can use yet. Cigarette butts, so I know he hung around a long time outside before he acted." He stopped, his expression darkening as he stared at the house. "Something else, but I'm not sure it's connected." Lance turned and strode away once more. "Then someone stole a pickup over across from the bus depot. Old truck, nothing special. I was figuring, it being close to homecoming and all, probably some teenagers joyriding. Except"--Lance paused and released a shuddering sigh of frustration--"that doesn't make sense either. And I found more of the same cigarette butts.

"The mayor is all over me about this. What with Joe getting run over at the intersection, Harvey doesn't want the town putting any blame on him for a crime wave in Sunny Hills." Lance made a wry face and scrubbed his fingers through his hair, then turned to face Dusty. "I could really use you on this one."

"You've got it. How about Monday morning? I'd like to have a look at what you've got. We'll figure it out."

Twenty-One

Arlene pulled up in front of the police station and looked over at her brother. Dusty was grinning like a kid, all anticipation and eagerness.

"You sure you want to go back to work so soon?"

"I am so sure, sis. Can't think of anything I want more." He glanced quickly at her, flashing a mischievous grin. "Okay, well, maybe one thing...but yes, I'm sure." He got out, closed the door and stooped to see her. "Besides, Lance can use the backup right now."

Arlene nodded. "Okay. You take good care of each other."

"Always have." He chuckled, waving as he walked away. "I'll have Lance or Randy drop me off after work. Thanks for the ride."

She watched him go into the building, then pulled onto Main and headed west from town. Fall Festival was a week away, and the Gazette wanted to take advantage of the excitement of town preparations.

Arlene tuned the radio to her favorite station and hummed along to Hank William's "Hey Good Looking", her fingers tapping on the steering wheel. It was a clear, bright morning; puddles of rain from the night before sparkled in the sunlight and everything seemed fresh and renewed.

Clarissa Johnson waited at the corner to cross. *Must be headed to the library*, Arlene thought as she slowed to a stop. Miss Johnson waved, but it didn't seem to be at Arlene. Glancing across the street, Arlene saw Jester waiting. He nodded to Arlene, then took Miss Johnson's hand as she reached him. *That's sweet.*

Pearl Jenkins raked heaping piles of bright colored leaves off her lawn. Her huge straw hat bobbed with every movement. *How many years has she worn that very same hat?* The wind caught the edge of a pile, sweeping a spiral of gold, red and orange across the road in front of Arlene's car.

Mayor Harvey's home came into view as she rounded the corner out of town. Arlene slowed. The big white house set back from the road, accented by a line of tall maple trees and a magnolia that hung over the roof to the rear. Lester Harvey had inherited the place from his mother and if it wasn't the biggest house in Sunny Hills, it was certainly one of the fanciest.

Today it seemed even more breathtaking that usual. The freshly mown lawn was an even emerald, every shrub and tree was newly mulched with deep red cedar that accentuated the red roof and accents on the house itself. The flowerbeds were ablaze with mums and huge pots of flowers lined the driveway and up to the entry.

Wow. Arlene shook her head in admiration. *Elizabeth Harvey is going all out for Fall Festival this year. About time her husband showed some real pride in this town.*

Arlene sped up, the scenery slipping past like a familiar tapestry. A gravel road turned off to the left toward the Martin's farm. Their fields stood fallow now, only the stubble of the last harvest remaining.

And around the next turn, backlit in a ray of sunlight as if heaven itself was spotlighting its simple, country beauty, the steeple of Sunny Hills Church came into view.

It really wasn't outside town so much as it would seem at first glance. Here on the corner of Main and River Road, it remained within easy walking distance of everyone in town.

Arlene pulled into the parking lot, hoping with a sheepish guilt that Pastor Brady wouldn't ask why he hadn't seen her the last couple of weeks. *He'll understand about Dusty coming home and all.*

Pastor Brady met her at the door, his wide smile a welcome greeting. "Arlene. Good to see you."

"Thank you for seeing me. Almost Festival time again."

"C'mon in." He ushered her to his office. A notebook lay open on his desk where he'd been working on his sermon for the following Sunday. "Coffee?" he offered. "Not great, but it's hot and fresh. The missus makes me a big pot every morning."

"That would be lovely, thank you."

"What's this I hear about Dusty being home?"

"Yes, he sure is."

"An answer to many prayers." The Pastor handed her a cup of coffee and took a seat behind his desk.

"Yes it is. I wanted to talk to you about the potluck dinner. Any idea what's on the menu this year?"

"Never completely sure, you know. We do get so many nice surprises each year." He rubbed his hands together, obviously relishing the church's annual participation in the Fall Festival. "Miss Johnson is bringing her prize winning pumpkin rolls. That's always a big favorite. And Mrs. Brady and the church's Women's Group are going to make roast beef and fried chicken, Mrs. Jenkins is making her famous Cheesy Tater Bake, and we'll have pumpkin pie and apple pie, and I am sure a nice dish from everyone in the community for everyone to share the bounty of the season."

"It's always wonderful," Arlene agreed. "Momma's been planning this for weeks."

"Well, your mother is a fine cook."

Arlene nodded appreciatively. "And what else would you like to tell Sunny Hills about?" She tapped her notebook with the eraser of her pencil.

"We got the ferris wheel again this year. Not to worry, it'll be running all afternoon and into the night. That way there's time for the kiddies to have a turn before bedtime." His pale gray eyes sparkled.

The ferris wheel. How long had it been since she had ridden it? The vision of Lance sitting beside her in the little seat, swaying atop the giant wheel beneath the moon whispered through her mind and Arlene smiled.

"And I know how the younger folk do love a slow turn or two come nightfall," the Pastor continued with a wink.

Arlene felt her cheeks flush and looked down quickly at her notes, clearing her throat. "I guess that should do it." She got to her feet, hand extended. "Thank you Pastor Brady."

He shook her hand warmly. "Fifteen tables, Arlene." He accented with a gesture. "That's how many tables the ladies are planning to see filled with food this weekend. Gonna be a fine evening."

"Yes. Yes, I'm sure it will be."

~

Lance leaned back in the booth, sipped his coffee and flipped quickly through the Gazette to Henrietta's column. No mention of Arlene? Or him? He breathed a deep sigh of relief and rolled his eyes heavenward. *Thank you, Miss Winston.*

He turned back to the front page and scanned through the articles. A nice piece by Arlene on Ox Nickerbocker's apple harvest, pumpkins, and the hay maze the farm would be putting up in the football field for Fall Festival.

Lance smiled.

'Mayor Harvey Announces School is Ready for Fun' the headline read. Lance's eyebrows crawled upward. It had Jack's byline. That made sense, Harvey probably still wasn't talking to Arlene.

He scanned the article. Slowed down and read it again. "Shit." He dropped the paper atop the table.

"What's up, Lance?" Ellie wiped her hands on her apron and refilled his cup.

He shook his head in disbelief. "Seems old Lester Harvey found some money somewhere in the town budget. He went and cleaned up the school for Fall Festival."

"He what?" Ellie's disbelief echoed his own. She slopped coffee over the saucer and onto the table. "Shoot. Now look at this mess. Gary sweetie, clean this up for me? I'll get you a fresh cup, Lance."

Gary came over and quickly wiped the spill up. "What's wrong?" he asked quietly.

Lance looked up at the boy. "Well, our good mayor hasn't had a dime for that light we need here at the intersection but apparently he did something right for a change." He shook his head again. "Dang if I understand it."

"What...what is it he did exactly?" There was hesitation in the boy's voice.

Ellie set a clean cup and saucer in front of Lance. "Now there's a good question."

"According to Jack's article, our illustrious mayor contracted with somebody and got the school grounds cleaned up, everything painted and mulched and ready for Fall Festival." Lance tapped the paper with his fingers. Something just didn't set right with him.

"But, but how can he say that?" Gary sounded strained and Lance looked up sharply. "That's not right. That's not right for them to put that in the paper." He backed away, scowling darkly. "I'll be back in a little while, Miss Ellie." He yanked off his apron and headed for the kitchen. "I gotta talk to Miss Sinclair over to the paper."

"Who's the kid?" Dusty asked, sliding into the booth and staring after Gary.

"His name's Gary Jones. Caught him trying to lift Henrietta Winston's purse over to the Corner Market," Lance explained. He watched out the front window as Gary raced across the street and took off up the street. *Something's really wrong here.*

"He's a good boy," Ellie added, filling Dusty's cup. "Works here every morning and night for meals. Does my books too. Smart kid. Never saw anyone who could do numbers like that boy."

Dusty's eyes narrowed and he stirred sugar into his cup until Ellie left to catch another table. "He show up in town before the robberies?"

Lance looked up, a line drawing between his brows. "Yeah, yeah he did. But you can just quit thinking that, he didn't do it."

"Why not? Seems a little hot-headed to me."

"I don't know what's got him riled up this morning, but he's a good kid. I like him. Reminds me of us at that age." He grinned at his friend and deputy. "Besides"--he sipped his coffee--"he doesn't smoke and as much community service as I've got him doing, plus him helping out since Joe broke his leg, that boy doesn't have <u>time</u> to get in trouble."

"Oh, I dunno." Dusty grinned and lounged back in his seat. "Never seemed to take us too much time." He chuckled.

~

"Arlene?" Jack poked his head around her door. "You've got a guest." He shot her his most charming smile, eyebrows waggling, then backed out and disappeared up the hall.

Arlene stared at the half-open door for a moment, but no one entered. "Come in?" She offered.

"Miss Sinclair?" Gary Jones shy face peered around the edge of the door.

"Oh, Gary. Nice to see you." Arlene motioned to chair near the wall. "Come on over."

He brought the chair over in front of her desk and perched on the edge of the seat. The kid looked so uncomfortable and nervous it was all Arlene could do not to go hug him.

"What's wrong?"

"I don't actually know. Just...there's an article in your paper today. And it's wrong."

"An article? One I wrote?"

He shook his head. "No, I don't think so. I didn't get a good look though."

"Okay, tell me what's wrong."

"It says that the mayor paid some people to fix up the school for the Festival."

Arlene nodded. Jack's article. "And you don't agree?"

"He didn't pay anyone. He had me do it."

Arlene leaned forward, frowning. Gary was obviously distraught. *What on earth has Lester Harvey done this time?*

"He had you do what, Gary?"

"Fix up the school. I worked all weekend. Painting and mulching and cleaning. He said it was part of my community service, and if it was, well that's all right and all... but...he shouldn't be telling people he paid someone else to do that work. Should he?"

Arlene sat back and released a deep breath. More money not accounted for. *Or misrepresented*, she fumed. The school...and what about the Mayor's house? It looked like a million bucks. *What did he do? Spend the school appropriations on his own place? Would he actually do that?*

She looked over and met Gary's worried blue eyes. "Don't worry, we'll get to the bottom of this. You did the right thing letting us know. We don't want the paper printing stories that aren't accurate.

"Might take me a little while to get the facts on this so we can print exactly what is true, but I promise you, I will find out and we will print it." She scribbled a quick note, then smiled at Gary. "And I'll speak to Sheriff Carter, I think maybe he can cut your community service at the park now. Sounds like you've done your share there."

Gary smiled for the first time since he'd arrived.

Twenty-Two

Sunny Hills Fall Festival had begun. Flags were displayed on every corner, banners waved above the streets and decorations adorned every store window.

Arlene smiled and waved as the floats rumbled past up Main Street. A turquoise blue Cadillac Coupe DeVille convertible proudly displayed this year and last year's Fall Festival Queens in their prom dresses and tiaras. Noisy tractors pulled flatbed floats decorated by the Sunny Hills High School, the local 4H club, and the Chamber of Commerce. Sunny Hills Savings provided a shiny black Studebaker for Mayor Harvey and his wife, and they sat in back and waved to the townsfolk while bank employees walked alongside and threw candy to the eager kids lining the street.

Flags fluttered on the breeze and everyone came to attention as the VFW marched proudly past. Arlene felt tears of pride welling in her eyes to see Dusty, resplendent in his dress uniform, striding in the center of the line. Hands clutched at her arm, and she looked over into Katie's beaming face.

"Oh," Katie moaned, clasping her hands to her heart. "Isn't he just so handsome? I'm so glad he got home in time for the Festival." Katie's eyes were wide and shining and as the VFW approached.

Arlene saw Dusty cut his eyes toward them and a flicker of deep dimple in spite of his sober 'military' face.

A hay wagon pulled by a team of gleaming gray draft horses followed and Arlene watched the parade out of sight, then headed back toward the town square and her mother's booth. Caroline Sinclair's bright purple and gold striped tent made a bold statement among the more understated white, blue and yellow canopies of other booths.

My mother, the town fortuneteller. Arlene had to smile at the thought, and smiled even wider when Caroline appeared in front of her booth in her perennial gypsy costume, right down to huge gold hoop earrings and a bright purple scarf tied over her hair.

"Hi, Momma."

"Arlene, come on in. You can be my second customer."

"Second?"

"Well, your father is always my first, you know." Caroline Sinclair beamed up at Clint where he busied himself hanging Chinese paper lanterns around the outside to light in an hour when the sun set. The entire square, the school, and the churchyard would all be ablaze with light and activities.

The Mayor would have the pumpkin-carving contest at his house. Elizabeth Harvey loved that. Of course, it provided an excuse for her to show off their lovely home, not to mention the exquisitely and intricately carved pumpkins she would have on display. And her ladies group would be there, naturally, serving hot-spiced cider and cocoa. *The Queen and her court*, Arlene thought. *Shame the King is a Fool.*

"Sheriff Carter." Caroline's voice shook Arlene from her reveries and she turned to see Lance approaching.

"I do hope you're going to come by and let me read your fortune sometime tonight?" Caroline's innumerable gold bracelets clinked as she waved him over.

Lance ducked his head, rubbed his chin and met Arlene's eyes with a smile. "Yes ma'am. I'll be by a little later, once we get the parade squared away and I make sure everything is running smoothly." He strolled toward Arlene, and she couldn't decide where to look first...at the little swagger in the way he moved, the slight roll of his broad shoulders, the laughter in his brilliant blue eyes.

He is fun to look at.

"Hi Arlene."

"Lance." She stopped close before him.

"You gonna be around here a while? I thought maybe we could get some pumpkin roll, hot cider, check out that ferris wheel." A smile curved on his lips. "To make sure it's safe."

Arlene bobbed her head, gaze locked on his. "Might be a real story there if it got...stuck...or something."

Lance waggled his eyebrows. "Could indeed. Can I meet you...?"

"Harvey's in an hour?" she suggested. "I have to cover the pumpkin carving."

"I'll see you there."

~

"That's great. That one will go with the article for sure," Arlene told the photographer.

The pumpkins from the contest were amazing, but not nearly as much fun as capturing the mess the younger kids had made in the process. Rinds, seeds, and inner pulp spread across the tables, dripped onto the ground and slopped out of buckets. Children with orange stained fingers and the occasional seed stuck to arms or hair, giggled as they accepted their awards then dashed off in search of games or food.

"Now that is a fine looking bunch of jack-o-lanterns," Lance drawled.

Arlene rolled her eyes, jotted down the final name and tucked her small notebook into her pocketbook. "Everyone safe and accounted for here?"

"Everything's just"--he paused, looked her toe to head, and smiled--"perfect."

Lance offered his hand and Arlene slipped her fingers through his, marveling at how natural it felt. How safe and right.

He escorted her across the darkening lawn where Christmas lights danced in the trees and tiki torches flickered in precise lines along the flower beds and down the driveway.

"Care to accompany me over to the church? I'll treat you to some pumpkin roll and hot cocoa."

Arlene smiled up at him. "Sounds good to me, and then what do you propose for tonight's entertainment?"

Lance looked down the road toward the church steeple. "Well, they do have that old ferris wheel."

~

The scent of popcorn permeated the air, mingling with the smoky aroma of tiki torches and the big harvest bonfire in the church lot. Laughter danced on the cool evening breezes. Arlene pulled her blue sweater closer, but Lance's hand was warm around hers and she didn't mind the chill. The bright lights of the ferris wheel rotated lazily against the deepening night sky.

"Ready?" Lance asked as he handed their tickets to Deacon Sanders.

Arlene stared upward at the huge wheel and squeezed his hand.

"Not scared of being all the way up there alone with the big, bad sheriff?"

"Oh, I don't know," she murmured. "I hear tell he's not nearly as scary as folks might think he is."

Lance chuckled. "Well, we'll find out. This would be our seat."

He helped her into the gently rocking metal carriage and the handle clanked down in front of them. The wheel moved forward a few feet while the next people were loaded. Arlene felt butterflies building as excitement fluttering in her stomach. The movement of the wheel, slowly taking her closer to the moonlit sky and Lance so close beside her was exhilarating.

She looked out across the glow of the bonfire in the field adjoining the church, bright orange against the night. Ribbons of Christmas lights glimmered between the trees in the square. They rose higher, Arlene shivered and Lance moved closer. She delighted in the security, the warmth of his body, his arm resting behind her on the back of the seat.

The tiny, intimate world of Sunny Hills grew smaller as they rose, then slowly drew nearer once more as the wheel circled back toward the ground before sweeping them upward again.

It spun the circle, a gentle rocking accompanying their increasing speed, the lights whirling past faster and faster till Arlene's hair blew back off her face and she squealed with the thrill of rushing through the air. Lance laughed with delight and closed his arm around her and she snuggled close against his body.

Gradually the ride slowed, their seat rocking as they finally came to a halt atop the giant wheel. Arlene giggled under her breath, the wonderment and excitement of the moment overwhelming her. On top of the world, with Lance at her side. *What could be more perfect?*

Lance shared her emotions, or maybe, she thought, he heard her thoughts. Leaning forward he tipped her face in his hand and softly kissed her.

The moment lingered, timeless, until the lurch of the ferris wheel starting separated them, breathless and longing for more.

~

Caroline Sinclair escorted a pair of giggling teenagers to the front of her booth. "Remember what I told you now." She spread scarlet nailed hands dramatically, and the kids' eyes widened before, laughing even harder, they dashed into the park. "Madam Caroline sees"--she droned in a thick theatrical accent---"it is time to reveal your future, Lance Carter."

Lance rolled his eyes, grinning broadly as Arlene pushed him toward her mother. He shoved a fiver into the donation can perched on a stool beside the door. Funds raised at the Festival would be used to replace the town's emergency aid fund emptied last year to help the Williams' family when their house had burned down.

Caroline gestured him inside and Lance leaned close to Arlene as he passed. "You owe me for this one."

"You two have fun. I'm going to check out the fun house in the gymnasium." She strolled away with a sway of her hips that made her soft cotton skirt swirl around long, shapely legs and Lance had to fight the urge to follow like a homeless puppy.

"This way, Sheriff Carter," Caroline encouraged and he turned and ducked under the canopy and into the tent. The flicker of the Chinese lanterns hung in the trees outside danced against the canvas and the lights inside were dim.

Lance took a seat on the folding chair and leaned an elbow on the purple swathed card table. *The 'crystal ball' is a nice touch*, he thought wryly. *Trust Mrs. Sinclair to do this up right.*

"Now, I'm only doing this reading for fun. You understand that, right? I don't believe in this stuff."

"Of course not, Sheriff," she murmured, laying a deck of fancy tarot cards before him. "You cut the deck, give it back to me when you think it is right."

Lance gave it a quick cut and set it on the table in front of Caroline who promptly began laying cards across the table in a pattern. She paused, scarlet lips pursed and arched brows rising as she studied the cards.

"This is your past. The events and perceptions that shape you. This"-- she tapped a card with one long-nailed finger--"shows something from your past will soon influence your future."

She turned another card, laying it with infinite care upon a line, then sat back in her chair. Lance squirmed uncomfortably. This was taking a lot longer than he'd planned. It was supposed to just be for fun, but Caroline Sinclair seemed to be taking this very seriously. She tapped a card, shook her head and tapped another, her gaze sweeping across the spread repeatedly.

"Interesting," she said after a moment. "More complicated than I expected, Lance." Her bright eyes flicked up to meet his. "You been keeping secrets from us, boy?"

"Aw, c'mon, Mrs. Sinclair. You've known me all my life." Lance hid behind a crooked grin. "So what do you see?"

"This is the card of change. In relation to these others it indicates a life-changing difference in a relationship."

"Who with?" Lance leaned forward, uncertain if he was eager to hear her prediction or scared.

"The cards don't give names, hon," she explained indulgently. "They show the way. Now you have choices to make. To embrace what's coming...or deny it."

"Dang." He rubbed his chin thoughtfully.

Caroline touched a card at the end of another line. "Now this tells us you--"

"Sheriff Carter," Randy burst into the tent, face flushed and breathless.

Lance came to his feet instantly. "What's wrong?"

"Hardware store. Glass is busted out. Might be a robbery."

Lance nodded. "Thanks, Mrs. Sinclair. If you see Arlene before I get back, tell her I'm real sorry." He grabbed Randy's shoulder. "Find Dusty."

Twenty-Three

The area surrounding Gleason's hardware seemed quiet as Lance eased the police car to the curb. Situated a block off the main square of town, the party-goers had little reason to pass except heading to or from the Festival.

Shards of glass glimmered in the glow of Lance's flashlight as he edged along the wall. The window in the front door was broken just above the handle.

Yep, looks like a robbery.

Inside, everything was dark and quiet. Lance held his breath and concentrated on sounds from within the store. Laughter and music from the Festival made it difficult, still, there didn't seem to be any movement, no footsteps, sounds of things being moved.

He tried the knob. Locked.

Reaching through the jagged opening, Lance eased the door open from the inside, then glanced back hurriedly at the sound of footfalls.

Dusty nodded as Lance met his eyes, then motioned toward the back. Lance jerked his head in agreement and watched his deputy vanish into the shadows along the side of the clapboard building.

"Stay here," he whispered to Randy. "Make sure no one comes in or out."

Stepping carefully over the scattered glass inside the doorway, Lance moved into the store. A bit of glass crunched underfoot and he froze for an instant. When there was no response, Lance breathed more easily.

He flicked the beam of his flashlight over the checkout area. The register was intact and appeared untouched. Lance shone the light across the surrounding aisles, moving with increasing speed into the store.

Nothing knocked over. Anything that might have been taken was not obvious. Something was wrong here. A tiny alarm sounded in the back of Lance's mind.

Dusty squinted as the light played across his face.

"Find anything?"

Lance shook his head. "Nope. Looks like someone just busted out the door, but the devil if I can see where they robbed the place. You?"

"No one back there, that's for sure." Randy jerked his head toward the back of the store. Back door was open though. Looks like they came straight on through."

"Okay. Lock it up back there. Mr. Gleason should be helping over to the church. I'll have Randy bring him over to board up that hole in the door. Meet you out front."

Dusty nodded and headed toward the rear. Lance strode purposefully to the entrance. Randy was crouched just outside the door, rising as Lance appeared.

"All quiet?" Randy asked.

"Yep. What are you doing?"

"Found this." Randy held out a small plastic bag containing a snubbed out cigarette butt. "Same as the ones you found over to Jonas' I think. Oasis brand."

Lance scowled. Same as the ones around Arlene's car. *Arlene.*

"Find Gleason, tell him about the door. I gotta check something." Lance shook his head in frustration and ran for the car. *Damnit, what's all this got to do with Arlene?*

~

The front of the school was decorated with children's art projects: construction paper scarecrows, turkeys made from handprints, and paintings on the windows of apples, corn and pumpkins. Laughing families filed down the wide concrete steps.

In the front hallway, lines of kids waited their turn at bobbing-for-apples and the Principal handed out big popcorn balls. Arlene took note of it all. This would be tomorrow's article after all.

Lights in the big gymnasium flickered off and on to help set the 'mood' for the annual spook-house. Cobwebs of string and long streamers of crepe paper hung from doorways and draped overhead. Good-natured screams came from behind the maze of partitions that formed small rooms, each with its own theme.

Arlene laughed at muslin ghosts dancing overhead on strings, obligingly stuck her hand through the holes in another room to touch various 'slimy' items, and giggled at the antics of parents and children squealing in mock terror.

At the next corner Arlene took a left around a divider swathed in black cloth and kids' drawings of their skeletons into a small cubbyhole containing the coffin on loan from Dawson's Funeral Home. The lights cut out and Arlene screamed happily along with everyone else in the gym, her shriek changing to surprise as she felt an arm slide around her waist. She stepped back, bumping into the casket, which caused her to yelp again. The disembodied hand caught the back of her neck, and Arlene gasped as someone kissed her. Lips pressed hard against hers, then just as abruptly pulled away. Her hands groped in the darkness, touched a man's arm but she couldn't seem to actually get hold of him. Where was he? Whoever it was turned her in a dizzying circle, thrust her backwards...and was gone.

The lights in the gym flashed back on, accompanied by more whooping from the crowd, and Arlene looked around the tiny cubicle.

No one?

"I am so going to get you for this, Sheriff Carter," she muttered under her breath. *Who else would be sneaking up on a defenseless girl and smooching her in the dark?* Arlene giggled at the idea; her guilty pleasure at the thought of kissing Lance fading slowly into niggling doubt. Somehow this kiss just hadn't *felt* the same.

Mrs. Martin and her trio of carrot-topped kids entered from the direction Arlene had come. *Time to leave, let them enjoy the coffin.*

The coffin... Her eyes widened in genuine horror and Arlene reached a trembling hand to take the single red rose laying atop the casket. Heart pounding, she pushed her way from the room and out the side exit of the gymnasium.

She needed fresh air. She needed to think.

Arlene glanced toward her mother's striped awning across the street, hoping Lance would come out soon. She couldn't wait. Her fingers closed around the stem and she bounded down the stairs leading from the exit just as the patrol car pull to the curb.

~

Lance swung out of the cruiser, slamming the door behind him as he caught a glimpse of Arlene standing at the side exit staring numbly toward him.

"Arlene?"

Her pace quickened and Lance strode toward her until he reached her, caught her in his arms and pulled her close. She trembled slightly, pressing her face against his shoulder for an instant before she stepped back.

"Where were you?" She tried to keep her voice calm and even, but Lance could hear the edge of nervousness.

"Someone broke a window at the hardware store, I was just checking it out." He leaned down to look closely at her in the wavering streetlight. "What's wrong?"

"Nothing." She shrugged, making a small wry face. "Just, I thought"-- Arlene drew a deep breath and plunged ahead--"Someone kissed me, in the fun house. At first I thought...I thought maybe it was you, but..."

Lance stiffened, his stomach clenching. *Someone kissed Arlene. And it wasn't me.*

"And?" he growled.

"But then when the lights came back on no one was there and...and there was this." She held out a single rose. Her smile as she looked up to meet his eyes quavered slightly. "My secret admirer?"

Lance caught her elbow, steering her toward the cruiser. "I'm taking you home."

"Now Lance, don't be silly. It was just a silly prank. Nothing to get all worked up over."

"You know better." He glared at her, catching her wrist and forcing her to look at the rose she still clutched. "It isn't a joke any more, Arlene. And I won't rest till I find out what is going on here."

She lifted her head, lips forming a tight line, and Lance saw the reporter taking control as the momentary worry in her features slipped away. "Was it another robbery?"

"What?"

"At Gleason's? You said someone broke in."

"No. I said a window was broken. That's all. Now come on. Let me see you home."

"If it wasn't a robbery, then why did they break the window?"

"That's another little mystery for me to solve." He stared at her hard. "Me, Arlene. Me, and Dusty and Randy. Not you." He let his hand slide down to cover hers, his voice softening. "I want you to stay out of this one. I'll give you the story if that's what it'll take. I'll tell you anything I can. But please, Arlene, please...I don't want anything to happen to you."

"Oh, don't be silly, Sheriff. Nothing's going to happen to me. Nothing ever happens in Sunny Hills." Arlene chuckled softly, but the laughter didn't make it to her eyes. She reached up and gently pushed his hair back from his forehead. "Okay," she murmured. "Take me home, if it will make you feel better. But I want the story. All of it."

Lance shook his head ruefully, then nodded. And that did light the smile in her eyes.

Twenty-Four

Kent Jordan hung back in the deep shadows alongside the gymnasium and watched Arlene and Lance get into the patrol car.

Damn Carter, anyway. Looks like the Sheriff is real tight with Arlene. Not that I blame him, dang if she isn't just as good a kisser as I remember.

She slid across the seat and Lance closed the door behind her. Kent nodded to himself. Yeah, Arlene was the answer. Punish her. Punish him. *Ten years of my life. And someone's gonna pay for that.*

~

Lance stared narrowly at the big colonial that housed Arlene's apartment. Golden light from the wide front porch spilled across the lawn. Arlene's smaller side porch remained darkened. All quiet. And yet... Something made the hair on the back of Lance's neck stand on end.

What's different here? He opened the car door, then glanced quickly back at Arlene. "Stay here a minute. Just let me check things out."

For an instant he thought she was going to argue with him, instead she nodded. "Okay. But tell Coco it's you. Don't need him waking the Murphy's baby if they're upstairs."

Lance's heart lurched. *Coco. That's what's wrong. Why isn't he barking?* He straightened slowly and closed the cruiser door. "Lock the doors. I'll be right back."

Edging toward Arlene's porch, Lance scanned the area. No signs of anyone around the house. The street was empty, as was to be expected, most everyone would still be at the Fall Festival for a little while yet, enjoying the weekend and the chance to visit with friends and neighbors, listening to the local bands, waiting for the evening's festivities to reach their climactic finale.

Front or back? Front or back? Lance glanced back at the car, grateful the dark hid him from Arlene as he slid his gun from the holster. *If whoever is stalking her is inside and armed...* Lance took a deep breath and skirted around the house. *Back.*

The old gate squeaked as he touched the latch. Rather than risk it alerting an intruder, Lance climbed over the fence, cursing the slight rattle as he dropped to the ground. A dark shape at the foot of the back steps drew his attention and Lance dropped to a crouch as he crept forward.

"Coco?" Lance whispered as the Lab lifted his head groggily and crawled unsteadily forward. Coco's heavy tail thumped the ground with recognition. "You okay, buddy?"

He stroked the broad skull. The dog seemed dopey...drugged...but otherwise fine. Coco panted, a foolish, happy look on his face. "Glad to see me, huh?" Lance straightened. "Stay, Coco. Atta boy."

Lance took the steps in two strides and checked the door handle. Locked. *Then how did Coco get out...?*

The dog door. Lance dropped to one knee and checked the heavy flap. It opened easily to his touch. No way was he crawling through there. He'd be an easy mark for anyone inside the house.

A sudden crack sounded in the dark and Lance leapt from the porch, his hand tightening on his revolver. Light flickered overhead, bright and sharp against the clear dark sky. Lance sighed heavily, relief flooding through him.

Fireworks. Another boom followed by the smaller popping of shells going off. The closing display celebrating Sunny Hills' Fall Festival coming to an end. Lance caught another deep breath and started toward the front of the house. *Great, way to overreact. That could have blown everything.*

The front door opened with the slightest touch. Not locked or latched. Easing the door open, Lance stepped into the darkened interior of the apartment. The steady ticking of the mantle clock sounded like a heartbeat. No other sound. If anyone had been here, they weren't here now.

"No, you did this before the fun house, didn't you?" Lance growled under his breath. "Now how do we know it was you?" He flicked on the lights and holstered his gun.

Eyes narrowed, Lance scrutinized the entry. Where to begin? He didn't have to go far. A single rose lay on the seat of the chair near the wall in the foyer.

"Dang, while I'm looking at Gleason's you're here, making your mark. Why?"

"Good question." Arlene's voice close behind made Lance jump. He spun around to face her.

"Thought I left you in the car."

"My house." She met his gaze with steady determination, but Lance saw the tight white around her lips. Arlene was scared no matter what she said. "I saw the lights go on, so I figured I'd see what's going on." She looked around quickly. "Where's Coco?" Her voice broke. "Where's my dog?"

"He's okay," Lance soothed. "Out back. Looks like he's been given some tranquilizer or something. But he's okay."

He pulled Arlene into his arms, felt her heart pounding against his chest. "And so are you." He held her out at arm's length and stared into her green eyes. "And I'm gonna keep you that way. You get your stuff. I'll put Coco in the back of the car. I'm taking you to your folks'."

"I am a grown woman, Sheriff Carter. I don't need to go running home. I can handle this. Reporter. Remember?"

"You are a beautiful woman. And strong. And more bull-headed than any woman I know. But dang it, Arlene, I need you home. I need you safe.

"If you won't do this for your own sake. Please, honey, do it for me."

Arlene closed her eyes, lips tight as she drew a long breath. Opening them, she nodded. "Okay. Okay, Lance." She looked around the apartment, eyes bright with tears. "It isn't home any more anyway."

~

Arlene reached over the seat to scratch Coco's ears and tried to regain her composure. Lance had called her honey. And this time she knew, it was no mistake. And what was worse, she'd let him not only make his mark on her heart...but gone along with his 'plan' for her safety.

Since when do I let other people convince me what to do? She looked up as he slid across the car seat and closed the door. Looking into his blue eyes, she knew she couldn't worry him like this. Not without a darn good reason. *And Mr. Stalker, you are an exceptionally good reason. The only question is, how do I find out who you are without having poor Lance fretting about me every minute?*

Well, that's what this is, isn't it? She chided herself. *I'm going home for no better reason than to keep Lance from worrying so I can get some answers without him right behind me every inch of the way.*

The cruiser pulled away from the curb and Arlene stared determinedly out the front windshield. "We're gonna have to talk about this, Lance. Something's going on, and we both know it." She glanced over at him; saw the little muscle in his jaw jerk. *Paydirt.* "You can't keep me in the dark about this. It kinda involves me now, doesn't it? Or shall we turn around and go back home?"

Lance released a pent breath through clenched teeth. "You know better, Arlene."

"So, you gonna tell me what is going on?"

"I don't know." He stared straight ahead for long, silent moments and Arlene could tell he was chasing answers, looking for what to say. He pulled the cruiser over beside the road and turned to face her. "I don't know anything right now. Except whoever is behind these robberies seems to be connected to you. Otherwise, why all the roses?"

Arlene leaned toward him, eyes dancing impishly. "Maybe he just wants to make you jealous."

Lance's face darkened. It didn't matter she meant it as a joke; he obviously didn't see it that way. "Gawd Arlene. What if it is me he wants? Then me just being with you puts you in danger." He scrubbed his fingers through his jet-black hair. "I won't do that. But if it's you he's after...damn." His hand closed on her shoulder. "I'll get Dusty to keep an eye on you. That okay? It won't get your folks all upset if Dusty is with you. We can come up with some reason you need to stay at their house for a few days."

"I'll come up with something," she assured him.

"And you won't go off alone without Dusty or me one, right?" Lance's fingers closed over hers. "You're at least gonna try to stay out of trouble, aren't you?"

Good thing he added that last part, now she could answer without lying to him. "Promise, I'll try to not get into too much trouble. Least ways, not without you."

Lance leaned forward and kissed her forehead. "Can't say I believe you completely, Miss Sinclair, but that'll have to do, I guess."

Twenty-Five

Gary yawned and dumped the wheelbarrow of pumpkin hulls and scraps onto the compost pile at the back of the Harvey's property. Most of the debris from the previous night was cleared now. Chairs lay in neat stacks waiting for him to carry them to storage.

Just gotta put those tables and chairs away and get the lanterns down and I'll be done. He stifled another yawn. *Stayed up too late last night. Shucks, it must have been nearly eleven o'clock by the time I got to bed.* Not that it hadn't been fun. Gary grinned at the thought. Sunny Hills was a pretty fine little town. *I wouldn't mind calling it home.*

Good thing Mr. Sinclair had come to the store early. He hadn't figured on the mayor expecting him to clean up everything at the park <u>and</u> his house, and Mr. Joe still needed help getting things open in the morning.

Gary tipped the wheelbarrow up and leaned it against the rear of the house. The sound of the phone ringing filtered from the kitchen window. He pulled the water hose loose and turned on the spigot to rinse the wheelbarrow.

"Lester out there?" Mrs. Harvey called out the window.

"No ma'am."

"Lester!" The sound of her voice moved from the kitchen toward the front of the house. "Lester, some gentleman on the phone for you."

Gary turned the water off and began recoiling the hose, pulling big, even loops of green around his arm.

"This is Lester Harvey."

His voice was so clear Gary glanced up to be sure the mayor hadn't come outside. Instead, he was leaning against the kitchen counter with his back to the window. Gary looked over at the tables, still spattered with residue from the pumpkin carving.

Shoot, need to hose them down too. Still holding the water hose, Gary bent to turn the water on again.

"Yeah, that was a fine race," Mayor Harvey proclaimed with a chuckle. "Now that just about brings us even, doesn't it? Tell you what, you take the money from last night and roll it onto the big NASCAR race next weekend."

Racing? If there was one thing a southern boy wanted to hear about, it was racecars. Curious, Gary stopped, still clutching the handle, water flowing unheeded across the lawn.

"Yeah, yeah, I know I've been in the hole a little lately. But you know me. You know I'm good for it.

"Who? Fonty Flock. All of it on Flock to pull this one off, he's having a dang fine year."

The Mayor's voice faded as he moved away from the window and Gary shook himself and hurried to the driveway to hose down the tables.

~

Lester Harvey pursed his lips, lost in thought as he hung the phone back in the cradle. *All right, this'll be the one.* The last win had almost pulled him even. *Just a couple of grand, that's all I need. One more win and I'll be in the green. Get me a good run going, I'll be able to put the money back, and no one'll ever know.*

Yep, that's all I need. Just one good run.

He rubbed his hand over his face and peered out the back at the youngster hauling the heavy picnic tables toward the storage barn. Good. Soon as he was done, Lester would drive the kid back into town and no one would ever be the wiser. This had worked out better than he'd ever hoped.

"This is shaping up to one fine day."

~

Caroline Sinclair flipped the page to the editorial section of the newspaper. Her eyebrows crept upward and a slow smile pulled her lips. "Well, well, well."

"What?" Arlene asked from across the table. "Someone's horoscope surprise you there, Momma?" She reached for the paper, but Caroline pulled back, swinging around and rising as she folded the page down.

"Nope, the horoscopes are just perfectly in line with the universe, sweety." Caroline smirked at her daughter over the top of the paper. "But my goodness, this article is interesting."

She could see the wheels spinning in Arlene's mind. The newshound perked up, eager for the bait.

"Well, let me see."

"Here ya go." Caroline cleared her throat and began reading. "Fall Festival and Henrietta heard about a lot more than the annual games, fireworks and fabulous food.

Mayor Lester Harvey and his wife, Elizabeth, opened their lovely home to Sunny Hills. The church potluck was a rousing success as always, and Henrietta heard many compliments on the wondrous dishes prepared for the festivities.

But a certain well-known man in uniform provided the finest attraction of the evening as he was seen strolling with one of the Gazette's own top reporters. Not the first time either. We'll be watching this one because Henrietta hears strains of romance on the air.

Until next time, remember it's not just what you see but what Henrietta hears." Caroline rolled her eyes up to meet Arlene's gaze. "Now whatever do you suppose she is referring to?"

Arlene's mouth opened and snapped closed, the pink of a blush burning across her cheeks. "What are you hinting at, Momma?"

Caroline continued to stare with unblinking expectation.

"Fine," Arlene sighed. "So she might have seen Lance and I visiting at the Festival. That doesn't mean anything, you know."

"Of course not. How about the sparkle I see in your eyes now days? The way you light up when he comes around." She walked around behind Arlene's chair and wrapped her arms around her daughter. "Does that mean anything?" she whispered.

~

Lance opened the door to his office and stared with a mixture of confusion and amusement at the scene before him.

Dusty leaned back in Lance's chair, ankles crossed and feet propped on the desk, reading The Gazette. Randy Taylor sprawled in the other seat, a bottle of wine topped with a big bow in hand.

"Okay, you two. What's this all about?"

"What?" Dusty snapped the paper and thrust it toward Lance. "You mean to tell me you didn't *know* you're dating my sister?"

Lance scanned the article, shaking his head and chuckling as his deputies burst into laughter, no doubt at the look on his face.

"So," Randy drawled. "Has our Sheriff lost his heart? You gonna make it official?" He slid the bottle of wine onto the desk in front of Lance. "Need some help popping the question?"

"Dang, you two just don't know when to quit do you?" Lance replied with a crooked grin.

Dusty winked and flicked the edge of the newspaper with his fingers. "There's the truth in black and white. You serious about my sister?"

"We've barely had a chance..." Lance shrugged ruefully. "And until whoever is behind the robberies and break-ins is caught, I don't expect we're gonna have much time for romance or anything else."

"Well you sure look like a man in love." Randy swung to his feet and slapped Lance on the back. "Got that moony, calf-eyed look for sure."

Dusty burst out laughing again. "Nah, he always looks like that."

"Get out of here, the both of you, before I put you on school crossing detail till next June."

The two backed toward the door, still grinning. "Least ways, we'll be done in time for the wedding."

~

"Morning, Arlene." Debbie snapped her bubblegum and smiled brightly. "Anything I can do for you?"

"I need to talk to Sheriff Carter. Is he in?" Arlene glanced hopefully toward Lance's office door.

"For you, I'm sure he is." Debbie wheeled around the corner of the desk and rapped on the door. "Sheriff? Miss Sinclair is here to see you."

"Arl...Miss Sinclair?" came Lance's disembodied voice from beyond the door. "Sure thing, send her right in. Thanks, Debbie."

"Come on in," Debbie rolled out of the way, pushing the door open and motioning Arlene inside.

Arlene left the door ajar. There were going to be enough rumors without giving anyone more to talk about.

Lance hurriedly shoved a bottle of what appeared to be wine under his desk and grinned sheepishly. "Morning, Arlene."

"Morning." She ran her string of pearls back and forth under her fingers, flipped her hair behind her shoulders and took a seat on the edge of the chair. "I need to speak with you about Gary Jones," she managed with cool formality.

Lance took his cue, easing down to sit behind his desk. "Certainly. Something wrong?"

"You might say that." She took a deep breath and met his intense blue eyes. Mercy, he did have the most beautiful eyes. Arlene tore her gaze from his, licked her lips and tried again. "Just how was he supposed to serve his community service?"

Lance's eyes narrowed. "He's working at the park. You know that."

"Anything else? Work at the schools, say?"

Lance released a deep breath. "No. Why?" The muscle in his jaw jerked. "What's the mayor done now?"

Arlene nodded knowingly. "He didn't hire out the work over at the school. He had Gary do it. All of it."

"That lousy..." Lance bit off the curse she could sense coming. "Guess Gary has done more than his share of community service then. I'll talk to him about it this afternoon."

"Thanks. If you should find out just where that money Harvey says he paid for that work went...well, I'm sure the people here in town would like to know."

A small smile curved on Lance's lips. "I'm sure they would." He looked down, biting his lip as he pushed a copy of the Gazette toward her. "I expect that's not the only thing folks are going to want to know about."

Arlene's heart did a cartwheel. "Saw that, huh?"

He nodded. "You okay with this? I mean, if you don't want to see..." He exhaled nervously. "If you want..."

She reached across the desk and put her hand over his. "I don't mind if you don't."

Looking up into her eyes, Lance flashed a bright smile. "Miss Sinclair, I don't rightly care what anyone thinks...except you."

She felt a flush warming her cheeks and couldn't help but return his smile. "I think we're okay then."

"I think so too."

"You're still at your folks' house for now?" The concern in his voice matched the worry etched on his face.

Arlene nodded. "For now." She shrugged and twisted her fingers anxiously, trying hard to keep any trace of concern from her demeanor. "I am glad I bought the house. I think as soon as I can get it ready, I'll just go ahead and move over there."

Lance nodded, some of the tension easing from his expression. "That'd be a fine idea. Tell you what, I'll round up that good-for-nothing brother of yours, and a few other people and we'll try to get the place painted this weekend. Would that be okay with you?"

Arlene smiled and got to her feet. "Going to bring the wine?" She cut her eyes to where he'd tucked it out of sight and Lance hid an embarrassed grin beneath his hand.

"You could call me tonight, if you like, and we'll make the plans."

Lance rose to face her, eyes dancing the way they often did when he looked at her. "Why thank you, Miss Sinclair. I think I might just do that."

Twenty-Six

Gary stared out the window of the diner at the pouring rain. It echoed the storm raging inside him. Heaving a sigh, he resumed wiping down the empty tables.

"All right," Ellie drawled, moving around the counter to take a seat. "Git on over here, Gary boy. Looks like a bear's got you by the rear. Wanna tell me about it?"

Gary dropped dejectedly down on the stool beside her, and shook his head mutely.

"Might feel better if you talk to someone," she encouraged. Ellie glanced around at the nearly empty diner. "We got some time. C'mon, what's eating you lately?"

"Nothin'. I just..." He frowned, staring at the dish towel he twisted in his hands. "It's nothing anyone can do..." His face crumpled, and he turned away, hating that she would see it.

"Well now, I thought we were friends. Aren't we?" Ellie's hand closed on his shoulder, but he didn't look toward her. "Wouldn't a friend want to help? Come on, what's going on?"

Gary raised his head and stared grimly across the counter toward the kitchen. He couldn't face Miss Ellie. He didn't want to. "I wasn't just passing through when I came here. I mean to Sunny Hills, you know. I was looking for something. For someone." He looked sidelong at the woman. "I was looking for me."

Ellie's brows drew together in a puzzled frown. "Whattcha mean, honey?"

He shook his head sadly. "Doesn't matter. I've looked everyplace I can think of here in town. No one seems to know anything. Maybe it's just too late." He sighed. "I don't belong anywhere." The tears burned in his eyes and he blinked them back and shoved his hair back. "I really like it here. I wanted to belong here."

Strong hands grabbed the back of his stool and spun him around. Ellie leaned forward, staring into his eyes. "You tell me straight out, Gary Jones. What are you talking about?"

"I was adopted as a baby. My mother and father were...well, they were older when they adopted me. Last year Mama had a bad stroke. My Pop spends every minute with her. It isn't he doesn't love me, Miss Ellie. Just, well, he needs her more. He told me my birth folks were from Sunny Hills and maybe I should come find them. Maybe I belonged with them now." He shrugged. "I was hoping he was right."

"You know their names?"

"No ma'am. Just my birth mother's first name and that I was born here."

Ellie pursed her lips, thinking hard. "There has to be a way--"

The bell on the door jangled and a gust of cold wind accompanied the sound. Gary and Ellie looked over as the Sinclair's rushed in from the rain.

"All right," Ellie whispered. "Soon as I get them started, you and I are gonna finish this talk." She glanced back at Clint, Caroline, and Arlene as she got to her feet and Ellie smiled. "I think maybe we've found just who you need for this."

~

"Ya'll done here?" Ellie filled the coffee cups and began stacking the empty plates with practiced ease.

"Can't eat another bite." Arlene smiled up at her friend. "And it sure is nicer in here than out there."

As if to accentuate her point, a peal of thunder shook the front windows.

"You got a busy day planned?" Ellie inquired.

A twinge of suspicion niggled at Arlene's gut. Something underlying the seeming innocence of Ellie's question whispered to Arlene. Something interesting. Arlene sipped her coffee and studied Ellie over the rim.

"I'll be headin' back over to help Joe soon as we finish up here," Clint Sinclair offered, sopping up sausage gravy with his last bit of biscuit. "Nothing much is going to be going on anywhere till this rain lets up some."

"True enough," Ellie agreed.

"It'll be past before noon," Caroline Sinclair said confidently.

Arlene rolled her eyes in bemusement, then looked back at Ellie. "What's up?"

Ellie took a deep breath. "Would you mind talking to Gary for a minute?"

"Of course not."

"The boy in some kind of trouble, Ellie?" There was fatherly concern in Clint's tone. Arlene knew that sound; her dad had grown fond of the young man.

"Not any trouble of his own making," Ellie assured.

"I would purely love to meet this boy," Caroline said. "I have heard so much about him from Clint and Arlene."

"I'll call him over in a minute." Ellie pulled a chair over to the booth. "Here's the thing, he's looking to find his mother and father. Seems he was adopted out as a baby, and all he knows is his folks were from Sunny Hills. It's real important to him, Arlene. There anything you could do to help him?"

"Goodness sake," Caroline exclaimed, catching Arlene's hand in hers. "You're so good at finding things out. You call that boy right over, Ellie."

Arlene nodded slowly. "Would he mind?"

Ellie's face split with a bright grin. "I pretty sure he's just waiting to be asked." She hopped up and disappeared into the kitchen.

Arlene pulled her trusty notebook and pen from her purse and took a deep breath. She looked up at the sound of Gary's shy, quiet voice.

"Hey, Miss Sinclair."

"Hi Gary. You want to sit down so we can talk? You know my dad," Arlene continued as Gary pulled up the chair Ellie had left. "This is my mother."

"Nice to meet you, Mrs. Sinclair."

Caroline shook his hand numbly, her intense gaze locked on his face until she finally pulled herself together and managed to plaster on a polite smile. "Well goodness. It is so nice to meet you." She shot a quick glance at Arlene, took a deep breath and composed herself. "I have heard such nice things about you."

"That's good to hear, ma'am." His blue eyes turned expectantly to Arlene. "Did Miss Ellie tell you? About me, I mean."

"She says you're looking for your birth mother and father and you think they were from Sunny Hills," Arlene replied.

"Yes ma'am. I was born here too."

Arlene frowned. "No, you'd have to have been born in one of the cities, hon. We don't have a hospital here. Maybe over to Hilton Falls?"

"No ma'am. Here. I'm sure."

Arlene tapped her notebook with the end of her pen. "How old are you, Gary?"

"I...I told Sheriff Carter, I'm almost eighteen." He stared down at his hands, not meeting her eyes.

"I can't help you if I don't know when to look. How old are you really?"

He looked up, biting nervously at his lower lip. "I'll be sixteen the end of the month," he whispered.

"I thought so," Arlene replied quietly. "You didn't seem to be thinking much about the draft. Why'd you lie to the Sheriff?"

"I didn't want him to send me back," Gary pleaded. "My Pop can't take care of me any more. I just wanted a chance to find someplace... To find where I belong." He looked from Arlene to her parents, over his shoulder at Ellie, and back to Arlene. "Please, please don't send me back. Not till I know. Please."

"Young man," Clint Sinclair leaned forward on his elbows, fixing Gary with a serious stare. "You should be in school at your age. Getting a good education."

"I know that, Mr. Sinclair. Shoot, I like school. Honest."

"He is just a whiz with numbers," Ellie piped up, patting him reassuringly on the shoulder. "Really smart."

"Thank you, Miss Ellie." He straightened his shoulders and Arlene had to smother a smile at how hard the youngster was trying to look like a man. "And I will go back to school, sir. I just need to find out who my parents are first. See if maybe...maybe I could stay here. Maybe... maybe they might want me now.

"I'm a good worker. You know that, Mr. Sinclair. And I wouldn't be any trouble to them." His wistful gaze fell on Arlene and she felt her heart melt. "When I look in the mirror, I want to know whose eyes are looking back. You know? And, is my birth father good at math too? Or did I get that from my mother? It's not so much to ask, is it?"

"No. No, I don't suppose it is. Okay, you think you were born here. What else?"

"My birth mother's first name is Virginia. My adopted mother is her aunt or cousin. Her and my Pop only had one baby that died at two. They couldn't have any more and they were really happy to have me. But I don't know her last name or my father's name."

"When's your birthday?"

"October thirty-first." Gary flashed a quick grin. "Suppose I was a trick or a treat?"

"You're a Scorpio, that's a good strong sign. Always curious, passionate, looking for answers." Caroline smiled and patted his hand. "You'll get to the bottom of all of these secrets."

Gary frowned. "I'm not the only one with secrets around here." He shook his head. "The mayor is up to something. He's lying to folks."

"Because of the work at the school you mean?" Arlene asked.

"That's just a little part of it, best I can tell. I work over to his place too. Not sure I was supposed to, but he said I was. Anyway, I got a good look at his books...the town budget and all. He's playing with the numbers."

"What makes you think that, son?" Clint Sinclair asked.

Gary leaned across to the next table and got one of the paper placemats. "Can I borrow your pen?"

Arlene nodded and Gary began to write columns of numbers down the back of the placemat.

"Miss Ellie told you I'm pretty good at math. Fact is, I can remember almost any figures I see," he explained as he jotted things down. "Now, you look here. This line was the town fund for the school improvements. You consider the mayor didn't pay me a cent, but there's this withdrawal."

Clint tilted the finished page so he could see it clearly. His brow furrowed. "Well, this doesn't look right."

"No sir," Gary agreed, with a tentative smile. "Didn't look right to me either. I mean, look at this line. I think that's where the money for that stop light is supposed to be. But this doesn't add up."

"I am certain you three can figure all of this out." Caroline got to her feet and Clint rose immediately to help her with her coat. "Now look there, the sun is coming out already. What did I tell you?"

She beamed as if she had ordered the sunshine herself and Arlene couldn't help but smile in spite of a pinching in her gut that told her Momma was up to something.

"Are you leaving, Momma?"

Caroline gave Clint a peck on the cheek and patted Arlene's shoulder. "I'll leave you all to your numbers and whatever poor Lester Harvey has done stupid this time. I just thought of something I need to see to. I'll see you both for supper. Gary, it is so nice to meet you at last. I am just certain we'll be seeing you again soon."

Her Cheshire cat smile sent tingles up Arlene's spine, but before Arlene could speak, Caroline waved jauntily and swept out the door. *What on earth is she up to?*

"Look at this, Arlene." Her father's voice commanded her attention back to the paper. "Dang it, the boy may be on to something here."

Twenty-Seven

Caroline marched along Main Street nearly oblivious to her surroundings. She knew them well, every store, every street. Instead her thoughts raced to new places and possibilities she hadn't considered.

Who else's son could that boy be? He's the spittin' image of his father at that age. Now who would know? If Gary really had been born in Sunny Hills, there was only one answer.

Caroline stopped in front of a small, ivy-covered house tucked beneath the arms of a massive magnolia tree. A sign next to the curved driveway swayed in the gusts of wind. *Doctor J.D. Grayson.* Caroline smiled. It didn't matter that Doc was retired, the sign wasn't.

She followed the cobbled walkway to the back and rapped firmly on the heavy wood door. "Coming, coming," called a muffled voice from inside.

The door swung open and a thin, silver-haired man peered at her over the top of his spectacles. "Caroline? What a pleasant surprise."

"It's good to see you too, Jefferson. Mind if I come in?" Caroline looked into his pale blue eyes and remembered the man who'd given her kids their shots, set Dusty's broken arm, and treated every sniffle and bump. How time had flown. "How have you been?" She took off her coat and hung it on the rack beside the door.

"Fine. Course its been hard gettin' used to being home every day." Doc took a puff of his pipe. "Went into town just yesterday to have a look at Joe. Can't be too careful at our age, you know."

"That was right nice of you. How's he doing?"

"Good, good." Doc motioned to the small, homey kitchen just off the back. "C'mon in. Got a fresh pot of coffee on, would you like some?"

"That would be lovely."

Doc poured steaming mugs, chatting as he busied about the kitchen. "When's Clint going to call me about fishin'?"

"Soon, I'm sure. That man is as crazy about fishing as you are."

"I know he's been busy helping Joe out at the store. But you know those fish won't wait forever." He winked amiably. "Now I know you didn't come over here to ask me about my health much less discuss our obsession with fishing. What's on your mind?"

Caroline stared thoughtfully at the rim of her coffee cup as she set it back on the table. "I never could fool you, Jefferson. I was wondering, do you remember when Virginia had her baby? I know it was some time back... probably what? Fifteen, sixteen years?"

"Now Caroline, you know you never forget a baby coming into this world." Doc chuckled as he took a seat across from her. "Now which Virginia do you mean? Virgy Rodgers? Or Ginny McKay?"

Caroline nearly choked on the coffee she was sipping. Mercy, she'd never thought about there being two potential mothers. She considered the question for a split second.

Virgy with her curly light brown hair and sweet, freckled face. She'd been married to Max Rodgers since high school, and all four of their kids had their mom's freckles and brown eyes. Plus her oldest girl, Karen, had to be real close to Gary in age.

Nope it has to be Ginny. "The McKay girl. You delivered her baby didn't you?"

Doc nodded. "I surely did. Delivered him right in my office." His usually warm smile faded. "Nelson said there was no way he wanted folks knowing about his daughter's mistake. He was trying to get her into one of those homes for unwed mothers up to Atlanta, but the baby came early. And he came fast." The old physician smiled wistfully and shook his head. "Never saw a baby in more of a hurry to get born." He sighed. "First thing, Nelson shipped poor Ginny off to her grandparents'. Never did hear who the father was. Nelson McKay wouldn't even give me a name for the birth certificate. "Wonder what became of that baby."

"Oh, I think maybe I know. And I suspect I know who the father is, too." Caroline smiled.

"Been reading those dang cards of yours again, Caroline?" Doc chuckled.

"Of course." She chuckled. "But it doesn't take tarot cards to figure this one out. I've seen the boy and he is the spittin' image of his father at that age."

"You sure?" Doc scratched his head. "Ginny died in Atlanta years back. I was sure that child was adopted out. Where'd you see him?"

"Here in town. And I've never been more sure of anything in my life." She thought of Gary; the sad lonely look in his blue eyes. "It's a dang shame his father never had a chance to know that boy. A shame for both of them." She sighed and got to her feet. "Thanks Jefferson. I appreciate it. Oh," she added, slipping into her coat as Doc held it for her. "Do you happen to remember what day Ginny had her baby?"

Doc laughed aloud. "Never will forget. Had him smack-dab on Halloween."

Caroline nodded to herself. That nailed it. Now she knew where Gary belonged. She just had to prove it.

~

Arlene stared at the phone on her desk, willing it to ring. Her article on the upcoming High Meadows trout-fishing tournament sat all but forgotten in her typewriter.

"Come on, Gary, call," she whispered to the silent phone. As if on cue, it jangled to life nearly sending her jumping to her feet. "Hello?"

"Okay, Miss Sinclair. The Mayor dropped me over at his house just like I said he would and his wife just left for her garden club meeting."

"Gary, I'm not sure I want you involved in this."

"Seeing as he's taking credit for work I'm doing for free, and it was my friend who got hurt at that intersection on account of there's no light, I figure I'm already involved."

There was a hard edge to his voice Arlene had never heard before. The boy had grit.

"I'll be right over."

Arlene hung up, threw on her jacket and strode out the door.

~

"See," Gary gestured to a small desk near the kitchen window. "That's the ledger right there."

Arlene slid it cautiously from between the other books and laid it on the desk. It fell open to a paper-clipped page. Arlene frowned. It looked very official, very orderly. Every column in order with precise figures and totals, notes on what had been spent and where.

"Look," Gary bent over the desk, sliding his finger down the rows. "If you add the figures in the right column to these, it looks pretty good. But the totals are off. See? You don't balance this kind of a spreadsheet the way he's doing it.

"Not only that but look at the list of expenses. Some of these just aren't right. He didn't use this money for the school renovation. You and I both know that. Or this money at the park."

Arlene nodded. "Okay, I think I've got it." She took a deep breath. "Tell you what, we need the Sheriff to see this. There has to be some way to get this out in the open."

"We can't just take the books."

"No. That would be stealing." Arlene raised an arched brow and pulled her small Kodak from her oversized bag. "But a picture's worth a thousand words."

~

Lance could barely conceal his amusement as Arlene eased her office door closed behind him. Dropping down to sit on the edge of her desk, he flashed a crooked grin.

"Aren't you worried about your reputation, Miss Sinclair? Being alone in here with a"--he waggled his eyebrows and leaned toward her--"man in uniform?"

Arlene planted her hand firmly in the middle of his chest and pushed him back, sashayed around her desk and took a seat. "This is a business call, Sheriff Carter." Her smile faded and she took a deep breath as she pulled a folder from a drawer. "And it affects us all."

Lance lifted the folder from her hands and flipped it open, scowling thoughtfully as he turned the pages. "What is this, Arlene?"

"Record of the town books. At least the way the mayor keeps them."

His heart clenched. Page after page of photos of every sheet in the town ledger. Lance scrubbed his hand over his tightening forehead. "Why are you showing me this?"

"It proves what Harvey is doing, Lance. Look at this." She flipped through to a specific page and tapped the photo with a perfectly manicured fingertip. "Look at what he says he spent on the school. He didn't. You know he didn't. Gary did that work."

"How did you know about this?"

"Gary saw the books when he was working--"

"Gary?" Lance rose to his feet, a flame of annoyance burning through him. *Tarnation, she's done it again. And now she's dragged that boy into this mess with her.* "You got him involved in this?"

"Lance, this is evidence--"

"Yes it is. Evidence of you taking a minor age kid, entering a private residence and appropriating these files without proper authorization." He threw the folder on her desk and watched the color rising in her cheeks, lighting fires of indignation in her green eyes. "It's illegal, Arlene. Inadmissible in any court. I can't use it."

"But you've seen it. You know that man is stealing from the town," she protested.

"Arlene--"

"Do something to catch him. He's a criminal, Lance."

He took her hands in his and released a deep breath, struggling with the turmoil inside him. She was right. What Harvey was doing was criminal...so was what she did. Did she always have to be so confounded right even when she was wrong?

"I can't do it this way. I'm sorry. And I want you to keep Gary out of this. That boy's had enough trouble in his life; I can feel it in him, Arlene. Just don't..."

"I won't."

"He's too young to get into something like this."

Arlene's lips pinched tight. "Younger than you know."

"What?"

"He's not going on eighteen like he told you."

Lance frowned, eyes narrowed.

"He's not even sixteen yet." Her fingers closed over his. "He's not going back to Harvey's. I won't let him get in trouble on my account. And you're right; he's had a bad time of it lately. I'm going to try to help him every way I can." She lifted her chin. "But I'm going to find a way to stop the mayor. Innocent people are getting hurt by whatever it is he's doing here, Lance."

"I'm not letting it go. You made your point. Just trust me a little, Miss Sinclair? Give me time to get to the bottom of this legally?"

Arlene nodded, her blonde hair swinging around her shoulders like golden light. "All right, Sheriff." She rolled her eyes and smiled impishly. "Can I get an exclusive interview once you do?"

Lance chuckled and headed for the door. "I can probably arrange that."

Twenty-Eight

One last piece to the puzzle. Caroline pulled up in front of Nelson McKay's house and sat in her car for a long moment collecting her thoughts. The McKay's had left Sunny Hills for Hilton Falls shortly after Ginny moved to North Carolina with her grandparents. She was lucky Doc had kept in touch with him all these years.

Spirals of brightly hued leaves swept across the rolling lawn. The call of children's voices drew her attention to the next-door neighbor's yard where a rough and tumble game of touch football was in progress. A freckle-faced youngster dashed across in front of her car, nabbing the ball in mid-flight and racing back toward his friends.

Caroline smiled wistfully. It had been such a long time since Dusty and Lance were this age. She missed those days. Her smile faded. If she was right, Nelson had cost Gary's father the chance to share so many years and moments with his son.

Resolve firmly in place, she left the car and marched to the front door. Miss Manners would be appalled at her brazen approach Caroline thought with a certain amount of pride. To heck with etiquette, some things were more important. Family for instance.

She rapped firmly on the door. The faint sound of a television came from inside, but there was no response to her knock. Caroline lifted the heavy pineapple shaped knocker and let it fall.

"Nelson?" She called, impatient to get this ordeal over with. "Nelson, it's Caroline Sinclair."

"All right, comin'," called a gruff voice from inside. Nelson McKay opened the door and stared at her with open suspicion. "Why Caroline, to what do I owe this pleasant surprise?"

"May I come in? I'm not sure just how pleasant you'll find what I need to discuss with you."

He stood to the side, motioning her into his living room, then crossed ahead of her and flipped off the squatty television. "Have a seat. It's been a long time."

"Yes it has." Caroline took a seat, hands folded in her lap. "Fact is, I had an interesting experience yesterday. I met the nicest young man in town and darn if that child didn't make me remember when our kids were growing up. Lance, Randy and Dusty always out playing ball and Ginny and Heather cheerleading." She smiled in spite of the burning in her heart. "Do you remember, Nelson?"

He nodded slowly. "Of course I do."

"What happened, Nelson? One day they were laughing, normal kids. The next Ginny went to live with her grandparents and your family moved here."

"I got a good job here, making a lot more than I could in Sunny Hills. You know that."

"I know that. Now you want to tell me the rest? About how that boy I just saw at Ellie's Diner is Ginny's son? Your grandchild. How is it that boy doesn't know who his father is? He looks just like his father, doesn't he?"

"From the minute he came into this world. Just like him." He bit his words off, his mouth twisted and down-turned.

She shook her head, fighting between tears and rage. "Oh, Nelson, what did you do?"

"That boy got my Ginny pregnant. He was no good. No good, or he wouldn't have touched my daughter. But she said she loved him." He slammed his palm against the arm of the sofa. "What did she know about love? She was barely eighteen years old."

"They were young. They made a mistake. And you're wrong; he was a good boy. He's a good man. Did you even give him a chance to do right by her?"

His angry eyes glared holes in Caroline. "I didn't want him around my daughter. I wanted to kill him. I made darn sure she never spoke to him again." His voice cracked. "Ginny agreed to go away after the baby was born if I didn't hurt him. And we moved away. I never saw him again." Tears glistened in his eyes. "Ginny never forgave me, you know. The missus and Ginny put that baby in a good home. Some family member I think. They never told me where. But Ginny wouldn't come back. She wouldn't see me. My wife, MaryLou, said give the girl time. But then Ginny died. She never forgave me and there was no way to make it right."

"You have another chance, Nelson. He's in Sunny Hills looking for his family." Caroline took a deep breath and steadied her nerves. "You're part of that family, if you want to be."

"Does he know?"

"Not yet. But he will. He has to." She got to her feet. "They both have a right to know. You've been alone a long time now. Maybe it's time you thought about changing that."

He stared at her for a moment before standing. "I hope you're right. I hope he's made a good life since then. I don't know that I want to see him. But I thank you for telling me about Ginny's boy."

"Will you come visit? Get to know them?"

Nelson McKay held the door for her, his expression guarded but no longer cold. "I'll think about it."

~

Lester Harvey crammed his hands into his coat pockets and stared through the barbershop window at the beckoning flicker of the television inside. He didn't need his hair cut. *Shoot, haven't got all that much to spare.* He leaned closer to the glass peering with interest at the sports on the screen. *Can't hear a darn thing out here.* Unable to withstand its hypnotic call, he pulled open the door and slipped inside.

"Howdy Lester." Hank Greeley nodded a greeting, scarcely missing a beat in his rhythmic snipping. "Can't imagine you're needing a trim already. Come to see the news?" He nodded toward the television.

Harvey rubbed his chin thoughtfully and edged toward the line of chairs where waiting customers watched the sporting news. "Don't rightly know," he hedged. "What are ya'll watching?"

Frank Perkins leaned back in his chair. "Just finished the weather. They said its gonna be raining the rest of the week." He chuckled and poked Harvey in the ribs with his elbow. "Like my arthritis hadn't already told me that."

"Doesn't look like weather." The mayor squinted at the picture.

"They're talking sports now." Hank brushed the last loose hair away with brisk efficiency. "Not much to talk about since the series ended."

"I don't know about that," Perkin's argued amiably. "The stock car season isn't over yet and football just started." He hooked his thumbs in his overalls and peered expectantly at Harvey. "How 'bout you? You following the sports?"

Harvey cleared his throat nervously and sat down. "Well, a little."

The sports announcer droned scores and statistics, the camera fixed on his face. Short clips from the weekend's football matches suggested the upcoming games to watch. The scene changed. A picture from the NASCAR track accompanied the report of the season's overall standings.

Harvey held his breath. *Good, good.* Flock remained at the top of the ratings. And the big race coming up on Sunday. A thousand bucks and Flock to win. Finally he was in a position to get back on top.

Rubbing his hands together, he got to his feet. "Nice seeing you fellas. I'd best be on my way."

The barber raised his brows, surprised by Harvey's sudden departure. "See you in a couple of weeks for a trim, Lester."

~

"That'll be $14.92, sir."

Kent pulled a ten and a five from his wallet while the old man packed the last of his groceries into the bag. "Keep the change," he growled, keeping his head lowered so the grocer wouldn't get a good look at him. Not like anyone in this little hole-in-the-wall town was likely to know him. But there was no reason to take chances.

Tugging his baseball cap lower, he shoved the front door open and pulled up short.

"Damn, damn, damn!" he cursed under his breath.

Across the street, a police cruiser was parked alongside the faded red '38 Ford pickup he'd stolen. *That dang Lance Carter snoopin' around. Good thing I left it alongside the diner; let him look over there for a spell.* Pulling the collar up on his jacket, Kent turned sharply around the corner of the market and strode purposefully in the opposite direction.

He'd need some distance between himself and the diner before Lance and his boys got to roaming the streets looking for him. Get back to the motel and lay low for a day or two.

He needed a new plan. Time was running out. Pretty soon Carter would be on his tail and he wanted to get his shot at getting even and be out of here before the rubes in Sunny Hills figured things out.

~

The plates on the old truck weren't local. Lance walked around it with an appraising eye. It sure fit the description of the one stolen at the bus depot. And Pierce County tags.

"That's the one," Randy announced, climbing out of the cruiser.

Lance glanced back at the diner, then scanned the street in both directions. "You really think the dang fool would park it here right on the street and then go in to eat?"

Randy's lips pinched together and he shook his head slowly. "Doesn't seem right. Still..."

"Yeah. Tell you what, you watch out here. I'll go in and see if Ellie's seen any strangers. You holler if he comes out the back."

Randy nodded and moved along the side of the diner where he could see both the truck and the rear of the diner.

Lance opened the door to the diner and offered what he hoped would pass for a friendly, casual smile. "Hey, Ellie." He quickly scanned the familiar faces. "Listen," he said quietly, pulling her aside. "You seen anyone you don't recognize in here?"

Ellie frowned, her quick gaze darting to the side windows and spotting the police car. "What's up?"

"Got us a stolen truck there. Have you seen anyone?"

"Nope, not a soul, Lance. Maybe they went on over to the barbershop?"

"Maybe. Although I didn't see a soul over there except Hank and Jester sitting out front talking. Okay, thanks Ellie." He flashed a genuine smile, relieved not to have to confront the thief with so many innocent folks there. "Anything?" he called to Randy as he stepped back into the parking lot.

Randy shook his head and returned to the truck. Lance tried the passenger side door and leaned inside. The keys were still in the ignition and a pack of cigarettes peeked from the visor over the driver's side. A surge of adrenalin rushed through him as he flipped down the visor.

Oasis. He looked up into Randy's curious eyes.

"Looks like things are starting to fit together."

Twenty-Nine

Caroline sat in the kitchen staring without truly seeing the tarot cards she turned before her. She had the truth. The answers Gary Jones sought were hers now.

But I can't tell that boy. He asked Arlene for help. It has to be Arlene. She drew a deep, shaking breath. *Oh dear lord, I have to tell her. And then what?*

She flipped the final card. Her flattened fingers fluttered over the neat rows with a trembling touch. "Come on, tell me. Tell me what I need to know."

The High Priestess, the Star, the World. Caroline shook her head and stared with tear-filled eyes at the alignment. It wouldn't be easy. There was so much pain here. She touched the final card. In the end...healing.

"Hey Momma, where were you all day?"

Arlene. Caroline squeezed her eyes closed, then opened them and began resolutely sweeping her cards into a single pile. "Hi, sweety. Come sit down." She wrapped her cards carefully and put them into their box. "I have some water on for tea."

"That'd be nice." Arlene slipped off her heels and padded in her stocking feet across the kitchen. "It was a long day. Coco out back?"

Caroline nodded. "That dog does love to watch the squirrels." She waited as Arlene got the cups and teapot and brought them to the table. "I have something to tell you and I don't quite know how."

Arlene stopped pouring, staring at her mother with a puzzled frown. "What is it, Momma?"

"You're serious about Lance, aren't you?" Caroline patted her daughter's slender hand.

Arlene tossed her head. "Now what kind of question is that?" She started to laugh, then stopped. "Momma?"

"Things can't always be the way we expect them to be. The way we think they will be. Sometimes, there are things that-- Well, things no one can control." Caroline took a deep breath. "Lance is going to be a father."

Arlene's eyes widened, her mouth dropping open. "He what?" she squeaked.

"Well, no. No, not like that. I mean I suppose what I meant to say is actually Lance is a father."

"Okay, this doesn't make any sense, Momma. Did your cards tell you this?"

"No of course not. That boy at the diner, he's looking for his parents. So I went to talk to Doc yesterday."

"Gary?" Arlene dropped back in her chair, staring numbly straight ahead before turning confused eyes to her mother. "What made you think...?"

"Honey, you may not remember, but I do. And that boy is the spitting image of Lance at that age. You look at him. He's got his daddy's eyes."

Arlene's face softened, tears bright in her green eyes. "He does. Oh, why didn't I see that? He really does. And the way his hair is always falling in his face." She sniffled, a wistful smile fighting to push away the sorrow. "Does Lance know? Why didn't he say anything?"

"He doesn't know. No one ever told him."

"No one told him? Lance has to know. He has the right to know." A couple of deep breaths and Arlene regained her composure. "I have to tell him." She got to her feet. "Whose...who was his mother?"

"Ginny. Virginia McKay. She never told Lance. Nelson McKay wouldn't allow it. I think he knows that was wrong now, but this isn't going to be easy for anyone. Not for Nelson. Or Lance. Surely not for that boy."

Arlene bent and kissed Caroline's cheek. "Thanks, Momma. It'll be all right. Let me get my jacket and bring Coco in. Then I'll call Lance. I think he and I have some things to talk about now."

~

Lance leaned against the front of his car, long legs stretched before him, and watched the entrance road to the park for Arlene's car. There it was. He swung to his feet as she pulled into a parking spot.

"Hey," he greeted and kissed her on the cheek. There was something wrong. She avoided his eyes even as her fingers wound through his. "Okay, what's going on, Arlene?"

She glanced up and her expression scared the fire out of him.

"The time we've had together lately...I've really loved it."

"So have I." He brushed her soft golden hair away from her face, saw her lips trembling. "That's not going to change. I want to spend more time with you. You have to know that."

She nodded tersely, her soft hand stroking his cheek. "I'm glad. But I have something to tell you, Lance, and it's going to change...everything."

"Nothing can change how I feel about you." He caught her upper arms. "Honey, you're scaring me a little here. What can be that bad?"

She shook her head. "Not bad. I just...there is no easy way say this." Her eyes met his. "Lance, Gary Jones is your son."

"What?" He stepped back and stared incredulously at her. "What the heck are you talking about?"

"Remember Virginia McKay?"

He stiffened. How long had it been since he'd heard her name? "Yes." Memories rushed at him...Ginny's smile...hot kisses...two kids so in love control wasn't an option. Then she was gone.

She went to visit her grandmother and never came home. The McKay's all left for Hilton Falls.

Standing in the rain three years later staring at her obituary. "Oh hell." He stared into Arlene's gentle green eyes and felt the ache in his heart rising into a knot that threatened to choke him. "He's my son?"

Arlene nodded mutely, her hands closing tight over his.

"Does he know?"

"No. He doesn't know anything, Lance. Nelson McKay sent Virginia out of state, and they gave the baby to relatives. Best I can tell, they were good, decent folks but older. He's on his own now, Lance, and he came here looking for his family.

"I told him I'd help him find them. We can't give him back his mother, but...he could still have you."

Lance shook himself, tingling fingers shivering across his skin colder than the brisk north wind gusting across the park. "My son. I have to tell him. How's he going to understand this? All these years...

"Nelson McKay knew. As much as he didn't like me, how could he do this? How could he live with knowing he took Ginny's son--<u>my</u> son--and never even tell me?" He forced a ragged breath into reluctant lungs. "What do I do now?"

"You tell Gary." Her arm slipped around him. "I'll go with you."

He nodded numbly, surprised at the rush of relief her words sent through him. "Thank you, Arlene. Thank you."

~

Lance held the door as Arlene entered the market.

"Hey Joe."

"Miss Arlene. Lance." Joe grinned broadly as they entered. "It's a mite close to closing, but if you two need something--"

"No. Thanks, Joe." Lance couldn't seem to find the words. What was he supposed to say? Where's my son?

Arlene came to his rescue; her voice quiet, calm and casual in tone. "No one here to help you close up? Where's Daddy and Gary?"

"Well, I sent your father on home. Gary's getting me a crate of oranges from the back. Then we'll be closing."

"How about we help you get locked up? We'd like to borrow Gary for a bit, if you don't mind."

Joe made a wry face. "No problem. Tell you what, you put the awning down for me, Lance and I can manage the rest." He patted his leg. "I'm getting around pretty good now."

Lance hurried outside, catching great gulps of cold air as he lowered the awning and locked it down for the night. *Damnation.* How could he be so afraid of facing a teenage boy? He shoved the door open, pulled down the shade and turned the 'closed' side of the sign outward.

"Thanks Lance." Joe called. "There ya are, Gary. Just put the crate right over there next to the bin. I'll unpack them."

Lance's heart plunged into his gut. He stared mutely, as if seeing the boy for the first time. How had he missed it? *My son.* A wave of-- something--something he'd never felt before rushed over Lance and it was overwhelming.

"What's this about?" Gary set the crate down, his gaze darting from one to the other. "Did I do something?"

"No, of course not." Arlene smiled reassuringly. *Thank God for Arlene.* "Lance and I just need to talk to you about something. Could we go outside?"

Gary nodded, wiped his hands nervously on the thighs of his jeans and fell into step between them. "I'll be back after the diner closes," he called to Joe.

"That's fine, Gary. Don't forget your coat; it's getting cold out there tonight."

Gary grabbed his jacket from beside the door and shrugged it on as they headed outside.

Lance opened the back door to the patrol car. "Let's sit in here and talk."

Gary stared at the car suspiciously. "No thanks. I can talk out here." He crammed his hands into his pockets.

Lance chuckled nervously. "Promise, you're not in trouble."

"Tell you what," Arlene volunteered, sidling around Lance. "I am freezing out here. So I'll just sit in back and you two can take the front."

"Good grief, no," Gary protested, putting himself between Arlene and the door. "Can't let a lady be seen sitting in the back of a police car. What's she thinking?"

He climbed into the back and slid across the seat.

Lance grinned. This was a good kid. He opened the front for Arlene, closed it behind her, then slid into the back beside Gary. *Now what?*

"What're you doing, Sheriff?" Gary frowned at him.

"I want to talk to you." He swallowed hard. "And I don't want to do it across the seat. Now Miss Sinclair told me about your being adopted and why you came to Sunny Hills."

Gary frowned, his gaze darting to Arlene. "Yeah."

"You're looking for your father."

A mask of sorrow descended over Gary's face. "Yes sir, but I don't think I'm going to find him."

"I think you will, Gary." Lance stared into the boy's blue eyes, like looking into his own soul. "You have found him. Gary, it's me."

A myriad of emotions raced across Gary's face. "Y-you? You're my father? Why didn't you...?"

"I didn't know, son. I swear to you. I never knew. I just found out." Lance cast pleading eyes toward Arlene.

"I just told him, Gary. Right before we came here. He didn't know any more than you did."

"Why? You mean my birth mother never told you she was going to have a baby?" Confusion and pain shone out of Gary's eyes and pierced Lance's heart. "She slept with you so she had to have loved you a little bit. You seem like a good guy now, but what? Were you a creep back then?"

Lance laughed nervously at the blunt question. "I don't think so. And we did love each other. I'd have married her in a flash if she'd told me, but we were just out of high school. Not so much older than you.

"I don't know why she made the choices she did. We'll find out together, if you like."

"Can we do that?" The confusion was replaced by hope. "Can we ask her?"

"We can ask her father."

His face went cold. "But not my mother?"

Arlene shook her head. "No, she was in an accident. She died just a couple of years after you were born."

Gary grew silent for long minutes. His expressive face showed the depth of his emotion, the questions and grappling for answers that was going on in the boy's mind. Then, suddenly, he raised his eyes to Lance's face, but Lance didn't blink. He would sit there, under this boy's intense scrutiny, for as long as it took, hoping in the end he would measure up.

"You really are my father?"

"Yes, Gary, I am."

"No doubts?"

Lance lifted his chin. "No doubts."

Gary nodded and grew quiet again.

The silence was consuming all the oxygen inside the squad car. Lance couldn't stand it any longer. "I'm sorry. I'm sorry I've missed so much of your life, son." He paused, hoping Gary would speak. Would say something. Tell him how they could begin again. When Gary made no comment, Lance added, "I want to try to make it up to you, if you'll let me. We don't have to miss anything else."

Gary nodded again, but didn't meet his eyes. "Can I go now? Miss Ellie will be needing me."

"Yeah, sure." Lance tried to hide his disappointment behind writing his home number on a business card and handing it to the boy. "Anytime you want to talk call me." Gary nodded once again, shoved the card in his pocket and got out of the car.

Arlene reached across the seat and squeezed Lance's hand. Despite her touch, Lance watched Gary walk across the street and into the diner without a backward glance and felt that now, in the most important moment of his life, he had failed.

Thirty

Lance stared out his office window toward the intersection. Joe's Market. Ellie's Diner. *Gary*.

"What do I do now? Huh?" He asked himself and sighed heavily. Well, if this was hard for him, how much harder did it all have to be for Gary?

As if on cue, a slender dark-haired figure crossed the street and passed Lance's window headed for the front of the police station. In his rush to reach the door Lance knocked his chair over, grabbed it, set it upright and managed to yank the door open without, he hoped, looking totally like a wild-man.

"Sheriff Carter?" Debbie's brows arched slowly upward, then she shot a quick glance back toward her desk. "You have someone here--"

Lance forced the air in and out of his lungs, his gaze locked with Gary's. He nodded tentatively and saw the kid flash a nervous, optimistic grin. Lance nodded, more confidently this time.

"Gary, this is Miss Debbie. She's the heart of this office. Debbie, this is"--Lance felt himself smiling and was helpless to stop it, even if he's wanted to. Which he didn't--"this is my son."

Debbie handled it like the pro she was. Her mouth dropped open, then she promptly closed it, flashed a bright smile and wheeled around the corner of the desk, arms open wide. "Well sweety, aren't you just the spittin' image of your daddy? Can I get a hug?"

Gary allowed a sheepish hug, color creeping up to his ears. "Thank you, ma'am." He looked back up at Lance. "Could we...talk?"

"Yeah." Lance slapped the boy on the back. "Come on in. Debbie, no calls. Miss Winston's cat gets up that tree, you tell her I'll have it down before dark. Unless we've got blood, no one interrupts."

His secretary chuckled. "Yes sir. No calls."

~

Gary paced around the room, sat down, popped back up and resumed pacing.

"It's all right, Gary." Lance took a seat on the edge of his desk, watching the obviously distraught boy. "Look, we don't have to talk here. We can go somewhere else if that would be easier for you."

Gary turned to face him. "No. I just--I don't know what I'm supposed to say."

"You don't have to say anything. We'll just take this a little at a time."

"You haven't been anything but nice to me, Sheriff, and I appreciate it. I just--I mean I've been waiting so long to find out who my parents were...and now that I know. I don't know what to do.

"I love my mother and father. I do. They've been good to me. I just...I needed..." Tears welled up in his eyes. "I needed you."

Lance got to his feet and closed his hands on Gary's upper arms. "I wasn't there when you needed me growing up. But I'm here now. And I will be here for you the rest of my life."

"Can you tell me who my birth mother was?"

Lance nodded. "I can do better than that. I called her father last night. Would you like to go meet him?"

A wash of emotions raced over Gary's face. "Does he know...about me?"

"He knows. Look, it isn't easy for me either. He was part of the reason I never knew about you...and, frankly, I'm angry." Lance stopped, waiting till he could control the emotion in his voice again. "And I'm hurt...that I missed knowing you. But you have a right to know what happened. And he said he wanted to try to make things right now. So if you want to meet him, I'll take you over there...right now." He got to his feet and pulled on his jacket.

The decision to take Gary to meet Nelson McKay didn't come easily. *So much pain because of that man's choices. Time for it to end.*

He glanced over at Gary. "Anything you want to ask me before we go?"

"You sure? You sure you want...to be my dad?"

"I've never been more sure of anything."

~

Getting out in front of the McKay house, Lance looked around. It seemed like a nice neighborhood. A big pumpkin sat beside the front steps. Scarlet leaves drifted down from the huge oak tree.

He and Gary walked to the front and Nelson McKay immediately opened the door. Lance was a bit taken back by the older man. The years hadn't been kind. He stared uneasily at Lance and Gary.

"I'm sorry. Lance, I never knew..."

"That's the past, Mr. McKay. We can start over if you're willing for the sake of my son...your grandson."

Lance meant what he said. Nothing would give them back the years they had lost. Gary deserved the best they could give him from this moment on.

McKay held out a trembling hand. "C'mon in. I'm glad you both came." He closed the door behind them and motioned to the living room.

The color had drained from Gary's face, except for flushed red splotches high on his cheekbones. Lance patted him reassuringly on the back, urging him toward where the older man had taken a seat in a big recliner.

"Mr. McKay, this is your grandson, Gary Jones."

"Hello Gary." Nelson extended his hand and Gary shook it. "It's nice to meet you. Go ahead and have a seat. Do you want anything? Tea? Juice?"

"No. No thank you, sir." Gary sat beside Lance on the sofa.

"I don't quite know what to say to you." McKay ran his hand through his hair.

"You could tell me about my family." Gary's voice was barely above a whisper.

McKay nodded. "Yes, yes I can." He rose with aching slowness, took a couple of photos from the mantle and handed one to Gary. "This is wife, MaryLou. She died a couple of years ago."

Gary stared at the picture. "She looks sorta like my mama. The same eyes. Same hair."

"Yeah, she might have. Your adopted mother was her cousin, I think. I never met her. But my MaryLou was a sweet, kind woman and I know she loved you even if she didn't get to know you." McKay bit his lower lip and held out the second photo. "This is our daughter, Ginny. Your mother."

Gary's eyes widened, filling with tears. "I know her," he choked out. "My mom...Mama has a picture just like this up over the fireplace. Right next to the one of baby Alice," His breath came in ragged hiccups and Lance put his arm around the boy's shaking shoulders. "Mama called them her angels. She said they were always"--his voice broke--"always watchin' over me."

Lance's heart melted with the boy's muffled sobbing. He looked up and saw tears running down Nelson McKay's cheeks.

"I'm sorry. I was trying to protect my baby girl. I know you can't understand, but I never meant to hurt you." He looked up and met Lance's steady gaze. "Any of you."

"She's so pretty. I never really looked much." Gary asked softly, gently stroking the image behind the glass. "What happened to her?"

"About two years after you were born she died. In an accident."

"I'm sorry. I wish I could have known her."

"I wish you could have too." The old man took a seat, leaning forward with his elbows on his knees, studying the boy appraisingly. "What do you like to do, Gary?"

Gary looked up with surprise, then flashed a tentative smile. "I like to play football. I'm pretty good. And baseball."

"Play any musical instruments? Piano?"

"Guitar. I like to play the guitar."

McKay smiled, his eyes crinkling. "Bluegrass?"

Gary cocked his head to the side, smiling broadly. "Well, can't say I've ever tried. But I expect I could learn it."

"I play the banjo." McKay shook his head. "Haven't brought that thing out even once since my MaryLou passed on. But I'll tell you what, if you'd like to learn some bluegrass, I'll buy you a good guitar and you can come over any time you want and we'll play."

"I'd like that, Mr. McKay."

McKay's face softened. "You look just like your daddy there, but you've got your mother's smile. And you don't have to call me mister if you don't want to. You could..." He cleared his throat. "You could call me Granddad."

"I never had any grandparents. My folks being so much...older and all. Yes sir. I'd like that." Gary looked over at Lance. "Would it be all right for me to come here? To visit and play"--His gaze darted to McKay and back to Lance--"with Granddad?"

Lance saw the pleading in the old man's eyes that just matched the hope in the boy's. He nodded. "That'd be fine, son. I think that's a fine idea."

Thirty-One

Arlene poured more paint into the pan and studied her handiwork on the porch trim. Things were coming along wonderfully. The yard bustled with activity and her lovely new house was beginning to become the home she'd dreamed of bright in a fresh coat of paint.

"Hurry up there, sis," Dusty teased. "The fellas have almost the whole exterior finished and you're still on the porch."

"Hey, smarty pants." Katie retorted, strolling around the corner. "You guys just slap on the easy stuff. It takes a woman's touch for the delicate things." She brandished her small trim brush in a quick twirl, sidling between Dusty and the edge of the porch. With a quick grin she turned and flicked paint across the end of his nose. Then, seeing the look on Dusty's face, she squealed and made a dash for the porch with Dusty close on her heels and Arlene laughed aloud.

"What's going on over here?" Lance rounded the corner with Gary at his side. The boy's face and hair were speckled with rich sage-green and lit with a wide cheerful grin.

Arlene used the corner of a cloth to dab at a smear on Lance's chin. "You two are a mess."

Lance waggled his eyebrows and bent to give her a quick peck on the lips. "Yeah, but the house is looking great, isn't it?" He straightened and draped an arm around Gary's shoulders. "Gary did a great job on those columns, didn't he?"

"Yes, you sure did."

"Thanks Miss Arlene. Dad's a lot faster, but I think I'm getting the hang of it."

Arlene saw Lance puff with pride at the mention of his new position-- 'dad'. He ruffled Gary's hair, then grabbed another gallon of paint from the line of cans along the walkway.

"Come on, son, let's finish it up."

"How're Randy and Jack doing on the windows?" Arlene dabbed her brush in the white trim paint.

"Great." Lance squinted up at the roof. "Soon as Gary and I finish around back, I'll tackle the trim up there."

"We're actually going to get this done in one day." Arlene couldn't keep the squeak of excitement from her voice.

Lance nodded. "And tomorrow, we'll get the inside done. You'll be moving in before you know it."

Arlene sighed. "Not that I haven't enjoyed staying with Momma and Daddy, but I will be *so* glad to have my own place." A wide smile crept across her face. "My house. My very own house."

Lance chuckled. "You deserve it, honey. C'mon, Gary. We'd better hurry up and get her moved in here."

~

"Looks like we've just about got it," Jack said, peering intently at the knife-edge line between the crisp linen-cream walls and the brilliant white ceiling. He backed down the ladder a step and dabbed his brush into the pan Arlene was holding. "One little speck here."

"Someone's at the door," Arlene fairly chirped with excitement at the sound of the doorbell. "Oh, geeze, I hope the paint's dry." She set the pan carefully on papers and headed for the entry.

"Thought you already had half the town here helping out," Jack teased as she opened the door.

"Oh my goodness," Arlene exclaimed pulling the petite brunette into her arms. "Heather!" She stepped back, still holding her friend's hands in hers. "What on earth are you doing here?"

"Mom told me you were fixing the place up this weekend, so I drove up to see if I could help." Heather giggled. "You have no idea how thrilled I am you are going to be living here." She caught a quick breath. "I love the color..." Heather bounded past Arlene into the living room.

"You like it?" Arlene spun in a giddy circle. "I thought with a deep yellow cream rug..."

"It'll be breathtaking," Heather agreed. She looked up. "Oh, hello Jack."

Arlene glanced up and saw the gape-mouthed surprise in Jack's face. Her gaze darted to Heather and then back to Jack. *So, the sparks are still there.* She'd thought they belonged together ever since Jack got back from college...but then Heather had moved away and...

Jack managed not to fall off the ladder in his gaping, closed his mouth and slowly climbed down. "Heather. Didn't know you were coming to help out here."

"Well, it was kind of a surprise." Heather rolled her eyes, looking demurely around the room. "Nice job."

"Thanks." He drew a deep breath and turned to Arlene. "Where next?"

"Still got to do the bedrooms."

"Have you done my old room yet?" Heather fairly beamed with anticipation.

"Nope." Arlene squeezed her hand. "Want to pick the color?"

"I ummm..." Jack wiped his hands on a towel, uncharacteristically at a loss for words. Arlene smiled to see his usual suave charm shattered. "I'm finished here. If you'd like some help--in there. With the painting, I mean."

"That'll be great," Heather shot back over her shoulder. "Better bring your ladder. I don't think we're the ones who'll be needing the help."

Jack blushed clean to his ears and Arlene covered her mouth to stifle the urge to giggle. House painting was turning out to be much more interesting than she had ever imagined.

~

That was easier than I expected. Kent suppressed a self-satisfied smirk and checked the rearview mirror. No one from the truck stop slop-joint followed. No sound of alarm. Probably no one even saw him hotwire this piece of junk.

He wasn't real partial to big sedans like this Buick, but it met his other criteria. Old, nondescript...ordinary. No one in Sunny Hills was likely to notice it. The truck had suited him better, but he wouldn't be needing this old tank for long.

Yeah, I'll settle up here, get me a nice ragtop. Just gotta find a way to get what I need without anyone the wiser.

He rounded the corner back onto Route 129 and headed for Sunny Hills.

~

Lance closed the can of paint then folded the drop cloth over on itself. Elegant pale, almost ice blue graced the walls. Coupled with the pristine white trim and the glowing patina of the hardwood floors Arlene's bedroom was gorgeous.

Lance grinned in spite of himself. *Arlene's bedroom.* He wondered how it would look when she got moved in.

"Kinda nice, huh?" Gary nudged his arm, looking around the room with obvious pride in their handiwork.

"Yeah, it sure is." He looked over at the kid and a slow realization tingled through him. Blue would make a nice boy's room too. But Gary didn't have a room of his own. Just a place in the back of Joe's market.

"That's gonna change," he murmured to himself.

"What? Don't you think Miss Arlene will like it?" Gary asked, obviously confused.

"I'm sure she'll love it. I just noticed how much paint we have left over. You go ahead and clean up. I need to talk to Arlene about something."

~

Arlene stepped out onto the back patio and looked across the dappled late afternoon lawn. Lance laughed and joked with Dusty and Gary where they were scrubbing the paintbrushes and rollers clean. The drop cloths lay in a twisted heap amidst the thick blanket of leaves.

Inside and out, the house's fresh paint offered a warm welcome. *Just beautiful.*

"Okay, everyone ready to eat?" she called.

"Shoot yeah." Randy banged the lid onto the paint cans.

"Kitchen isn't dry yet." Jack pushed an armload of newspaper he'd used to catch drips into the garbage. "I can't even push the stove back into position for you."

"I know." Arlene tossed her head. "I planned on that. Ellie has fresh fried chicken and potato salad and all the trimmings ready and waiting for me to pick up. How's that sound?"

Gary let out a whoop. "That sounds great!"

Arlene chuckled. "Okay, let me run get it. Think ya'll can hold down the fort till I get back?"

"We'll make sure it all gets cleaned up," Lance assured.

Heather laughed. "And we'll make sure there's actually a place fit for eatin' when you get back."

~

Arlene parked at the Corner Market and headed across the street. Ellie's Diner was always busy Sunday night before church and today was no exception, the lot filled to capacity.

A screech of tires to her left forced Arlene to glance toward the corner just as a cream and white sedan careened toward her. Her heart lunged upward as she screamed and leapt back onto the curb.

The car sped away without stopping and Arlene sank back against her car, shaking.

"Arlene! Arlene, you okay?" Ellie screamed, running out the front of the diner and across the road. She threw her arms around Arlene and held her close while Arlene clung to her friend and fought for control.

"I'm okay. I'm okay." She assured Ellie after a moment. "Oh dear Lord, Ellie, we've gotta get a light here." She felt tears welling in her eyes and gulped air in an effort to calm her nerves.

Ellie glared down the road. "And that creep didn't even have the common decency to stop and make sure you were all right." She huffed, put her arm around Arlene and herded her across to the diner. "Come on, honey. Let's get you something to drink. You want me to call Lance?"

"No. No, I'm all right." She sank down on a stool at the counter and glanced around at all the worried faces. "I'm okay," she reassured them then rolled her eyes and forced a disarming grin. "Besides, I've got to get home and feed some hungry painters."

~

Kent pulled the Buick into the narrow alley behind the seedy motel and backed into the hidden spot near the dumpster. He gripped the steering wheel tight, trying to control the shaking of his hands.

I nearly hit her. Damnation, I nearly killed her. He crammed a cigarette between his lips and managed to get a match to it. *Too close.* He wanted her to pay but not this way. *Not like that.* Pay. Sudden realization brought a wry smile to his face. *Damn right she's gonna pay. And when she does, that self-righteous cop of hers is gonna know. He'll know what he did to me wasn't right.*

Thirty-Two

"You sure you're okay?" Lance held Arlene's face in his hands, brushing her hair back and searching her eyes worriedly.

"I'm fine, really." She put her hands over his, easing his grasp. "Really," she reassured and stepped back. "It just scared me mostly. It was like the car was...aiming for me."

"Any idea who it was?"

"I've never seen the car around town before, and it's getting dark enough...I'm sorry, Lance. I was so surprised, I really didn't even think..."

His hands closed on her shoulders. "It's okay. I'm sure it's just that we need the light there. No one would try to hurt you, hon. Why would anyone even want to?"

"Maybe it was Mayor Harvey," Gary muttered angrily. "If he found out how Miss Arlene knows he's been fixing the town's books..."

"Fixing the books?" Jack echoed, leaning across the picnic table eagerly. "Arlene? You holdin' out on us?"

Arlene rolled her eyes, then fixed her coworker with a narrow glare. "Don't even think it, Jack. This one is mine."

"I can't imagine old Lester Harvey having the guts to even think about trying a stunt like this." Randy shook his head. "Besides, we know his cars."

"And he doesn't have anything at all like what Arlene described," added Katie.

"Ya'll quit worrying about it," Arlene admonished. "Let's eat. Besides, it's getting chilly out here."

Gary reached across the table and grabbed a drumstick. "Maybe it was the Mayor's bookie."

"What?" Lance scooped potato salad onto Gary's plate and then his own, then passed it to Arlene.

"His bookie. I heard the mayor placing a bet the other day. Maybe it was his bookie's car?"

Lance exchanged a quick look with Arlene, then shook his head firmly. "No. No, I'm sure it was just someone passing through who didn't realize how dangerous that intersection can be. Right, Arlene?"

She nodded quickly. "Right. Now, how about if I feed my hard working painters--"

"Great, I'm starving," said Dusty with a wink.

~

Lester Harvey stared at the Monday sports section of the Gazette. *He lost. How could he lose? Thompson wasn't supposed to win this race. How could he lose?*

Panic engulfed him, churning in his gut. Another thousand. He'd lost it all. *Now what? Think Lester, damnit, you can change this. Just one win. Just one and you can fix it all.*

But what? The money wasn't there any more. He'd emptied his savings; cleaned out every town fund he could get his hands on...even if he could find more money...no, he needed something bigger. Sometimes you had to play big in order to win big.

Where'd he made his money before this streak of bad luck? The off-circuit track. It wasn't legal to bet on those dirt track races, but this was different.

I need this one. Not like I'll ever have to bet on these little unsanctioned races again. No, just this one more time.

He wiped sweat from his upper lip, and picked up the phone in a trembling hand. He'd have to ask Brennan for a marker.

He'll give it to me. I'm in to him for too much for him to turn me down. He knows I'm good for the money. Just this one race and I can even things up with him. Brennan's too smart to let a sure thing like this go by.

"Hello, this is Lester Harvey. Let me speak to Brennan."

~

"Hey, Ellie," Lance called as he entered the diner. "Gary working?"

"He sure is. You're a little late for lunch there, Sheriff." Ellie flashed a quick smile. "Hang on, I'll get him. Gary," she called, heading into the kitchen.

"Hey Dad." Gary wiped his hands on a towel as he came around the counter. "Did you come for lunch?"

"Nope, not today. Actually, I had something I wanted to talk to you about.

"Lunch rush about over, Ellie? Mind if I borrow him for an hour or so?"

Ellie nodded. "Sure, you two go ahead. I'll see you around supper time, Gary."

"Yea ma'am. I'll be here." Gary followed Lance to his car and slid into the front seat. "So, where are we going?"

Lance turned out onto Main. "Home."

~

Arlene eased the bedroom door closed behind her, carried the empty paint can to the kitchen and set it next to the garbage can. She pulled her ponytail loose to let her hair fall around her shoulders and tugged the hem of her sweater down. Her heart was dancing with a giddy delight she'd never expected as she saw Lance's car pull in the driveway.

She looked quickly around his living room. It was small, and very 'male', she thought but the sofa was comfortable if worn and things were clean, if not really tidy. Toward that end, she scooped the newspaper and a couple of magazines off the coffee table and dropped them into the magazine rack beside the sofa.

What would people think if they knew she was here in Lance's house? *They'll think you helped a friend get a nice surprise ready for a very special kid. And if they think otherwise--then who cares what they think anyway?*

The kitchen door opened and Gary peered curiously around until he saw Arlene.

"Hi, Miss Arlene."

"Hi, Gary." Arlene nodded to Lance and he grinned and winked at her.

"Come on in, Gary." Lance motioned to the living room. "Want anything to eat? A coke?"

"No, I'm fine, thanks." Gary wandered into the next room. "Nice place."

"Thanks." Lance offered Arlene a seat in the big bentwood rocker, then sat down on the couch and motioned to Gary to sit beside him. "Kinda small, but, well, it's always been just me."

He took a deep breath and looked at Arlene and she could see the nervousness rising in him. Strange, she'd almost never seen Lance like this. *Proof of how much this means to him.*

He wiped his palms on his thighs. "I was thinking"--he began, with another quick glance at Arlene before he fixed Gary with an intent stare--"it's about time that changed. It doesn't have to be just me any more. It could be both of us. How would you like to move in here, son? With me?"

"I know it isn't much to look at, not much of a yard and all...but, we could look for another place later. I'd just really like to have a chance for us--"

Gary's face split into a wide grin and he threw his arms around Lance. "I'd love that. I mean, would it be okay with Mr. Joe? I don't want to leave him in the lurch..."

"It'll be fine, Gary." Arlene smiled at his earnestness. "My dad is helping out there now and he loves it. Gets him out of the house. And you could still stop over and help Joe with the heavy crates and all."

Gary looked around eagerly. "I could sleep right here on the sofa. I don't need much room."

"Well," Lance hid a grin as he met Arlene's eyes. "I've got a little room down the hall here. We could probably squeeze you in. Come on, I'll let you have a look."

Arlene followed them down the hall, standing to one side where she could watch their faces as Lance opened the door. Gary's mouth dropped open, eyes widening with surprise and delight.

"Oh wow! For me?" He swung around to face Lance and Arlene. "You did this for me?"

"Arlene helped." Lance put his arm around her and pulled her close. "And dang, you did a gorgeous job, honey."

"Thank you. This is great. Thank you." Gary caught them both in a big exuberant hug, then ran into the room and bounced joyfully on the edge of the twin bed. He ran an admiring hand across the blue and burgundy Lonestar pattern on the quilt, grabbed the football resting against the pillows and tossed it in the air. "Man, I never knew how much I'd miss having a place of my own. This is the best."

"I'm glad you like it." Arlene beamed. She and Lance had worked hard at getting things ready for this moment. Lance had painted the walls with the leftover paint from her house. She'd finished the trim, gathered the bedspread, curtains and desk. Lance had moved in the bookcase and sports paraphernalia. She had to admit, it *looked* like a boy's room. "And to celebrate, I have a pot roast in the oven."

"Aww, that's wonderful. Thanks, Arlene." Lance gave her a quick peck on the cheek, blushing when Gary rolled his eyes and laughed at the display of affection. "Fine." Lance ruffled the boy's hair. "After supper, we'll drive Miss Arlene home, take you over to Ellie's for work, and then I'll pick up your things from Joe. Tonight...you can sleep right here in your own room. How's that sound?"

"Sounds great, Dad. Like everything I ever hoped for."

~

Moving. She's moving somewhere. Kent frowned, scooted lower in his seat and pulled the collar on his jacket up. Up the street he saw an anthill of activity in front of the big old colonial where Arlene had her apartment.

Lance and Dusty both had trucks parked in front and everyone bustled back and forth with armloads of boxes. "Tarnation, just my luck."

No way he could approach her now. Not with two cops riding herd on her. Arlene came out of the house with her dog bouncing along at her side, loaded the animal into her car and climbed behind the wheel. The trucks pulled away from the curb following Arlene's car and Kent watched as they headed south down Elm. He couldn't follow. *No way I'm taking a chance on them seeing me yet.* He slammed his fist against the steering wheel. Dang it, he'd come too far, too close, to lose track of Sinclair now. *The neighbors. Maybe the neighbors know where she's going.*

Climbing out of the sedan, he crossed the street and ran up the three steps to the porch, where he rang the doorbell to the main house.

"Comin', comin'," called a raspy voice from inside. An elderly man opened the door and looked Kent up and down. "What can I do for you, young fella?"

Kent plastered on his most winning smile. "Afternoon, sir. I was looking for Arlene Sinclair. I'm sure this is the address she gave me."

"You just missed her. She moved."

"Oh no. I was supposed to help. Dang traffic was terrible, but I didn't think I'd be too late. Don't suppose you know where the new place is, do you? I could run over and help unload at least."

"Bought a house. Over on the outside of town. Newberry? Newton? Norton? Something like that."

"Well, thank you. I appreciate your help."

"Good luck finding her. Sunny Hills isn't all that big."

"No sir. Not big at all." Kent headed down the steps, hands dug into his pockets. *So she bought a house. Well, there's only two realtors in this little hole-in-the-wall. And one of 'em is right up at the corner.*

It was only three blocks, Kent decided to walk rather than risk taking his stolen car onto the main road. The front window of the small brick building displayed photos of the newest houses either up for sale or just purchased.

Kent studied the photos. *There we go.* Nice looking bungalow on Newton. *Newton; that might be it.* By the time he opened the door a smiling woman in a bright pink suit was already on her feet and smiling.

"Afternoon. Can I help you?"

Kent nodded toward the poster in the window. "I was interested in that house. The one you just sold. It looks like the picture my friend sent me. Would that be Arlene Sinclair's new house?"

"Do you know Arlene?"

"Yes, yes ma'am...well, not exactly. I'm a friend of her brother's. We served together--"

"In Korea?" The woman clasped her hands together. "Oh, I heard Arlene's brother just returned. Were you in his unit?"

Kent cleared his throat, his mind racing. Okay, this was working better than he'd hoped. "Yes. Yes ma'am. So, *is* that Arlene Sinclair's house? Over on Newton Street? I'd really love to see that place."

The woman smiled brightly. "Yes, yes it is."

Kent nodded. "Thank you. Appreciate your help. You have a good day."

On the sidewalk in front of the realtor's office he lit a cigarette and studied the photo of the house a moment before he headed back to his car. Newton Street. He could find her now.

Thirty-Three

Arlene drummed her fingers on the edge of her desk and stared at the copy of the town books. *Not evidence, huh? He stole the town's money...how can this not be evidence? But why?*

Originally she'd thought Lester Harvey's embezzlement of town funds was personal--like all the work around his house. But Gary did those things for Harvey, and although it was an abuse of power and trust, it didn't constitute an actual crime.

But Gary said he heard the mayor placing bets. Bets on what? Is that where the money is going? She slammed her palms against the desk and bounded to her feet. "I've got to talk to Gary."

~

"Okay," Arlene closed her notebook and took a long sip of hot chocolate. "So he was talking races?"

"Yeah, I've heard him three or four times." Gary wiped his hands on his apron. "Once it was baseball, and then a couple of times it was races. The last time I heard him he said something about a dirt track race?" He looked up at her intently. "You want me to tell Dad about this?"

Arlene considered for a second. No way did she want Gary to keep secrets from Lance, but then again, Lance had made it perfectly clear he did *not* want her involving Gary in any more of her schemes to catch the mayor. "No." She shook her head. "I mean if your dad asks, of course you should tell him. But I just needed to find out what you heard." Arlene flashed a quick smile and squeezed his hand. "You were a big help, honey. Now I have an idea of where to start. Thanks, Gary."

"You're welcome, Miss Arlene."

Arlene nodded and headed for the door. A dirt track car race. *Time to talk to Dusty.*

~

Dusty pulled up in front of Arlene's house. *This is just stupid, Dusty old boy,* he argued against his common sense. *You didn't even call first. What on earth makes you think she needs to see you right now?* Shaking his head ruefully, Dusty headed for the front door. "Great, be just my luck I take after "psychic momma"."

He knocked and the door swung open almost immediately.

"Dusty," Arlene exclaimed and gave him a quick hug. "What on earth are you doing here?"

"I just--um--I just wanted to have a good look at our handiwork." He nodded appreciatively, looking around the porch. "Looks pretty good, if I say so myself."

"Oh come on," Arlene looked at him narrowly. "You didn't come over here to tell me the paint job is great. Which it is, by the way." She held the door open. "Come on in, I was just getting ready to call you."

"Me?" Dusty followed his sister into the living room. The blue sofa and love seat looked great against the linen-cream walls. *Dang, sis really did it up nice.* He dropped onto the loveseat. "So, what did you want to talk about?"

Arlene sat on the edge of the sofa nearest him and he could tell by the way she toyed with her fingers something flustered her. "I've been following a story. And the thing is, I've heard it's going down tonight at some dirt track outside Hilton Falls."

"You're covering car racing now?"

"Well, not exactly." She folded her hands in her lap. "But, I can't finish the story until I go to the races. You know where they happen."

Dusty grinned wryly. "Yes, I do. But there is no way I am telling you."

"Dusty, this is major. This could be my big chance." She leaned forward and touched his arm. Her eyes pleaded.

Dang it, she always had known how to make him do whatever she wanted. "All right. Look, these are mostly illegal races on backcountry roads. You know that? Lance and I have busted a few folks there more than once. It's no place for a lady."

Her lips twisted and the familiar sparkle lit her green eyes. "My place is wherever I choose. I'm a reporter."

"Aww, come on, Arlene, I can't let you go over there alone. Lance would kick my rear if anything happened to you."

Her eyes widened and her smile took on a devilish pleasure. "Oh, would he? Well, since our good Sheriff has not offered to accompany me on my fact-finding expedition to the underbelly of racing in our fair county, I guess we'll never know.

"Now, where are they running?"

Randy shook his head. "You're not going alone." He got to his feet. There was just no stopping Arlene when she set her mind on something. "Okay, you get changed. It's cold outside and it'll be even colder standing out there. Dungarees and keds. Nothing fancy, okay? I'll go home and get changed out of uniform. We can take my truck; probably no one there will recognize the truck or me. It's been a couple of years, after all.

"I'll meet you back here in two hours?"

Arlene nodded and smiled brightly. "It'll be worth it. You'll see. We're going to get answers to questions no one even knew to ask before."

~

Arlene watched out the side window as Dusty's truck sped down the county road through stubble covered cornfields and past barns and pastures of cattle already shaggy in their winter coats.

It was all she could do to contain her excitement. This was almost too good to be true. Dusty would take her right to where they were racing and, with any luck, headlong into whatever scheme the mayor was up to. *This is going to be big. I am finally going to get a story that'll get me noticed further away than Goose Creek or Hilton Falls.*

And maybe, just maybe, if it forced Lester Harvey out of office, Sunny Hills could return to its roots and become the peaceable haven she had always known it to be. *Shoot, we might even finally get that traffic light. That'll teach you, Mr. Mayor.*

"Sorry I was late." Dusty broke the silence as he wheeled the truck onto a narrow country road. "Miss Winston caught me heading back to the station. I had to get Fluffy out of that tree again." He chuckled and shook his head. "Some things just never change."

"And thank goodness for that." Arlene pursed her lips to hide a smile. "But I know what you mean. Glad Fluffy was cooperative this time or you could still be there."

"Yeah. Sometimes I think Miss Winston needs a yard with no trees at all." He turned south at the next intersection, a lazy plume of red dust drifting behind the truck. "It's right up there," he said at length. "Now just who or what are you looking for?"

"I'll know when I see it." Arlene pulled up the collar on her wool jacket, checked her hat and pulled on her gloves. Cars and trucks parked across a narrow field hidden from the main road by a heavy line of trees.

"Would you look at that?" Dusty chuckled, pointing toward the ragged line of cars. "Looks like your buddy the mayor is here."

Arlene caught a quick gasp. *Perfect.* "Better park over near the other side. We're less likely to be noticed."

"Good thinking." Dusty drove the length of the line and found an inconspicuous spot between a larger truck and the tree border.

"That's it, isn't it?" Dusty asked as they walked toward the side of the road. Innocent looking concrete blocks and bales of hay formed makeshift bleachers where fans gathered to root their favorite cars and drivers to victory.

Arlene glanced sidelong at her brother, brows raised in feigned innocence. "What?"

"The mayor. You're here trying to get something on him, aren't you?" He took her hand; a move she could tell was intended to convince those gathered that she was his girl. He leaned closer as he directed her to a seat. "Aren't you?"

Arlene searched the scattered crowd of faces. *Where are you, you old scoundrel? Come on. Show your true colors.*

Engines roared at the far end of the stretch of road that marked the starting line and Arlene half-rose, craning to see if she could catch a glimpse of her target.

"Race is starting," she offered enthusiastically, hoping to divert Dusty's attention. "Okay, so what is happening here? What should I be watching for?"

"Some of these folks are breaking more laws than you can shake a stick at. A lot of bookies like these set-ups. A lot of money can change hands here. Plus I'm watching for underage drivers. Kids don't belong in these races. People can get hurt. Killed. But a lot of times, they let 'em run.

"Most of the folks here are okay, though. Good ol' boys just looking for a place to let off some steam, test their skills. Prove their car is fastest."

"Well, I don't want to hurt your 'good ol' boys', I'm more interested in those bookies you mentioned. And all that money." Arlene caught a quick breath, her fingers closing tightly on Dusty's forearm as she caught a glimpse of a familiar ugly toupee.

The cars roared toward the finish and the crowd responded, rising to their feet, screaming with delight or disappointment.

~

Lester Harvey groaned and covered his face as the cars crossed the finish line in a cloud of red dust. Shaking his head, he dropped his hands and looked around quickly.

How could he lose? That guy should have won easily. He puffed his lips and tried to think. What now? It couldn't be over.

"Mr. Harvey," drawled a deep voice.

Lester's heart plunged. Clearing his throat, he turned. "Brennan. Well, that didn't go as well as I'd hoped."

"No, it didn't. I think it's time we discuss your repaying the funds I have loaned you."

"Now look here, Brennan, you know I'm good for it. Just give me another chance." Lester licked his lips, and looked anxiously around. "You know these boys will give us a good run."

Brennan motioned and two big men moved to either side of Harvey. "Run's over, Harvey."

~

A brightly painted red, white and blue car spun out approaching the finish, vanishing within a cloud of smoke and dust as other cars raced past. Arlene gasped as the car slammed into a wall of straw bales stacked along the fence line bordering the stretch of road that formed their track.

Her gaze darted back to the mayor. The man he'd been speaking with moved aside and two burly fellows grabbed Harvey by either arm. She pulled on Dusty's sleeve, directing his attention to the interaction at the edge of the track.

"That doesn't look too friendly," she noted.

"That's Wes Brennan," Dusty explained. "I'll give you odds he's old Lester's bookie. And you're right, no one's looking too happy right there." Dusty squinted, looking quickly across the race crowd then directly into her eyes. "Can I trust you to stay put till I get back?"

"Where are you going?"

"To my truck. I've gotta call Lance. I'm gonna need backup before something worse happens here than those gorillas of Brennan's scaring our mayor's toupee off." He squeezed her arm. "I mean it, sis. Stay put. I'll be right back."

He vaulted over the low railing and sprinted toward the parking lot. Arlene watched his receding figure. *No one else*, she noted, *showed more than a fleeting interest.*

The bookie's 'muscle' forced Harvey around the corner. Arlene looked toward the parking area, shook her head, and headed down the fence line. *This story isn't getting away from me.*

Thirty-Four

The throng of race-goers thinned beyond the makeshift stands along the roadway. Cars waiting their turn at glory formed a ragged line along the outside of their impromptu track. Someone up near the starting line hollered for the next set of racers.

"Hey there, can I help you, pretty lady?" A lanky young man in coveralls offered Arlene a lazy grin.

She peered past him after the mayor and his escort. "I'm trying to speak with Mr. Brennan." She indicated the direction he had gone and the man glanced that way with a scowl and a shake of his head.

"And here I thought maybe you just liked fast cars."

He sounded genuinely disappointed and Brennan and the mayor had stopped moving and seemed to be engaged in a rather enthusiastic argument, so Arlene took a moment to see where the conversation might lead.

"Are you a driver?"

The man brightened a bit. "Yes ma'am. This ol' girl right here is mine." He patted the hood of a Plymouth then stuck out his hand. "Name's Woody."

Arlene accepted his handshake and smiled. "Nice to meet you Woody. I'm a reporter with *The Gazette* and I would love to do an article on what you all do here."

His lips tightened and he looked around nervously.

"Don't worry," she assured him. "I won't mention any last names, or say where ya'll are running. But I think what you do, and why, would be of interest to people. Don't you?"

"Yes ma'am. We have a lot of good times here. But the last thing we need is a lot of heat turning up when we're just having some friendly races."

Arlene nodded. *Great, two stories in the making here.* "I understand. And I won't make trouble for you. I promise.

"Tell you what, let me finish up with Mr. Brennan and Mr. Harvey over there, and I would love to interview you and some of the others. Would that be all right?"

He leaned back against his car and pushed his ball cap back on his head. "I think we could do that."

"Thanks. I'd better get over there." Arlene started around Woody and found a gathering knot of drivers eyeing her narrowly. Woody waved them off and they wandered toward their cars. "Thanks again," Arlene acknowledged and hurried past the cars in hopes of getting close enough to overhear Mayor Harvey's conversation.

Brennan's goons picked Harvey up bodily and deposited him atop the fence and Arlene heard his squeaky protests clean across the field. "Now, come on Brennan. You know I'll get you the money. Here, here...look, I got the grand for ya didn't I? Well, didn't I?"

Arlene crouched behind an old Dodge and crept toward the front, where she could peek through and see what was happening. Gratefully, Brennan and his bullies seemed much too intent on Lester Harvey to even notice her. She pulled her notebook from her coat pocket and began to scribble notes.

"Where you gonna come up with this kind of cash, Harvey?" Brennan demanded, puffing on a fat cigar. "That little town of yours isn't big enough to support your habit." He blew a cloud of smoke at Harvey, then gestured to the big men who pushed the squirming man to his knees. "So I'm thinking we're gonna have to show you just what happens when you welsh on a deal with me."

"No, no!" Harvey pleaded.

"That'll do," ordered a commanding voice and Arlene caught a quick breath, heart racing as Lance strode out of the heavy shadows. Dusty and Randy followed close behind, closing in on the mayor and his bookie from all sides.

"Well, now Sheriff Carter," Brennan drawled. "What a surprise to find you over here. But I don't believe we are in your jurisdiction now are we?"

"Now there's the rub, Wes." Lance motioned to Dusty who took the mayor in hand. "See, the road where these old boys are running...that's actually the dividing line between Hilton Falls and Sunny Hills. I called Sheriff Peters over to Hilton Falls and his fellas are right there." Lance nodded to two uniformed policemen. "But it seems you and your boys...well, you're on my side of the road." Lance grinned. "You're under arrest."

"Thank goodness you showed up when you did, Sheriff Carter." Lester Harvey ran a shaky hand over his sweat-drenched brow. "Things were just quite out of control here."

"You're under arrest too, Lester. Seems to me, there's going to be one heck of an investigation into your gambling, and the missing town funds--"

"No," Harvey protested loudly as Dusty moved him firmly down the fencerow. "They threatened me! I'm innocent I tell you."

Arlene came around the front of the Dodge, smiling smugly. "I overheard a considerable exchange between these gentlemen, Sheriff. I would be happy to testify."

Harvey's eyes widened, his mouth opening and closing like a fish flopping on a creek bank. Lance grinned at Arlene, shook his head ruefully and handed off Brennan and his cohorts to the deputies.

"I'll be along directly." He sighed heavily as he took Arlene's arm. "I knew it. I knew you'd be knee-deep in this the minute Dusty called."

She patted her notebook. "I got my story. You got the mayor and Sunny Hills gets a chance at a fresh start."

"Honey, you worry me. One day you're going to get yourself in a fix you can't get out of."

Arlene smiled coyly and squeezed his hand. "And then you'll be there, just like you always are for me." She straightened her jacket and tossed her head. "Now I have another story to write here. You want to stay and watch me work, or just have Dusty leave the truck for me to drive home?"

Lance sighed and called after Dusty where he was pushing Lester Harvey into the rear of the squad car amidst a buzzing and somewhat antsy crowd of onlookers. "Ya'll go on. I'll keep an eye on Arlene."

"Good." Dusty chuckled. "Someone needs to."

~

"You did it." Jack slapped the folded paper onto the desk in front of Arlene then dropped down to sit on the chair. "You've got a great story there, Arlene. And I hear there is more?"

"Plenty more. Another article on the mayor's... problem. An entire series on how his gambling has impacted our town, the consequences from the loss of funds, the betrayal of trust. Plus one on the racing itself. And--"

Jack waggled his eyebrows and eased a slip of paper from his shirt pocket. Lips pursed, he considered the writing on the note. "So, I don't suppose you need this--"

"Jack," Arlene warned, leaning across the desk and attempting to snatch the paper he held just beyond her reach. "What is it?"

"Just a little...note...regarding what Mr. Solana thinks you should do with this article of yours." He grinned impishly as he met her gaze. "But I expect you already have your own plans, right?"

"Gimme that." Arlene grabbed the note from his fingers and lowered herself with practiced poise onto her seat. "Oh my gosh," she exclaimed, reading the slip. "It's going to the big papers. Savannah wants to run it." She barely managed to keep the squeal of delight out of her voice; no way she could conceal her smile. "They want a follow-up after the trials. With my byline." Arlene beamed at Jack and he nodded.

Rising, he leaned across the desk and planted a kiss on the top of her head. "I always knew you were a star." He strolled toward the door. "And there's more," he teased, pausing to lean against the doorframe. "Mr. Solana wants to see you in his office."

Arlene took a deep breath and got to her feet. "Guess I'd better see what the boss wants then."

She attempted to regain her composure en route to his office. It wasn't easy. The expose article on the mayor was only the beginning. The best was yet to come. Already she had her report on the race drivers, their cars, and their passion. It would run in the Sunday paper.

And wait till Mr. Solana sees this next one, she thought with a swell of pride. It was, without a doubt, the best thing she'd ever written. She rapped on his door before opening it and poking her head into the room.

"Called me, boss?"

"Come on in, Arlene." He gestured to the chair facing his desk. "That was good work on the mayor."

"Thank you."

"There's more, isn't there?"

"A lot more, most of it will come out at the trial, but he's already plea bargained. He'll have to pay restitution to the town funds, but you know how long that's going to take. And he had to step down..."

"Yeah. Big rally this afternoon over at Town Hall to discuss what all this means to the town. Deputy Mayor Richardson is stepping into the office until interim elections can be held."

"Is that what this is about?" Arlene eyed her boss curiously. "You want me to cover the meeting?"

"Actually, yes I do. But that's not why I asked you to come. You saw the note from the Savannah paper?"

Arlene nodded. "I'm really pleased with their interest."

"So am I, but that piece you're doing on the mayor's gambling and what it has cost him, cost the people here, cost our whole community...that's the one I want you to run with Arlene."

"Sir?"

"Soon as it's ready, you let me know." He folded his hands behind his head and leaned back comfortably in his chair. "That one is going to put you on the map, and I intend to see it gets the chance to do just that." He leaned forward, cold sober and serious. "Look, I may just be the editor of a little paper in a little town you don't think anyone will ever take notice of, but I got my start outside Sunny Hills. I know people, and I know reporting.

"You did it, Miss Sinclair. Congratulations."

Thirty-Five

Wisps of homemade spider webbing danced on the breeze. Candles, tiki torches, and luminaries flickered awaiting the approaching dark. Caroline Sinclair straightened her large gold hoop earrings, swished her long multicolored skirt, and took a seat behind the card table draped in purple set up on her front porch.

"Here you go, honey." Clint set her crystal ball on the stand in front of her and lit the jack-o-lanterns lining the steps.

"Got the apples ready?"

"Yep, a whole bushel sitting down there just waiting for dunking. Arlene's got the hot spiced cider and cocoa."

"Oh my goodness," Caroline exclaimed, looking worriedly toward the house. "Did I remember to put the birthday cake for Gary out of sight? What if he comes in? It would spoil the surprise."

"For goodness sake, Caroline, you put that cake in the pantry the minute Arlene arrived. Now quit fretting."

"Fretting?" Arlene came out of the house with the popcorn ball treats for the kids. "Momma, really everything is just perfect."

Caroline looked lovingly at her daughter. "I think it is such a sweet thing you are doing for that child, Arlene. Goodness knows that boy deserves something special this year. He's been through a lot." Caroline glanced toward the street.

Trick-or-treaters would be arriving soon. Friends. Neighbors. She loved this night. The one time each year when being 'psychic momma' was a bonus. But this year, other things were foremost on her mind. Dusty. Lance and Gary. Arlene. So many things were changing.

Arlene smiled, fairly beaming with delight. "I think so too, Momma. Lance has been so excited about having this little party for him." The sound of laughter and voices drifted through the trees like the final autumn leaves. "Here they come!" She hurried down the steps to the refreshment tables.

~

Children in bright costumes held hands with their parents or raced in small giggling groups around the Sinclair's yard. Arlene handed Jester Riley two paper cups of hot cider, chuckling to herself as he scurried across the lawn to pass the second cup to Clarissa Johnson beneath the discreet shadow of the tulip tree.

Some adults, notably her mother, wore costumes. Al Porter from the post office arrived in his traditional clown costume, complete with makeup, red nose and a squeaky horn and sat beside her father to oversee the apple dunking and make balloon animals for the children. Jeb Martin dressed as a cowboy, although with his carrot hair and freckles Arlene thought he more closely resembled Howdy Doody.

"Boo!" A decidedly adult size ghost greeted Arlene.

"Cider or hot cocoa?"

"Cider. I spill that hot chocolate I'll stain my outfit for sure," replied a familiar voice.

Arlene narrowed her eyes and considered the sheet-draped figure. "Randy? That you under there?"

"Shh, you'll blow my cover." He chortled at his pun, slipping the cup of cider underneath the fabric.

"Well, we wouldn't want that to happen," Arlene agreed with a grin.

A group of kids raced between her and Randy, grabbing cups of cocoa topped with marshmallows and popcorn balls wrapped in cellophane before they ran on, calling back enthusiastic 'thank you's'.

"Think I can get a hot chocolate before the kids snatch 'em all up?" drawled a soft voice and Arlene laughed aloud at Katie's Minnie Mouse costume.

"Aren't you just too cute," Arlene gushed.

"Well, I hope that brother of yours thinks so." She looked hopefully around the festivities. "Have you seen him?"

"Sorry, I sure haven't. Randy?"

The ghost shrugged beneath its shroud. "Dusty and Tyler are on patrol, just keeping an eye on things." The cup reappeared from beneath the sheet as he set it on the table. "Thanks Arlene. I'd better go round up my young 'uns too."

Arlene watched him snag his five year old from where the boy sat happily munching a caramel apple that left as much candy on the child's face as on the apple. Randy wasn't much older than her, but he seemed happy--content--with his wife and kids and quiet, settled life.

I can't imagine feeling that way.

"Arlene?" Katie's voice yanked Arlene back from her reveries.

"Sorry, Katie. I was just thinking-- But if you'd like to stay, I know Dusty is coming back after trick-or-treating ends." She leaned forward and whispered conspiratorially, "We're having a surprise party for Gary's birthday."

"Oh, what a wonderful idea." Katie beamed. "Are you sure you don't mind? I'd love to stay."

"The more the merrier."

"Thanks, that is so sweet."

"Sweet," whispered a muffled voice. "Isn't that a matter of taste?"

Arlene looked up in surprise, giggling at the sight of a grown man in a widely grinning Bugs Bunny mask. She cleared her throat, but couldn't avoid the obvious as the words came rushing out despite her stifled laughter. "What's up, doc?"

The man tossed his glowing cigarette butt on the ground and crushed it under his heel, then took a cup of steaming cider and a popcorn ball. "More tricks than treats before the night is over, I'm thinking," he murmured quietly and walked away, disappearing into the shadows around the back of the house.

A chill raced up Arlene's spine.

"That was odd, wasn't it?" Katie said, shaking her head. "Wonder who that was."

"So do I," Arlene agreed, staring in the direction the man had gone. "I really wonder."

~

Lance wiped water from his face and grinned foolishly around the apple in his teeth. He watched Gary sputter, snatching at the dipping and darting apples in the heavy aluminum tub until nearly his whole head disappeared beneath the water and Gary popped up with an apple of his own.

"Good job," Lance praised enthusiastically.

"You got one too?" Gary grinned and wiped his face on the hand towel Clint Sinclair tossed his way.

"Like father, like son," Clint drawled and Lance couldn't help but smile even wider.

"About ready to call it a night?" Lance looked around at the diminishing gathering. Parents escorted children toward home and called their thanks and appreciation into the night.

Clint leaned closer to the tiki torch beside his chair and glanced at his watch in the flickering light. "Yep, nearly eight o'clock. Time to call it a night." He got to his feet and stretched. "Closing up, folks. See you all next year."

"It was great, Clint. Thanks," Al said and squeaked his horn one last time. "Think I'll go relieve your daughter of one last cup of that cider before I head home."

Lance glanced toward Arlene. She was busy serving someone in a gray hooded sweatshirt and a Bugs Bunny mask. Lance frowned, squinting against the darkness. Who was that? Something pricked at his memory, sending tingles like a chill across his skin. *Just a coincidence.* Lots of folks were Tweety or Bugs on Halloween. *No one would be fool enough to show up here in public.*

The man strode casually toward the backyard. It seemed innocent enough; Lance clapped Gary on the shoulder. "Come on, let's get you some hot cocoa. That dang water nearly froze my nose off."

They followed Al to Arlene's table.

"Hi Lance, Gary," Arlene greeted them as they approached. "Glad you two made it before I ran out of cocoa."

"Or marshmallows," Gary agreed, tossing a handful into the top of his cup.

Lance took a cup, noticing the way the candlelight danced on Arlene's hair. *Come on, pull yourself together.* He couldn't help staring, she was so darn pretty. Her fingers brushed across his hand and he wanted to hold onto that touch and never let go. He gulped cocoa instead and burned his tongue. "Whoa, hot."

"Be careful," Arlene admonished.

Eyes watering, Lance looked away, blowing short breaths in an attempt to cool his mouth. A flicker of light within the inky dark under the heavy oak at the back caught his eye. He recognized the glow, a quick flare of yellow, dimming quickly to a small reddish gleam. Someone lighting a cigarette. *Odd.*

He peered intently toward the shadowy figure nearly lost in the night. Did whoever it was see he was watching? The glow dropped toward the ground, quickly extinguished within the black, and the person moved on. Prickles nipped at the nape of Lance's neck. He didn't like the feeling.

"Looks like we're done here," Arlene said. "Care to help me clean things up?"

Lance shook the niggling uneasiness from his mind and focused on Arlene. *Time to get things rolling here.* "Sure thing. Gary, can you bring in that punch bowl? I'll get this for you."

Katie and Arlene cleared the rest of the table and the four of them headed up the front steps to the house. Caroline slipped a black velvet bag over the crystal 'ball' that otherwise doubled as a floating candle vase on special occasions, folded the familiar table cover with its myriad of silver stars, and smiled.

"Put the card table up for me, Lance?" Caroline requested. "Arlene, you girls come in the kitchen and we'll get those things-ummm--put away." She winked at Katie, then led the way through the living room. "You boys just set that old punch bowl on the dining room table for me, would you?"

Arlene gave Lance a surreptitious glance and he nodded, put his hand on Gary's shoulder and gestured toward the darkened dining room. "Over there. Go ahead and put it on the table."

~

In the kitchen, Caroline hustled to bring out the cake Arlene had made. With the swirls of cinnamon-cream cheese frosting and filling, it looked perfect. Arlene put the candles in place around the perimeter.

"What can I do?" Katie whispered.

"Get the people waiting on the porch." Caroline motioned to the back door. "He is going to be so surprised."

Katie opened the door and motioned the rest of Gary's guests inside. Ellie, Joe, Dusty, Nelson McKay and Lance's parents came in followed closely by her Dad. Arlene put a finger to her lips, meeting their grins with a smile of her own as they gathered near the table.

Caroline lit the candles and swung open the door separating the kitchen from the dining room as the entire group hollered "Happy Birthday" at the top of their lungs.

Lance flipped on the dining room lights and Arlene carried the cake to the table while everyone sang happy birthday to Gary. The boy stood, wide-eyed and gape-mouthed, in mute shock.

"Happy birthday, son." Lance urged him toward the table and a slow grin lit Gary's face.

"This is great. Thank you." He hugged Lance.

"Blow out the candles," Arlene urged. "Make a wish."

"I think I already got all my wishes," Gary said, but he obliged by bending, eyes squeezed tightly closed for a moment before he blew out the candles.

"Gary"--Lance gripped his shoulder, directing his attention--"These are my parents, Maggie and Travis Carter. Your Grandparents." He smiled with a pride so warm in its strength Arlene thought he absolutely glowed. "Mom, Dad, this is your grandson, Gary."

"Oh sweety," his mom gushed, smothering Gary in a swift embrace. "I am so glad you found your Daddy. So glad we have you in the family now."

Lance's father shook Gary's hand and nodded to the table. "Nice to meet you at last. Now how about you get to those birthday presents so we can have some of this beautiful cake Miss Arlene made for you?"

"You made this?" Gary's eyes danced as he met Arlene's gaze. "For me? Thank you. It's great. Maybe we should eat it first?"

"Tell you what, sweety," Caroline offered, sliding the cake from in front of Gary. "I will slice this up and serve the cake while you get started on those gifts."

Gary beamed with excitement, slowly taking a seat at the table. Everyone gathered around the table, Lance held a chair for Arlene to sit beside him.

"This is from me." Nelson McKay extended a large box with a royal blue bow.

Gary eased the lid open cautiously, peeking inside before he threw it open and lifted out a guitar. "Thanks, Granddad."

"As I promised," Nelson McKay said with a wink. "But I still expect you to come play some bluegrass with me...not just this new-fangled stuff I hear on the radio nowadays."

"How about I'll learn your music and you learn mine?"

"Deal," Nelson McKay said.

"This one is ours," Travis Carter offered and Gary happily accepted the box producing two baseball mitts and a ball.

"This is great." Gary slammed his fist into the pocket of one glove. "Why two?"

Travis shrugged, looking up to meet Lance's gaze. "Your Dad always did love baseball. Figured you might too."

"Lance has done nothing since you two found each other but tell us how much he's missed of your life," Maggie said warmly. "Maybe this will let you two make up for some lost time."

"Thank you, that's really nice."

Lance leaned closer, placing a small velvet box in front of the teenager. "I thought and thought about what to get you. I'd give you my name in a heartbeat, if I could..."

"I know, Dad."

"But after I had you call your parents this morning, talked to Dan Jones, well...I know how much they love you. And you love them."

Arlene longed to take Lance's hand, ease the emotions she felt overwhelming him. *He had Gary call home. Oh, he can't lose him so soon. Having Gary means so much to him.*

"Yeah, I do. But...but I love you too." Gary's eyes filled with tears. "And I'm glad Pop is letting me stay with you."

"So am I, son. So am I." Lance clasped his shoulder warmly. "Now you have two families that love you. And this"--he tapped the small box--"is part of that tie."

Gary opened the box, frowning with puzzlement. He lifted a silver chain from which dangled a ring. His gaze flitted to Lance who reached over to touch the ring gently.

"It was your mother's. Ginny and I exchanged rings at our senior prom. It was special to her. Just like you are."

Lance sat back, flashing a crooked grin. "You'll get your own Sunny Hills High School ring in three years. Assuming you can catch up the work you've missed so far."

Gary slipped the necklace over his head, then jerked around to stare at Lance. "So far?"

"You start school Monday. Principal Scott says you're going to have to buckle down to keep up, but I'm sure you can do it."

"School?"

To Arlene's surprise, Gary's face lit with an eager smile. *He's happy about it?*

"Can't say I'm looking forward to the homework, but I've missed school. I don't even know anyone my age here yet. I've met a couple at the diner, but no one really knows me."

"It's good to have friends," Dusty agreed slapping Lance on the back, then lifted his plate. "Now, let's have cake."

Thirty-Six

"He had a really good time, didn't he?" Lance asked Arlene as they loaded an armload of Gary's gifts into the back seat of Lance's car.

"He sure did. It was great seeing him with your folks, but I think Dusty's claimed him as the little brother he always wanted--except he got me." She giggled and rolled her eyes.

Lance shook his head and caught her hand as she headed back toward the house. She moved into his arms with fluid ease, head tilted to one side as she searched his eyes. "He might make a better...uncle?" *Why doesn't she answer? Lance, you idiot. Maybe it's too soon.* "Someday?" he whispered hopefully.

Arlene continued to stare at him, eyes wide and suddenly bright. With a short release of breath, she turned and ran toward the house.

Damn. Damn, what'd I go and say that for? He slammed the car door and stormed across the backyard, seeking privacy in the deep shadows beneath the trees. *Now what? Face it, you old idiot, you're in love with her. Head over heels, puppy-dog in love with that woman. Now what am I supposed to do? What if she doesn't feel that way about me? But I was sure...* He swallowed hard, trying to get the lump out of his throat. *Give her time.* He looked toward the house. Dusty walked Katie to her car, bent to give her a quick kiss before he closed her car door.

Lance rubbed his fingers hard against his forehead. His head ached. His heart ached. *C'mon, pull it together. I can't let Gary see me like this.* He couldn't get his thoughts off her. What was that look he'd seen in her eyes?

Head hung in dejection; he wandered toward the old oak tree he and Dusty had used for a fort as kids. Acorns crunched underfoot. A flash of white amidst the dark caught his listless gaze. Lance paused, a slow frown gathering.

The man in the shadows. He knelt, brushing away the leaf cover until he found the cigarette butt. Pulling his pocketknife from his pocket, Lance carefully eased the half-burned cigarette into his handkerchief and strode quickly into the glow from the porch light.

Crushed though it was, the butt bore the now familiar brandmark. *Oasis.* Cold calm settled over Lance. The thief disrupting the peace of Sunny Hills slipped into a new and more terrifying persona--stalker. *Who are you? What the devil do you want here?*

Dusty paused on the bottom step, watching him with open curiosity. "Hey Lance. Whattcha got there?"

"Trouble."

Dusty rubbed the back of his neck dubiously. "You want to explain that?"

"Remember I told you the thief who robbed Jonas' place and broke into the hardware store left cigarette butts?"

"Yeah. And?"

"Well, I found the same brand at the bus depot where the truck was stolen. Whoever he is, he's sticking around here for a reason, Dusty. And tonight, he was here."

"How can you be sure?"

"I've never seen this brand anywhere else." Lance handed his handkerchief to Dusty who peered closely at the dingy butt.

"No, I know these," Dusty said with certainty. "Who could forget? Arlene complained the whole time Kent hung around her in college. Said they smelled nasty. Never discouraged him though. He just kept coming around."

Lance frowned, images of the past slowly coming in startling clarity. "Kent? Kent Jordan?"

"Yeah, this was his brand. He wouldn't touch anything else. Said he liked these better. You remember him?"

"Yeah. I arrested him for the robbery that put him in prison. So these can't be his. He went up for fifteen years."

Caroline Sinclair slipped out onto the porch, pulling her sweater close around her. "What are you two up to out here?"

"Just getting ready to take Gary home," Lance covered, recovering his hankie with the evidence--of what he had no idea but instinct told him it was indeed evidence--tucked inside. He met Dusty's gaze whose raised brows and pursed lips told him the deputy also suspected something was afoot. "I need to have a word with Arlene before we head out though."

"Officially, of course," Caroline quipped, shaking her head. She planted her hands on her hips and fixed Lance with a narrow gaze. "Which is not what either of you *needs* to be discussing right now. So, you want to tell me what's going on between you two, Lancelot, or do you want me to tell you?"

"What?" Lance asked defensively, his earlier discomfort slamming into him again. "You see something in the cards?"

"I'm not the 'psychic momma' for nothing," Carolina agreed with a smug grin. "But you don't need cards, horoscopes or a crystal ball to see something is going on between you and Arlene."

"Why'd she come flying back into the house like that?"

Lance sighed. "I think...I'm in love with Arlene." He looked up sheepishly, prepared to find much-deserved shock and dismay on his friends' faces.

Caroline raised an arched brow. "About time you figured that out."

"What?"

Dusty chuckled. "Shoot, everyone knows it except the two of you."

"I tried to tell her." Lance slumped. "She just stared at me, and headed back inside. Not a word. Guess she doesn't feel that way about me."

"Oh, don't be foolish, Lance." Caroline crossed her arms across her breast. "She's crazy for you, but look at what you're asking of her. Since she started writing that series about Lester and his gambling and all the trouble it has caused for this town she's been published in Savannah and Atlanta. Today there was a call about them running it clean up north someplace.

"Ever since high school, this has been her dream. Writing a story that will touch people. Making a difference. And she's finally got it almost in reach. And then the only other thing she's wanted all her life tells her he *might* be wanting her too. What's she supposed to do with that? What are you asking her to do, Lance?"

"I never thought of that. I just...I want her to be happy. If that means the city then"--he swallowed hard, trying to fight down the bitter bile rising in his throat--"much as I can't even imagine getting up every day without being able to see her...that's what I want for her too."

He closed his fist over the handkerchief. "But that's not what I need to talk to her about right now, Mrs. Sinclair. I'd better go talk to her--"

"She's already gone home. Came rushing inside and right out the front to her car." A gathering concern filled Caroline's face. "Oh this isn't good. It's that man isn't it? The one you two were talking about...before I came out." She tilted her head to the side, obviously in thought. "I keep seeing that rabbit. What's he done? What's this got to do with my daughter?"

Lance shook his head. "I don't know, but I'm going to find out. Could you call Arlene and just make sure she got home all right and then let me know? I'll get Gary and head on home."

"It was a wonderful Halloween party. And a great birthday for Gary. I appreciate everything ya'll did."

"It was mostly Arlene's idea," Caroline reminded him.

"I know. She's amazing."

"Be sure you tell her that when you finally quit moping and start talking." Caroline opened the door, glancing back one final time. "Better make it soon, son, if you're not already too late. And, I don't need any cards to know that either."

~

Arlene curled up on the end of her sofa, her thick chenille robe wrapped close around her, and patted the cushion for Coco to come up beside her. She scratched his ears and, sensing her mood, he laid his wide muzzle on her leg and watched her with soulful hazel eyes.

"Oh Coco, I'm so mixed up." She sighed, picked up the folded letter from the end table beside the couch and opened it. *Boston. They want the whole series in Boston.* The tingle of pride, satisfaction with her accomplishment, faded beneath the crushing fire in her gut, the wrenching ache in her heart. *And then Lance.* "Why'd he say that, huh?" she asked the patient Lab. "What if he's thinking..." She sniffled, dabbing her eyes on the thick folded cuff of her sleeve. "I mean, if he actually"--Could she say it? Say the word out loud? Make it as real as she'd always dreamed it could be--"Actually loves me, what would I do then?"

Coco lifted his head and pushed it under her hand. She obliged by stroking the soft chocolate-brown fur. Outside, rain pattered against the window and Arlene stared into the darkness beyond her warm little room and knew she wouldn't find sleep tonight.

Thirty-Seven

Lance punched his fist into the mitt. The new leather needed some breaking in before he and Gary played some ball after school. *After school.* He grinned. *My son will be coming home to play ball with his old man after school.*

And after work. He'd spent almost the whole weekend just getting Gary ready for school. *Time to get back to work.* He set the glove on the corner of his desk and picked up the phone. *Kent Jordan, Dusty said. Couldn't be him, but if it is... Surely Jeff will be back to work now that it's Monday.*

"Jeff McDaniel, please. It's Sheriff Lance Carter from Sunny Hills," he replied to the voice of the switchboard operator on the other end of the line. "Thanks, I'll wait."

He tapped the eraser end of a pencil against the blotter on his desk, thoughts racing as fast as the staccato beat. *Kent Jordan. Robbery.* He'd been a deputy then, ten...almost eleven...years ago. *Jordan tried to hide out here. He thought Arlene would help him...Arlene--*

"Hello? Lance?"

"Hey Jeff. Been trying to catch you all weekend. Fishing, I heard?"

"Yep, sorry Lance. Hope it wasn't too urgent. Got some great fishing in though. They're really biting this time of year."

Lance shook his head and grinned. *McDaniels and his dang fishing.* "Listen, I've got a question. Do you remember a guy named Kent Jordan?"

"Well, normally I'd say no."

Lance heard McDaniel's chuckle, but the sound sent a chill through him. "Normally? Jeff, I've got some strange things going on here in Sunny Hills. Things I think might be connected somehow to Jordan."

"Might be? You be careful then, Lance. Kent Jordan was released a month or two back."

"Released? It's been ten years, he's serving fifteen."

"He got an early parole."

"Damnation, Jeff. Why didn't anyone tell me?" *Arlene identified him. Shit.* "Thanks anyway. I'll let you know when I arrest that sonofabitch again." He slammed the receiver down, yelling even before he opened his office door, "Debbie. Get Dusty. Randy too. Now."

~

Quiet. The usual crowd gathered at the barbershop watching the television and swapping stories. Ladies hurried out of Libby's Beauty Shop, scarves protecting their newly styled hair from the elements. Kids played at recess in the school yard.

Zeb Tinker, walking his wife's Chihuahua, waved a casual greeting as Lance drove past him along Newton Street. Peaceful at Arlene's house too. He saw Coco bouncing merrily around the fenced back yard. *Good.* Lance felt a wash of relief. At least the big dog provided her with some protection.

Randy's voice broke in over the radio. "Lance? You there?"

"Yeah, anything?"

"Sorry, Sheriff. I walked the whole trailer park. No one has seen anyone new."

"Head on over and check the bus depot."

"Sure thing."

Lance pulled to the curb in front of Arlene's house. *I'm missing something. There has to be some clue. Something we can look for even if he's under cover.*

A white Studebaker passed.

Of course! The car. I've got to talk to Arlene. He pulled out and headed for the station.

~

Arlene sipped coffee and rubbed her fingers against her pounding temples. Her eyes burned. *Tired. Too many hours this weekend.* Too many long hours unpacking the boxes from moving. Too many hours trying not to think about Lance. She groaned under her breath and straightened.

Focus. There's work to do.

The phone jangled, sending shockwaves along her already frayed nerves. She snatched the handset up to her ear. "Hello?" Arlene shook her head to clear her thoughts and tried again. "Hello, this is Arlene Sinclair at the *Sunny Hills Gazette*."

"Hey Arlene. It's Lance."

Her heart slammed against her chest so hard she could barely catch a breath. *Deep breath. Stay calm.* "Hello Lance. What can I do for you?"

"I--I wanted--"

Interesting. It wasn't like Lance to stammer. Arlene felt an uncharacteristic satisfaction in his apparent discomfort. *Good, maybe I'm not the only one who had a miserable weekend.*

She heard him draw a long breath and waited, letting the silence between them draw out until it was insufferable. "Something you needed?"

"I'm sorry I didn't call. I just didn't...I don't want to pressure...didn't want you to think--"

"I assure you, I'm not thinking anything," Arlene snapped. She rolled her eyes. *I didn't just say that.*

"Well, that's good to know," Lance replied more quietly. "I just tried to spend the weekend getting Gary ready for school. That's all. How about you?"

"I was unpacking. Setting up the house, you know. But I'm sure you didn't call about that."

"No. No, actually, I need to know more about the car that nearly hit you the day we painted the house. Do you remember the make, the color?"

"Cream and white two-tone. And it was"--she paused to think, identifying cars was not her strong point--"a Buick, I think. Older though. 40s maybe."

"Did you get a look at the driver at all?"

"Not really. It was dusk by then, lots of shadows. And it happened so fast.

"Male. Not a teenager. Probably our age. Had a baseball cap on. That's about all I can think of. Why the sudden interest?" The newshound in her came awake. *What's Lance on to?*

"Nothing. Not sudden at all. Finishing a report. Just wanted to get the facts right."

He's stalling. He knows something; I know this tone.

"Have you ever seen this car around town before? Locally?"

"No. No, I don't think I ever have."

"Okay, well, thanks."

"What's up, Lance?"

"Nothing. Just got a report here..."

"Oh no you don't. Whoever he is, he nearly squashed me flat. Now if you know something, Lance, I deserve to know."

There was a momentary silence on the other end. "Yes. Yes, you do. Look, hon, I'm just following up a lead that the car might be stolen and might still be around here. If I find it, I'll let you know."

"Mmm hmm."

"Listen, Arlene, stay out of this one. You could be in way over your head. Just, do me a favor...no Miss Snoops on this. Stay home tonight. Stay safe."

The plea in his voice melted any residual anger she might have felt. No more doubts. How much he cared showed in his voice.

"Be careful," she replied, deliberately noncommittal.

"Yeah," Lance said softly. "You too."

Thirty-Eight

Arlene opened the brochure from the Chamber of Commerce and flipped it over. A small map of Sunny Hills scrawled across showing not only the streets and roads, but also the location of the schools, both eateries, town hall, various businesses, churches, and the old motel on the outskirts of town.

The motel. Her brows arched upward. If it wasn't a local car, as Lance had hinted, and might be stolen, then the question was did the motel have a place a car could be hidden out of Lance's keen view?

The old place had lost a lot of business when the interstate had gone through near Hilton Falls instead of Sunny Hills. There wasn't much traffic on the old route any more. *It might be a good place for someone to stay unnoticed.*

"Time to put all these pieces together." She buttoned her long wool coat and pulled on her gloves. "Miss Snoops indeed," she huffed with a smirk. "Wait till you see what a real newshound can do, Sheriff Carter."

~

The cold November air nipped at Lance's cheeks, but he hardly noticed. Their efforts to canvass Sunny Hills in hopes of locating Kent Jordan were proving fruitless.

Think, Lance, he berated himself, chafing his hands together. Where has be been that I know about? *The garage, the hardware store was probably his doing, and then the haunted house at Fall Festival. Arlene's--* Lance slammed his clenched fist against the hood of the cruiser. "Oh yeah, he has definitely been to Arlene's."

But that was her apartment and now her folks' house on Halloween. *Maybe Kent doesn't know she moved. Where else? The bus depot. He stole that truck at the bus depot.*

Dang it, Jeff, if I'd known this creep was out... He shook his head. No sense in letting it get to him now. Right now he needed his thoughts clear. He needed to find Kent Jordan before the creep got his hands on Arlene. Lance was more certain than ever Arlene was the target of everything.

The bus depot. That's how he got here after prison. But where would Kent go? He knew Arlene from college; he'd never lived in Sunny Hills so he wouldn't know anyone here in town he could stay with.
Where would Kent Jordan hide?

"Why didn't I think of that before?" Lance threw the car door open and slid inside, grabbing for the radio handset. "Randy. Dusty. Drop everything. I think I know where he is."

~

Arlene parked in front of the "Shady Grove Motel" and slowly got out. The neon sign shuddered in the gusting winter breeze. Long, grass huddled yellow around its base and tangled amidst the untended hedge of roses that once had framed the courtyard.

Creepy. Arlene shivered and pulled her coat close. Three older cars were staggered around the pot-holed parking lot. Another was parked near the motel office.

Obviously no one would park a stolen car in front. *Let's have a look around back.*

Edging around the last row of adjoined rooms, she made her way to the rear of the motel, stepping over a fallen brick wall and a jumble of discarded guttering and broken plumbing fixtures. The back area, overgrown and obviously in disrepair, showed little sign of recent use save for the rusted garbage bins.

Tracks. There were tracks through the dried grass along the fence and hedgerow protecting the rear of the motel. They passed the ugly storage shed and continued the length of the building.

Arlene followed the trail toward the garbage bins. She looked up at the trees and tall shrubs overshadowing the area, then back toward the motel. From here she couldn't even see the road or the main parking lot. *A perfect hiding place.* One more quick glance; no one in sight. *Good.*

She slipped past the big dumpsters. A flash of cream amidst the foliage. *Yes!* The cream and white Buick sat camouflaged and protected. "Gottcha," she crowed. A quick tug on the front door handle and the door opened.

Arlene leaned inside, crinkling her nose in disgust. The car reeked of stale cigarette smoke and sweat. She flipped the visor down. No papers or maps. *Nothing on the seats.* "Who are you? Why did you try to run me down?"

A husky voice answered from behind. "Now that, darlin', would be the question."

~

Kent Jordan flattened against the side of the motel and peeked around the corner toward his stolen ride. *That dang Sinclair.* He'd know her anywhere.

She leaned further into the car, allowing him a nice view of long legs despite her heavy coat hiding all her other obvious attributes. He sneered lecherously.

Well, whaddya know, she came right to me. And here I was figuring I'd have to try and chase her down tonight. Time to get what she owes me.

He pulled the Bugs Bunny mask from his coat pocket and slipped it over his head, then drew his gun and crept toward the car. Last thing he needed now was for her to look up and scream. She continued to search the car, muttering to herself about why he was after her.

Little does she know.

Easing close behind, he threw his arm around her throat as she straightened and jammed the gun against her ribs. "Now that, darlin', would be the question," he breathed against her ear and pulled her backwards out of the car, kicking the door closed with his foot. "Come on, let's go inside and have a little chat."

"Hey, buddy, I'm not that kind of girl."

"Yeah? What kind of girl snoops around behind an old flea-trap like this anyway? Poking your nose into other people's cars--"

"Well, it's not your car either, now is it?"

"Shut up," he growled and dragged her around the end of the motel and into his room. He pushed her bodily through the doorway and onto the bed, the springs protesting loudly beneath the sudden weight.

She groaned and bolted upright, face twisted with disgust. "What happened in here? Didn't the maid come today? Or last month even?" With a shake of her head, she got to her feet and stared at him. "Someone forget to tell you...Halloween is over."

"Cute." He waved the gun toward her. "Sit."

She shuddered. "Not on that, I won't."

He grabbed a chair and dragged it into the middle of the room. "Sit down."

Arlene swallowed hard, chin lifted defiantly, then obeyed. "What's this all about?"

"I got you a little present here."

He tossed a rose at her, the scarlet edges curled and darkened from frost. Arlene caught a quick breath as it slid to the floor.

"And now you're gonna give me one."

"Roses?" Arlene arched a brow and he glowered angrily.

"Not hardly. You owe me. Big time, lady."

"Owe you?"

She sounded surprised. What, had she forgotten so soon what she did to him? Kent snatched off the mask.

"Yeah, you owe me. Ten years of my life you and good old Lance Carter stole from me. I'd have graduated that spring. Had me a good job. You took that."

"You threw that away when you robbed that store."

"I figure you owe me"--he paused to calculate what he wanted--"at least two grand a year. That's twenty grand."

Her mouth gaped open, eyes widening. "Twenty thousand? Dollars?" A small giggle escaped her. "That's a lot of carrots there, Bugs."

Kent snarled, his hand tightening on the butt of his revolver. "Damn it, Arlene. You're a big time reporter now. I've seen what you're doing. You owe me!"

She drew a deep breath. "And how do you propose I get this money for you, even if I could? You are holding me prisoner in here."

Dagnabit! She was right. Now what? *Think. Come on.*

"That loony mother of yours will get it. You can call her and tell her to. Then I'll pick it up and be gone before your boyfriend even figures out what happened."

Her face flushed with indignation. "I don't have a boyfriend."

"Don't kid yourself, sweet-cheeks. I may have been locked up, but I'm not blind. You've got that cop right in your pocket and you're so sweet on him it makes me gag." He yanked the heavy phone across the room and dropped it onto the end of the bed near her. "Think psychic momma needs a hint from you? Or will she know to get the money if you don't call?"

Arlene glared at him, lips tight. *Good, go ahead and get mad. As long as you bring me the money.*

"You are going to regret this," she announced.

"Only thing I regret is getting involved with a snoopy busy-body like you." He shoved the pistol against her back. "Let's get this over with."

Thirty-Nine

A seldom-used side road into the old parking lot of the "Shady Grove Motel" provided Lance with a less conspicuous entrance than driving straight to the door would have. He glanced through the passenger window beside Randy and watched Dusty pull his truck up in front of the office, leaving the truck-bed blocking the main exit from the rear.

Got it covered, Lance thought with satisfaction. He pulled the cruiser over beyond the last of the buildings and nodded to Randy as he climbed out.

"This guy has to be staying somewhere and this sure looks like a likely candidate."

Randy pushed his cap back on his head and scratched his chin. "Good thing you thought of it, I sure wouldn't have. I don't think anyone in town has used this place since old man Parker died."

"Dusty has things under control up here, let's have a look in back."

Lance grimaced and squeezed through a gap in the rusted fencing, his boots crunching on gravel and dried grass. He motioned Randy toward the far end and studied the maintenance area for an instant.

Where could Jordan hide a car? A storage shed at the other end might conceal it from where he was standing, but not from anyone in the side parking lot.

His eyes narrowed. The garbage bins were big and separated by a gap wide enough to drive through. Lance nodded. *Looks like a good place to start*.

The brush grew thick and tight against the first dumpster. Lance eased past it and followed the opening between the bins. *There it is.*

It was all he could do to stifle a victory whoop. Two-tone cream and white, just as Arlene had described it. He opened the front door and peered inside. No papers or clothing. Nothing to identify owner or thief. *Except...*

The ashtray bulged with cigarette butts. Oasis.

Gottcha.

Lance closed the door softly, looking swiftly around for any sign they had been discovered. Everything remained quiet. Nothing moved but a squirrel chasing along the rickety fence line.

Now to go to the office and find out which room Jordan was using.

Randy gestured wildly, pointing up the far side of the motel toward the front. Lance jogged the length of the long row. "What?"

"Down there." Randy waved and Lance looked in the direction indicated. Dusty stared back at him from the front of the motel, face stern and lips pinched he leaned against the hood of a familiar sedan. Lance's heart went into overdrive.

Shoot, Arlene. What have you gotten yourself into now?

~

Kent Jordan. How long had it been since his name even crossed her mind? *Ten years. He's been in prison ten years. They should have kept him there.*

Now the lunatic wants twenty grand? From me? The words rushing through her mind spilled out in a burst. "From me? You want all that money from me? Are you out of your mind? Do I look like I have that kind of money?" Indignation overcame caution and she jumped to her feet, fists on her hips. "You grew up in Hilton Falls. You should know better, Kent Jordan. I'm not with the New York Times or Smithsonian. I write articles for the *Sunny Hill Gazette.* Do you <u>really</u> suppose I make enough money to just up and give you twenty thousand dollars?"

Kent's face reddened and he was nose to nose with her even as she rose. Teeth bared, he stared unblinking into her eyes. "You owe me! You had to go sticking your nose where it didn't belong." Grabbing her arm with his free hand, he shoved her back and down. "Now sit! This time you won't be running to ol' lover boy Lance. This time you are going to do just what I tell you to do."

Arlene lifted her chin defiantly, though her heart pounded a warning and it was increasingly difficult to catch her breath for fear she would let him see or hear the fear welling inside. "How is this going to help you? Holding me here? You're just making more trouble for yourself, can't you see that?"

For an instant she saw fear in his eyes. The gun wavered, and Kent moved away an arms-length. "I don't want trouble. I just want my life back." His lips tightened and he slammed the phone into her lap. "I want what's coming to me. You owe me. Now don't make me do anything we'll both regret. You--"

His head jerked up and he frowned as the sound of approaching voices. "Not one word, or so help me, it will be your last."

~

Dusty moved to the side as Lance stormed out of the motel office. "Which room?"

Lance shook his head, face set and jaw clenched. "Night manager checked in someone fitting the description. This guy isn't sure which room he put him in." His hand settled on the butt of his service revolver. "He hasn't seen Arlene at all."

"Then where do we start?"

Lance could hear the worry underlying Dusty's quiet words. He understood the feeling all too well. *If he's hurt her...*

He pushed the thought from his mind. *Don't even think it. It'll just distract me.* Lance jerked his head toward the far end row of apartments. "He said he thought Jordan was in one of the rooms in that last unit." Lance paused, staring at Dusty and Randy for a long moment. "Be careful. He might try to run. If he does, we'll get him. But if he has Arlene..."

"We'll get him, Lance." Dusty looked as sober as Lance felt. Hard and cold. "She's close. I know she is."

"Good. Be careful." He took a deep breath, turned and marched toward the trio of dingy blue doors highlighting the last row of rooms. "One room at a time. Try to keep it down, we don't want him to know we're here."

At the first door they stopped again. Dusty knocked. No answer. Lance used the manager's key to unlock the unit and they kicked the door open.

No one. The room was dark and empty.

A knot clenched in Lance's gut, wrenching and twisting. *C'mon Arlene. Where are you?* He jerked his head and Randy slipped inside, checked the room and shook his head. *Nothing. Two to go.*

They moved to the next door. Unbidden prayer whispered through Lance's mind. He'd owe Pastor Brady a visit this weekend if they could pull this one off. *Please. Please let her be all right.*

The key clicked in the lock.

~

Kent's grip on her shoulder tightened painfully. The sound grew closer. A door slammed open in the adjacent unit.

Arlene's gaze never left Kent's face. *Wait. Wait for him to move the gun.* If he just lifted it away. Even for a second.

It's Lance. It has to be.

Kent raised the gun, swinging it toward the door, and Arlene knew her chance, her only chance, had come.

She hadn't grown up roughhousing with her brother and his friends without learning a thing or two. Her foot sailed up and forward, connecting solidly with Kent's crotch.

His eyes went wide and he made a mewling sound as he dropped to his knees. Without hesitation Arlene seized the heavy, black motel phone and swung it in a sharp arc, connecting with the side of Kent's head.

The internal bell in the phone gave a loud jangle, followed immediately by the thud of Kent's body hitting the floor.

Dropping the phone to the floor, Arlene leapt to her feet, kicked the gun away from his limp hand and ran for the door even as it flew open.

Lance, Dusty and Randy piled through the doorway. In a single swift movement, Lance had her in his arms, only then did he stop to consider the motionless form on the floor.

"Looks like we got here just in time," he murmured. He flashed a relieved half-smile. "Might not have been anything left of old Kent if we hadn't."

Dusty chuckled aloud and flicked his handcuffs open. "Always warned you Arlene was enough to give any man a headache."

Lance allowed a short, breathy laugh before pulling her around where he could get a good look at her. Arlene saw the tension fading from his expression.

"Are you all right?" he asked, his fingertips a warm caress as he stroked her hair back.

"I'm fine. He didn't hurt me."

"Didn't I ask you to stay clear of this?"

Arlene nodded. "I'm sorry. I just had a hunch--"

"And of course you had to follow it up without telling me, without making sure it was safe--"

"Lance, you know better. You know I can't always play it safe."

"More important than what could have happened to you? Honey, what if we hadn't found you in time?" His voice cracked.

Kent Jordan groaned and stirred. Dusty pulled the man to his feet. "We'll be running ol' Kent here over to the station, Sheriff."

Lance gave a curt nod. "Fine, take the cruiser on back, Randy. I'll drive Arlene home."

Arlene watched them half-carry, half-drag Kent Jordan out the door, then turned to face Lance. "You don't need to drive me. I'm fine. I'm pretty sure you just arrested my 'secret admirer' and he won't be coming back. There's nothing else to worry about."

Lance sighed, his beautiful blue eyes searching hers. "There's still one more thing between us, Arlene." He ran his hands down her arms until his fingers found hers and she felt them intertwine. "I guess I've known I'd always love you since you were in pigtails."

Arlene's heart soared, taking flight on his words. "And I've loved you since the first time you pulled them."

"You know you scared the hell out of me today. I don't want to lose you. Things have changed so much the last couple of months and"--he took a deep breath and pressed her hand to his heart--"and now I can finally say it. I love you. I want to marry you.

"I'm not asking for your answer now. I know me having Gary changes things some and...and I know you've had a lot of changes in your life too. I don't want to stand in the way of what you want. Of what makes you happy."

"Oh, Lance." Words wouldn't come. She'd waited so very long and now everything she'd thought she would say seemed lost beneath a tidal wave of emotion. What could she say to this? That she loved Gary too? That she'd figure it out somehow? "Lance..."

He bent, stroking her face with his free hand before his lips touched hers and he kissed her. Kissed her with all the longing and love he possessed inside.

He straightened, his forehead resting against hers. "I've talked to Tom and Jack and your mom." He chuckled softly. "I know you have job offers. Savannah. Atlanta. Shoot, honey, I wouldn't be a bit surprised if you had the *Times* knocking on your door before long. I'm not asking you to give it up. It's always been your dream." Lance nodded and stepped back, his hand still strong and warm around hers. "But my offer stands. I'll always love you, and when just me and Sunny Hills is enough to make you happy...I'll be waiting for you.

"You just let me know."

Tears burned hot as they slid down Arlene's cheeks and she threw her arms around his neck and let him hold her.

"I've made my world out of writing. Out of always having the right words. I hope I can find them now," she whispered.

Forty

The late summer sun cast long shadows across the lawn. Birdsong filled the air, perfumed with lavender and roses. Dappled shade from the oak tree blazed with the color of lantana and daylilies growing in wild profusion despite the heat and at the corner of the house Arlene's beloved golden-rain tree waved shimmering fronds in the soft breeze.

"Let's see you hit it in here, Dad," Gary shouted, running backwards across the yard. Lance tossed the baseball into the air and batted it toward the teenager.

"Good catch," Arlene called as Gary nabbed it and side-armed it back.

Coco raced toward them, hurtled into the air and snatched the ball in mid-flight.

"Coco!" Gary took off after the delighted Lab and Lance tossed the bat down in the grass and walked over to sit beside Arlene on the swing.

"How're you two doing?" He stroked gently across her rounded belly before leaning forward to kiss her tenderly.

"We're doing just fine. I think this baby wants to be a football player," she teased.

"Maybe she's just dancing in there." Lance grinned and kissed her again.

"Hmmm, well the paper says Henrietta hears it's going to be twins." Arlene flashed a wide smile. "What do you think about that?"

"Who's she been talking to, psychic gramma?" Lance laughed. "One, two...it's going to be perfect no matter what." He sat up, tracing small circles on her tummy and staring intently into her eyes. "About got that next article done?"

"Yes, just taking a break to watch my two favorite fellas play keep-away with Coco." Arlene leaned back, setting the swing into motion.

"Ah-ha, I knew you taught that dog to do that on purpose," he joked. His smile faded until the tender warmth remained only in his eyes. "Keeps you busy, working at the Gazette and free-lancing for the big papers. It's not what you planned. But are you okay with that?"

"Oh Lance." She smiled contentedly. "I always wanted the big story. I got it, twice over. I wanted to do something--special. And I did. I married the man I've loved all my life."

She looked up as Coco streaked around the corner at Gary's side.

"Mom," Gary called, Coco bouncing at his side eager to continue the game. "Okay if I get a snack?"

Arlene nodded. "All right, sweety. Supper won't be for a couple of hours yet. You two can run it off."

"Yeah," he replied enthusiastically. "Come on, Coco. Want some peanut butter?"

"Hey," Lance stopped Gary. "Leave some room. After supper we're going into town."

"Cool." Gary grinned and scruffed the dog's ears. "Come on, Cocoa." They raced up the steps, the screen door banging behind them.

"Town?" Arlene asked, arching a brow. "What are we doing in town?"

"Oh," Lance drawled teasingly. "Thought I'd take you for sundaes at the soda shop. And--I've got a surprise to show you."

"A surprise? Tell me, tell me." She tickled his ribs, delighting in his deep-throated laugh.

"Now would it be a surprise if I did? Okay, okay." Lance caught at her wrists and held her hands between his. "The light on Main Street is up." Pride shone in his face. "And since you are responsible for that, my dear, I wanted you to see it."

"The whole town pulled together to collect the money for that light," she demurred.

"It was your idea. Otherwise, council would still be sitting on their hands trying to work it into the shambles of a budget Harvey left us. You are amazing." He raised her hand and kissed her knuckles. "And that's why I asked. Sure you don't miss the glamour you'd have had in the big city?"

"It may not be New York or Atlanta, but I found some things that are way more important. I have the best of both worlds. I get some articles in the big papers...and I get to stay here, with the people and places I love."

"And I have you." She sighed happily, and stroked his hair back from his brow.

"Always have, always will," Lance whispered, sliding his arm around her shoulders so she could rest her head on his chest. "Is that enough?"

"Nothing can be better than that," Arlene murmured. "I have no regrets."

THE END

1740805

Made in the USA